WHITE BODIES

JANE ROBINS

ONE PLACE. MANY STORIES

HQ
An imprint of HarperCollins*Publishers* Ltd
1 London Bridge Street
London SE1 9GF

This paperback edition 2018

1

First published in Great Britain by
HQ, an imprint of HarperCollins*Publishers* Ltd 2018

ISBN: 978-0-00-821755-6

MIX
Paper from
responsible sources
FSC™ C007454

This book is produced from independently certified FSC™ paper
to ensure responsible forest management.

For more information visit: www.harpercollins.co.uk/green

Printed and bound in Great Britain by
CPI Group (UK) Ltd, Croydon CR0 4YY

For Carol

AUTUMN 2017

The evidence suggests that Felix showered. Beyond that, I know practically nothing about his final hours on this earth. All I have is the odd scrap of information and the patchy impressions of the bystanders, and it's like I'm at the theatre, looking at the stage and seeing only the supporting cast, the scenery and the arrangement of shadows. All the important elements are missing. There are no principal actors, no stage directions and no script.

The receptionist said this – that Felix's last morning was fresh and cold, that there was a frost on the lawn outside the hotel and a mist in the distance, where the woods are. She'd watched Felix sprinting out of the hotel, down the gravel drive, then turning left at the gate. 'I was arriving for work and I called out "Good morning!"' she said. 'But he didn't reply; he just kept running.'

Forty minutes later, he was back, dropping his head to catch his breath, panting and sweating. He straightened up and, now noticing the receptionist, said that he'd sprinted all the way to the golf course, running the perimeter and the long path through the woods back to the hotel. He thought that the sun glancing through the trees had been magical, as though life was just beginning (how extraordinary that he should say such a thing!). Then he took the stairs up to his room, two at a time.

He didn't come down to breakfast or order anything to be sent up, not even the continental breakfast that was included in the room rate. His colleague, Julio, said he was surprised when Felix failed to attend the first session of the conference. At the mid-morning break, Julio carried a cup of coffee and a biscuit up to the room, but found the *Do Not Disturb* sign hanging on the door. He thought Felix was unwell, sleeping maybe, so he drank the coffee himself and ate the biscuit. 'We missed him at lunch,' he said, 'and again in the afternoon session. By three o'clock I was calling his phone many times, but my calls went to voicemail.' Julio felt uneasy. It was so unlike Felix to be unreliable, so he went upstairs one more time to hammer on the door, then he summoned the hotel manager, who arrived with a key.

The two men were struck by the unnatural stillness of the room, its air of unreality; Julio said it seemed considered, or planned, like a *tableau vivant* with Felix as the centrepiece, lying on his back on the bed in a strange balletic pose, right arm cast out across the duvet, left leg bent, bath robe open like a cape, grey eyes gazing at the ceiling. His left arm was dangling down the side of the bed, fingers suspended above the floor, and the hotel manager, who had a degree in History of Art, was reminded of the pre-Raphaelite painting of the suicide of Thomas Chatterton. Except this didn't look like suicide; there were no pill bottles or razor blades or other signs.

Dr Patel arrived and the receptionist stood by the door while the doctor conducted her examination. Her professional opinion was that Felix had suffered a heart attack or had some sort of seizure after his morning run. She left, and the receptionist took photographs of Felix and of the room – the bedside table, the pristine bathroom, the opened shower door, the view from the window and, finally, the untouched hospitality tray. 'I know that was weird,' she said. 'But it felt like the right thing to do, to make a record.' Maybe she thought her photos might become important, that they'd suggest that something about the scene was wrong. No one else had that sense, though. When the results of the postmortem came through, they were in agreement with Dr Patel – Felix's death was due to heart disease.

As simple as that, he had collapsed and was gone – and for a while it seemed that he'd simply vanished. The world had swept over him like the tide coming in.

But then the funeral happened. I trekked out of London that day to a pretty Berkshire village with a Norman church sitting among gravestones and windblown copper-coloured leaves. When I saw it, I thought that Felix, who was born and raised in America, was having a very English final moment, though the mourners who were arriving in small solemn groups were from his international life. Solid men in sharply cut suits; flimsy, elegant women in heels. I watched them from a distance – in fact, from a broken bench set against the churchyard wall, where I was trying to calm down. Eventually, I slipped into the church and stood at the back.

My sister, Tilda, was the person on show and she walked slowly up the aisle like a melancholy bride. I tried hard, really hard, to get inside her head at that moment, and I conjured up a spectacular array of emotions – from profound grief and loss, to exhilarating release and relief. But nothing felt right. As always, I found her confusing, and I was reduced to noticing her expensive clothes. The black silk dress, the tailored jacket, doubtless costing a thousand pounds or more. And I watched her take a place in the empty front pew. On her right, in front of the altar, was Felix's coffin, under a cascade of white lilies; and to her left, on a wooden stand, a giant photo of his smiling face. A few minutes later, Felix's mother and father slipped in beside Tilda and then his brother, Lucas. There was the slightest of nods towards my sister who sat perfectly still, gazing at the floor.

The first hymn was a thin rendition of 'The Lord is my Shepherd' – but I found that I couldn't sing. Instead I slumped against the back wall, feeling faint and nauseous, overwhelmed by the occasion. Not that I was mourning

Felix, although the sight of his hunched up, grieving family was upsetting. It was more that I was sick with knowing too much. On the day of his death, I'd waited for the police to turn up at my flat or at the bookshop. It was the same on the morning of the postmortem. And now, at the funeral, it seemed certain that police officers were waiting for me outside the church, stamping their feet to keep warm, sneaking an illicit cigarette, and that as soon as I stepped out of the gloom into the autumn sun I would hear my name. Callie Farrow? Do you have a minute?

1

The branches outside my window are spindly and bare, and Tilda stands across the room looking like a waif-woman, saying, 'How can you stand it? All those broken fingers tapping at the glass.' She's opening the door, is halfway out. 'Anyhow, I want you to come to Curzon Street this evening. I'm ordering Thai food and a DVD. *Strangers on a Train*. It's an Alfred Hitchcock.'

'I know that.'

'Come about eight. There'll be someone else too. Someone I want you to meet.'

The invitation sounds innocuous, but it isn't. For a start, Tilda always comes to *my* flat for movie nights. Also, it's unknown for her to introduce me to her friends. In fact, she rarely even talks about her friends. I can name only two, and those are girls she's known since childhood. Paige Mooney and Kimberley Dwyer. I'd be surprised if she saw them more than once a year, so I'm curious and am about to say, 'Who?' but she's leaving as she's speaking, disappearing down the communal stairs.

*

At Curzon Street, I'm clutching my bottle of cider, knowing full well that Tilda won't have cider. And I've brought brownies.

She's waiting on the second floor, at the open door of her flat. Then she's greeting me with uncharacteristic enthusiasm, kissing my cheeks, saying brightly, 'Callie!' Behind her a tall, fair-haired man is in the kitchen area, sleeves rolled up, busying himself with things in cupboards. He comes to say hello, holding out a thin hand, and from the way he stands, so firmly inhabiting his space, I realise that he's accustomed to being there. Tilda gazes at him proprietorially, glancing at his hair, his shoulders, his bare forearms. She says, 'Callie, meet Felix. Felix Nordberg.'

'I'm opening a bottle of white,' he says. 'Will you have some?'

'No, I'm fine with cider.' I hold up the Strongbow bottle for inspection and take it to the kitchen counter, thinking that Felix seems to be in command of things. The kitchen, the wine. Then he starts asking me polite questions in a soft, moneyed voice that makes me think of super-yachts and private islands. Where do I live? Do I enjoy my work at the bookshop? I ask him about his work, which is for a Mayfair hedge fund.

'I don't even know what that means. Except that it's a sort of gambling.'

He laughs. 'You're right, Callie. But our clients prefer to call it investing, so we humour them.'

I sense that he's humouring me too, and I watch him pouring our drinks with precision, examining the label of a French Chablis, checking that the wine reaches the perfect level in the glass. And he's careful with my cider, treating it like precious nectar, even though it's in a plastic bottle with a gigantic red sticker saying £3.30. He hands Tilda her wine, and she flashes him a half-smile as their hands touch. Then Felix gets back to the kitchen cupboards, taking out plates and bowls, wiping them with a cloth and sorting them into piles, at the same time telling me how to short a market.

'Think of it like this. I'll sell you this plate for the current price of ten dollars, agreeing to deliver it to you in three months' time. Then, just before the three months is up, I'll buy-in a plate for nine dollars. You see? I'm betting that the plate market will go down and I'll make a profit of a dollar.'

'That's an expensive plate.'

'Felix likes expensive things,' Tilda offers from her position at the end of the sofa. She's decoratively arranged, her feet tucked up, hugging a velvet cushion with one hand, holding her glass with the other, and she's observing us, wondering how we're getting along.

I look at Felix, to see if he'll say *That's why I like your sister,* but he doesn't. He just grins as if to say *Got me there!* and opens the cutlery drawer, taking out the knives and forks and polishing them. I don't comment. Instead I ask Felix where he comes from, and how long he's been in London. His family is from Sweden, he says, but he grew up in Boston, USA and considers himself to be a citizen of the world. I snigger at the phrase, and he tells us that he's trying to get to grips with England and London.

'What, queuing and minding-the-gap and apologising all the time, that sort of thing?'

'Yes, all that. And the self-deprecation, and the way you guys make a joke of all situations, and find it difficult to accept compliments… Did you know, Callie, that those dark eyes of yours are enigmatic, soulful even?'

Feigning a serious expression, he looks right into my face and I feel embarrassed because he's so handsome and so close to me. But I feel he's including me in the joke, not laughing at me.

'Whatever.'

I move away, hot-cheeked, and as I pour myself more cider, I think that he's intelligent and funny and I like him.

Tilda says, 'Come and watch the DVD,' so I pick up my glass and head for the other end of the sofa, intending to recreate the movie nights at my flat, when we sit like that, at each end, passing brownies back and forth and making little comments like 'Keanu Reeves looks sad in this,' or 'Look at the rain outside, it's going sideways.' Nothing that amounts to conversation, but enough to make things seem companionable, like we're children again. But I'm too slow. Before I can establish myself, Felix has taken the space next to Tilda, making it obvious that I should be banished to the old armchair. So I flop down and put my feet up on the coffee table, while Tilda presses the start button on the remote.

Felix and I haven't seen *Strangers on a Train* before, but we both like it, the chilling effect of the black-and-white, the clipped 1950s voices and mannerisms, and we all have comments to make as the drama unfolds. Tilda, being an actress, and some sort of expert on Hitchcock, chips in more than Felix and me. Hitchcock put his evil characters on the left-hand side of the screen, she tells us, and good characters on the right. I laugh. 'So I'm evil, because I'm sitting over here, and you're good.'

'Except, silly, onscreen that would be reversed. So I'm bad and you're good.'

'I'm the most interesting,' Felix says. 'I'm in the middle, and can go either way. Who knows what I'll do?'

'Oh, look at Ruth Roman!' Tilda's suddenly distracted. 'The way her lips are slightly parted, it's so suggestive.'

I say, 'Hmm,' in a sceptical way, pouting, and Felix raises an eyebrow. But Tilda isn't put off.

'And Robert Walker is incredible as a psychopath. He does that clever thing with his eyes – looking so calculating. Did you know he died just after this movie, because he was drunk and his doctor injected him with barbiturates?'

'The other guy is using his wrists,' I offer. 'He's doing wrist acting'. Tilda laughs.

'I like the plot,' I say.

'Patricia Highsmith… She wrote the novel that the film is based on.'

The idea is that two strangers on a train could swap murders. The psychopath with the calculating eyes offers to murder the estranged wife of the wrist-guy, if, in return, the wrist-guy will murder the psychopath's hated father. The police will never solve the crime because neither murderer would have any connection to his victim. There would be no discernible motive.

'It's a brilliant idea for a film,' I say, 'but it wouldn't work in practice. I mean if you were plotting a murder and wanted to do it that way.'

'What do you mean?' Tilda is nestling into Felix.

'Well you'd have to travel on trains the whole time, planning to fall into conversation with another person who also wants someone murdered. It's not going to happen.'

'Oh, everyone wants *someone* murdered,' she says.

Felix rearranges Tilda so that her legs lie over his lap, his hands resting on her skinny knees, and I notice that they are beautiful people, with their fine bones, white skin and blonde hair, looking like *they* are the twins. They pause the movie to open another bottle of the same French wine and Felix says, 'Of course you're right, Callie, about the murder plot, but these days you wouldn't have to travel on trains to meet another murderer, you could just find someone on the internet, in a forum or a chat room.'

'I'll bear that in mind.'

'I suppose it's true,' says Tilda. 'The internet is where psychos find each other.'

*

We watch the final scenes, and afterwards I say I need to get home, but I'll go to the bathroom first. It's an excuse; I don't really need a pee. Instead, once I've locked the door, I ferret around, and find that there are two tooth-brushes in a plastic tumbler, and a man's shaving gear in the cupboard over the sink. Also, the bin is full of detritus: empty shampoo bottles, little nodules of old soap, wodges of cotton wool, used razors, half-used pots of lotion. I realise that Felix has been tidying up Tilda's bathroom mess, just as he was organising the kitchen; I'm happy that someone's looking after her, sorting her out. I reach further into the bin, and pull out a plastic bag wound around something hard. Sitting on the toilet, I unwrap it, expecting something ordinary, an old nail polish or lipstick maybe. Instead I extract a small used syringe, with a fine needle and I'm so shocked, so perplexed, that I head straight back into the sitting room, brandishing it, saying, 'What the hell is this?' Felix and Tilda look at each other, faces suggesting mild embarrassment, a shared joke, and Tilda says, 'You've discovered our secret. We've been having vitamin B12 injections – they help us stay on top of things. Intensive lives and all that.'

'What? That's crazy. You should be ashamed!' I'm incredulous, and am still holding the syringe in the air, defiantly.

'Welcome to the world of high finance,' says Felix.

'Really!' Tilda's laughing at my stunned face. 'Really… There's nothing to be alarmed about. Lots of successful people do it. Actors do it… Bankers do it… Google it if you don't believe me.'

Then she adds, 'Hang on… Why the fuck are you going through my bin?'

I can't think of an answer, so I shrug helplessly and say that I'd better be getting home. Tilda gives me a wonky face that says *You're incorrigible!* And she fetches my coat.

Felix says he hopes to see me again soon and as I leave he gives me a quick affable hug, the sort that big rugby-playing men give to nephews and nieces.

*

At home, I open up my laptop and start Googling vitamin injections. Tilda's right, it turns out, and I'm amazed at the weird things professional people do in the name of 'achieving your life goals'. I decide to let it go and to accept that Tilda and Felix live in a different world from me. Then I start to make notes on both of them, working in the file I call my 'dossier'. It's a habit that I've had since childhood – monitoring Tilda, observing her, checking that she's okay. I write: *Felix seems like a special person. He has a way of making you feel like you're in a conspiracy with him, sharing a joke about the rest of humanity. I'm astonished that she let me meet him and, now that I have, I'm pleased that she's met her match and that he is looking after her so well.*

2

On Wednesday, my sister phones and invites me to supper. I'm surprised because I thought she might be angry about the bathroom bin incident, but she doesn't mention it, and on my return to Curzon Street, I discover that Felix has made venison stew with juniper berries and red wine, and also a lemon tart.

'You're a genius!' I say, and he rewards me with a sexy *Get-me!* grin.

'Felix did the pastry himself,' Tilda says. 'He has pastry-making fingers, long and cold.'

He flutters his fingers while we assure him that we've never attempted pastry in our lives; we always buy ready-made. I notice that Felix has a knack for cleaning up the kitchen as he works, so that when I go to help out after the meal, there's nothing to do. The surfaces are clearer and cleaner than I've ever seen them, all the pots and pans dealt with and back in the cupboards. 'How do you do that?' I ask. 'It's like magic.'

'It comes naturally… Now, Callie, forget about cleaning, and tell Tilda that it would be a romantic idea to take a boat down the Thames on Sunday. Up towards Windsor and Bray, where the swans are.'

'What sort of boat?'

'Something simple and wooden. Kinda English.'

'It's okay,' says Tilda. 'I'm sold.'

She's looking at him upwards through her hair, a soft dewy gaze, and I feel a stab of pain, realising that she's totally in love with him. She notices me watching her and says, 'You should come too, Callie. Won't it be lovely?' This sort of sentimentality is entirely unlike her, and I can't help making fun of her as I reply, 'Oh yes, it will be very lovely… very lovely lovely.'

*

Felix hires a sporty red Peugeot, and on Sunday we pack a picnic to take to Berkshire. It's not far, an hour's drive, and when we arrive we're in another world – the river so wide and brooding, the tangled woodland coming alive with buds and the first tiny leaves of spring. The boat is just as Felix wanted, a little wooden tub, chipped red paint on the outside, all open, with a motor on the back. 'It's perfect,' I say, admiring the way it's bobbing on its rope, checking out the three benches, the emergency oars. We clamber in and chug along the river, turning our faces to the sun, and it's glorious to feel the fragile warmth. One minute a golden caress, then gone again. I lean over the side, trailing my fingers in the black water, and shiver. 'God that's cold!'

We pass by open fields and then Windsor Castle, by white-washed suburban mansions with lawns that run down to the water, and I spot a heron on the far bank.

Felix is steering from the back, and he says, 'Let's swim.' We're on a wide part of the river now, dense woodland on one side, a flat, empty field on the other. I look around, for people, but there's no one.

'It's too cold!' I protest. 'And not safe. Don't people drown in the Thames?'

But Felix and Tilda aren't listening. Instead, Felix ties the boat to an overhanging branch, and the two of them are ripping their clothes off, frantically, like they're in a race. Then they're standing up, totally naked, the boat rocking madly as they position themselves to jump out. Two spindly white bodies, Tilda gripping Felix's arm and screeching, 'I'm bloody freezing already! I can't do it.'

'Oh yes you can!'

In a sweeping move, he scoops up my sister, holding her across his chest in his arms, which I now notice are muscular and strong. She yells, 'No! No!' and kicks her legs in scissor shapes as he flings her overboard into the water, then leaps in himself. For the briefest, heart-stopping moment, they both vanish into the black; then they are swimming and splashing about, Tilda screaming, and I can't tell whether she's exhilarated or furious. But she calls out, 'Come on in, Callie! It's amazing.'

'You know you want to!' Felix reaches up, pulls the side of the boat down into the water, as though he's a monster coming to get me, grabbing at my ankle.

'I won't!'

My mind is racing, though, trying to figure out what to do. I don't want to strip off my clothes in front of them – I'm embarrassed about my roundish pinkish body, and afraid that they'll laugh at me. At the same time, I'm thinking how wonderful it would be to sink to the bottom of the river, swallowed up by the icy water. Also, I'm intoxicated by the compliment of being included and, for some reason that I don't quite understand, I want to impress Felix. So I sit on one of the benches and take off my parka coat and my sweatshirt and jeans and socks. Then I jump in wearing a t-shirt, bra and knickers, sinking down, just as I had wanted, shocked, numb and frozen, unable to think because my head is pounding. My feet touch the bottom, a thick slime with hard edges jutting out. I flinch, and float to the top, where I find that Felix is standing next to me, water up to his chest, and he leans into me, his hands gripping my waist. 'I have you in my power,' he says, raising me out of the water, while I pretend to struggle, my hands on his shoulders. Then he throws me backwards; in again, and under, right down to the bottom. When I emerge, I find myself screaming and laughing just as Tilda had done. I want to say, 'Do it again! Do it again!' like a child would.

But Felix has turned to Tilda, and I see that he can lift

her thin body much higher than mine, and can throw her into the water much harder. Then, when her head appears, it takes only a swift push with one hand to force her back down, so cleanly that she has no chance to protest, and there is no sign of her, no arms flailing, no disturbance in the water, and I worry that he's holding her down at the bottom far too long, forcing her into the hazardous mud. 'Stop it! It's too much,' I yell.

He releases his grip, so that she comes up limp and choking, her shoulders heaving. This time he takes her gently in his arms and carries her back to the boat. 'You shouldn't have done that…' she says, coughing out the words so weakly that I can barely hear, her head resting on his chest, her arm dangling lifelessly at her side.

Felix flops her over the side, into the bottom of the boat. 'You're fine. Now let's get dressed and have some food.'

I swim to the boat and heave myself up to look inside, to check that she's okay. Her eyes meet mine and she's blinking slowly, looking startled and empty. There's something insect-like in the way she is folded into herself in the corner, something maimed. I'm about to screech with concern but she changes her expression so swiftly that it's like a magic trick, and she's laughing and telling us to get into the boat before we freeze to death.

We take it in turns to use a linen picnic cloth as a towel, and as I watch Tilda drying herself I think I detect that she's still shaken, but it's hard to be sure.

Soon we're huddled in our dry clothes, eating

sandwiches, and drinking black coffee from a flask that we pass around. Tilda's smiling as she says to me, 'This is what it's like being with Felix – amazing! And I'm so pleased you joined us.' Felix says that he too is pleased I came, and he leans across the boat to touch my bare ankle, just for a second. At that moment, everything is sharper, keener, more intense than I've ever known. The sky, the trees, the water – even the ham in the sandwiches.

Later, when I'm back home, I open up the dossier and write: *Tilda is in love with Felix and maybe I love him too. As her boyfriend, obviously. He's so handsome and clever and romantic. My pulse raced when he stripped off all his clothes and I saw his white, muscular body, and he jumped into the river. I was amazed that he would do something so spectacular in front of me. I can't remember such an exciting day in my life as this. I just wish he hadn't forced Tilda under the water and held her there so long.*

1997

3

It's the hottest, brightest day I have ever known and we are running, so fast, hurtling down a steep hill, somewhere in Kent. Beneath us, the grass grows in tufts and mounds, and I'm trying to keep my balance, at the same time looking towards the bottom of the hill, at the grown-ups in the half-distance. They are sprawling on a blanket and passing a bottle from hand to hand. Mum is slightly apart from the group, drinking her wine, smoking and adjusting the skirt of the long yellow dress she made the night before.

She looks up to watch our race, shading her eyes with her cigarette hand, and we run faster until we're tumbling through blue sky into the field, my legs going so fast they're out of control, making me bump-bump at a million miles an hour, right past the picnickers, whose voices I can suddenly hear. Mum yells, 'Come on, Tilda!' because my sister is challenging a girl called Precious for first position, and they are neck and neck, belting for the finish line.

Tilda's blonde hair is flipping around and her elbows are jabbing outwards, until she is just about in front, and she shrieks, 'I'm the winner! I'm the winner!' For a fraction of a moment my heart is broken, then Mum calls out, 'Great job, Callie!' and I'm happy again even though I hear the note of consolation in her voice, because I am going to be last. At the bottom of the hill, the other children collapse into each other and I bump straight past them, accelerating instead of stopping, until I fall headlong into the black prickly bush that separates the picnicking field from the one beyond, the one with cows in it.

Now, the sunny day is gone and I'm on my knees in the bush with my hands pressed into the earth, trying to find a way to stand up, but I can't because I'm stuck in a mesh of branches which are spiking into my back. I think maybe I can scrunch myself up and inch out backwards, and I shift my hands into a good position so that my right palm presses into something hard and knobbly in the ground. As I grasp it, I hear someone laughing, saying, 'Look at Callie!' and the others running to the bush to watch me. I'm curious now about the object in my right hand, and am careful to keep hold of it as I scratch myself slowly into the light, rolling backwards until I'm sitting on the grass. I find that I'm holding something pale under dark crumbly soil, which I brush off with the tips of my fingers, tracing along crevices and points. Cradled in my hand, I have the skull of a small animal, and my eyes start to sting.

Precious says, 'That's gross. What is it?' and everyone

crowds in to see. Tilda thinks it might be a calf skull because of the cows in the next field, and Precious points out that I'm crying. 'It's because you came last,' she says. I smear the tears away, but don't really understand. Maybe I'm upset about being last, maybe I'm jealous of my trium-phant sister, or maybe I'm thinking of the dead animal. What I haven't mentioned yet is that I am remembering our birthday, Tilda's and mine. We are seven.

Tilda says, 'Don't worry about that thing, come back to the picnic and we can have our cake.' I take her hand, but have the skull in my other hand, clamped to my chest. When I give it to Mum she inspects it and wraps it up in a paper napkin saying it might belong to a lamb, and it's a beautiful discovery which she will put into a painting one day, but first it needs a good wash and if I want I can take it to school for the nature table. I hold my hands out while Mum pours water over them from a plastic bottle, then dries them with her skirt. The other children are standing around, watching, and then everyone is singing happy birthday. I lie on my back with my head in Mum's lap, looking upwards at Tilda who's standing with her legs apart and her face turned to the sky. She's singing, even though she's one of the birthday girls, and the sun shines through her hair, making it glimmer like a halo. At that moment I'm hurting with adoration of her. Then Tilda flops to her knees and I sit up, and side-by-side we blow out the candles.

The next day is Monday, which means school. I bring

in the skull, wrapped in a plastic bag, and we're drawing pictures of our weekend when our form teacher, Miss Parfitt, looks over my shoulder, saying, 'Interesting, Callie, expressive.' I explain that my gashed-up picture is the bush and the skull. Then she examines Tilda's drawing of a birthday cake and a yellow spider in the sky, which is the sun, and says in an absent-minded way, 'How lovely.' My picture is dark like my hair and Tilda's is gold, like hers.

Miss Parfitt is my favourite teacher, and she places the skull in the centre of the nature table like it's the most impressive exhibit, which it is, better than the crackly old bird's nest and heaps of dead leaves, and superior to the egg shells with faces and cress hair. I feel proud.

But two weeks later, the skull disappears from the display, and I cry in class as Miss Parfitt stands at the front with her arms folded, saying, 'Whoever took the sheep skull should put it back on the table, and no more will be said.' Days pass and nothing happens.

It's all I can think about. Mum and Tilda both know how upset I am and that I was looking after the skull on behalf of the dead lamb and its mother. To cheer me up, Mum makes a painting of the skull one evening after work, but I have to pretend to like it because the colours are too bright and it lacks tenderness. And, at night, when we're in our beds, I tell Tilda that I think Precious is the prime suspect because she doesn't like the skull and she doesn't like me. Tilda says she would like to punch Precious in the mouth, that Precious is a gobby attention-seeker who needs to be shown a lesson.

'And you'd be standing up for me,' I say.

'That too. I'm your guardian angel.'

I can't tell from her face whether she means it, or whether she just likes to think of herself as special.

For a couple of days we follow Precious around the playground chanting, 'We know, we know what you did,' and I think to myself, *And you have warty fingers and smell of biscuits.* Precious finally retaliates with, 'Don't think you can escape your weirdo sister, Tilda Farrow.' At this point Tilda does punch her in the mouth and I cry with love and gratitude while Precious runs and tells Miss Parfitt. (Years later Tilda said, 'Do you remember how horrible we were to Precious Makepeace?' I've looked her up on Facebook, but she isn't there.)

That night, alone in our bedroom, I take the pink Princess notebook that I received for my birthday and I write on page one: *My dossier.* I have learned the word from Mum who keeps a dossier on her favourite artists, making notes about their techniques and styles, trying to understand them and (Mum's words) 'absorb their essence' so that she can make her own work better. Then I start to write about Tilda, describing everything she did that day, how she looked and what she said. All the small things. The way she laughed when she punched Precious and then looked around to see if she had an audience. The pity in her eyes when she looked at me – her cry-baby twin. *She's braver than me,* I write. *And she's stronger than me.* Then I cross out my words, realising that while I idolise my sister, I don't know her at all, not deep down. If I want to *absorb her essence*, I'm going to have to write a whole lot more.

When I finish working on my dossier, I look at the pages and feel deeply satisfied, as though by writing about Tilda I'm less dominated by her.

4

Tilda's embedding me in the heart of her relationship – join us here, join us there, come bowling, come to the theatre. It's weird because I used to see my sister only once every three or four weeks and then only for movie nights. The latest development is an invitation to meet her and Felix at Borough Market to help look for a French cheese called Cancoyotte, which has to be served with champagne and walnuts, apparently. Also, she wants Lithuanian rye bread and sea salt caramel, and a micro-greenhouse that sits on your window-ledge and sprouts rocket and chard. Tilda explains her shopping list on the phone in a voice that suggests that her niche ingredients are incredible earth-shattering news, but I infer that the real agenda is for me to spend yet more time with Felix. I say yes straight away.

The anticipation of seeing him brings back that sense of an enhanced world, and as I make my way to the market, negotiating the London streets, everything seems to have a splendid clarity – magnolia trees, red buses, people walking labradoodle dogs (they're everywhere, those labradoodles!). When I arrive at the market, I'm still in that elevated state, my skin tingling, buffed by the sharp air – and I don't have to wait long, because Tilda and Felix appear on the pavement, walking towards me. Felix's eyes are smiling, as usual, and he does his hug-thing, squeezing me tight, and then the three of us set off into the crowds, shuffling up to market stalls, attempting to see around the heads to the actual produce for sale.

Tilda and Felix have their arms round each other's waists; they're behaving like lovebirds and, after an hour or so in the market, I find that I'm trailing behind them, struggling to be part of their conversation; and something happens – instead of being energised, my excitement is draining away so that I start to feel leaden and dull, and it dawns on me that I have somehow fallen into the role of stupid sheep, following them dumbly from stall to stall while they taste little morsels of chorizo and salami and bread dipped into rare olive oils. Felix asks questions about the production processes and the flavours in a distant voice, and I notice for the first time that his habit of talking softly means that people have to lean in to hear him.

At one point he makes a special effort with me, saying, 'Try this one, Callie; doesn't it have intriguing overtones, salty and sour at the same time?' and he pops a crumb of goats cheese into my obliging mouth. Tilda now has her arm hanging prettily through his, and she's looking at me, waiting for a reaction. 'It's bitter,' I say, 'not like cheddar.' Then we move on to a stall selling freshly pressed apple juice, where a bald guy is pouring juice into miniature paper cups.

'Hey beautiful,' he says to Tilda, 'give this a try.' And then the inevitable, 'I know you, don't I?'

Everywhere she goes, Tilda is recognised as the actress from *Rebecca*. Even when she's wearing big sunglasses. She tastes the drink, but doesn't say anything and, as she returns the paper cup, Felix ushers her away. The bald guy leans towards me. 'What's he? Her minder?'

We take a cab to Curzon Street, and Tilda and Felix go to the kitchen space to make a lunch out of their purchases at the market, while I sit on the sofa and flip the pages of the *Vogue* magazine on the coffee table, sniffing the free perfume and rubbing it onto my wrists and neck. I look up and notice that Felix is gazing at Tilda lovingly as she sets things out on plates; he's watching her when she goes to the bedroom. When she comes out again he says, 'Shirt looks good.' She's put on a floppy salmon-coloured blouse, bordering on see-through, and I'm sure that it's been bought by him, as a present. Even to my untrained eye, it looks expensive.

'Nice,' I add.

She sashays across the room likes she's Cara Delevingne on the runway, saying, 'Givenchy!'

'If you say so.'

I watch her put her arms around Felix, and give him a thank-you kiss, delicately, before she stands next to him, so close that their arms are touching, while they attend to the food.

I gaze at *Vogue*, but don't read. Instead I listen to their conversation, which is mainly Tilda asking Felix questions: 'What about Julio?' 'How far did you run this morning?' 'Do you like my nails?' 'Do you like these shoes?' His opinion of mundane things is evidently a powerful bonding force between them, and the atmosphere in the kitchen is intimate and exclusive. Then, out of the blue, Felix says, 'Oh, fuck it. I didn't buy sparkling water...'

His aggressive tone and furious face seem to turn the entire room from warm to cold with the sort of shock you get when a shower turns suddenly freezing. And they are totally out of proportion with the problem. I say, 'I'm fine with tap water,' and Tilda says, 'Me too.' But he's already halfway to the door, which he slams behind him, and we hear another 'Fuck!' before he descends the stairs.

'What was that about?' I'm up off the sofa, joining her in the kitchen area, where she's leaning back against the fridge, like his words have forced her there.

'God knows... Felix feels strongly about fizzy water I guess.'

I can tell Tilda's trying not to cry, which also seems an overreaction.

'Come on, tell me... It's not about the water, is it?'

She's shaking her head and tugging at her sleeves, pulling them down over her wrists.

'I know you want me to love him,' I say, touching her fleetingly on her arm, watching her flinch. 'And I do. I think he's wonderful… but that was weird. I mean, it was only water, but he was so angry, out of nowhere.'

'He's under a lot of pressure at work and it makes him like that sometimes. He snaps.'

'It was creepy though.'

Tilda shakes her head, indicating that I shouldn't criticise, and she says in a shaky voice, 'Wait and see, he'll be fine when he gets back.'

Acting instinctively, I lean over and pull her silk Givenchy sleeve right up to her elbow, exposing white skin splattered with yellow and blue bruises, little smudged ink-blots.

I grab her arm to inspect it more closely.

'Stop that!' she says. 'For fuck's sake!'

'Tilda! What's going on? Please tell me.'

She pushes me away, hard, making me crash into the kitchen counter, and pulls her sleeve back down. She runs into the bedroom, then the en-suite bathroom, slamming the door, turning the lock.

I'm amazed by what's just happened. What made me do that? How had I sensed that she had damaged arms? It seems inexplicable. There had been no bruises on her that day on the Thames. Then her body had been milky white, no blemishes other than the mole on her left shoulder.

I sit on her bed, staring at the shut bathroom door, working out what to say next – we're close, but I'm hopeless at communicating with her, forever driving her away with my crassness, my blunt way of talking. Gently, I call out, 'Are you all right in there?' But she doesn't answer. So I lie down, burying my face in her pillow, breathing in her smell, and wait. Occasional sounds emerge; splashing water, pacing about, and after a while she calls out, 'It's nothing, Callie, I'm fine.' And she comes out of the bathroom, looking refreshed and happy, but slightly insane, her eyes still rimmed in pink. I'm about to ask her again to confide in me, but I don't get the chance because at that moment there's a sound in the other room. It's Felix returning (he has his own key!). We both leave the bedroom and find that he's transformed – he's grinning, has a big bottle of fizzy water in his hand, and he thumps it down on the kitchen counter together with a set of car keys attached to a disc that says *Porsche*. Tilda reacts like an excited idiot, jumping on the spot, flipping her hair about, a quick look to see that I'm paying attention. 'You didn't!'

'Come and see.'

He throws the car keys for Tilda to catch, and they leave, his arm around her shoulders, me following, comparing the blondeness of their hair, the thinness of their hips, their totally modern beauty. Tilda says sweetly, 'So you forgot the water on purpose? So sneaky!'

A few streets later, and we're admiring Felix's new silver-coloured Porsche sports car. He opens the door, sits in the driver's seat and presses a button that makes the roof slide backwards. 'James Bond,' I say. I want to be massively impressed, but I'm still thinking about Tilda's arms. I clamber into the back and Tilda slips into the passenger seat, picking up a white envelope that has her name on the front, written in a spiky, tight script. She opens it and reads the card that's inside.

'My god! That's perfect.' She starts kissing Felix with an uninhibited enthusiasm that makes me look away.

'Come on,' I say. 'Take us for a spin.'

'Look, Callie.' Tilda turns around to face me, her face radiant, and hands me the card.

I read: *Darling T, come with me to France.*

On the other side is a picture of a white-washed villa on a hillside, a turquoise swimming pool at a tasteful distance from a vine-covered terrace.

'To this actual house?'

'Yes, that actual house.' Felix steers the car through the streets with one hand, the other arm stretched out, his fingers under Tilda's hair, brushing the back of her neck.

'We'll drive down to Provence,' he says proudly. 'And, while we're gone, my builders will come into your flat and do some work.'

'What sort of work?'

'A surprise.'

'Nothing too drastic?'

'No – what can I say – fine-tuning… You'll like it. It will be my gift.'

'Lucky me!'

That wouldn't have been my reaction – and I'm surprised that Tilda's going along with Felix's scheme. Wanting to change her home without consulting her about *how* strikes me as rather extreme. 'You're being swept off your feet,' I say.

'I am.' She's ignoring my disapproving tone, acting like the emotional dash into the bathroom hasn't happened, like her arms aren't bruised, and she laughs as Felix puts his foot on the accelerator. We zoom three hundred yards up Regent Street, then hit a traffic jam.

*

In the dossier I write: *I was shocked to see bruises on Tilda's arms. Was Felix responsible? I don't know. I can't work out whether he's a truly amazing person – organising surprise holidays and improving her flat – or a deeply dangerous one. Either way, Tilda's infatuated with him and I'm in pain. I don't know whether I still feel the elation that came from adoring him, or whether I'm now terrified that I've been manipulated.*

I go online and start Googling. I look up the dangerous elements in passionate romances, and what happens psychologically as relationships become increasingly abusive. Before long I come upon a website called controllingmen.com and I find myself reading for hours the hundreds of posts in forums called *the first signs* and *romance as control* and – most interesting of all – *what you can do to help a friend who has been targeted by a controlling man.* In fact, I'm so sucked in that I join the site, giving myself a username, and entering the forums that are visible only to members. It's addictive, and I'm up all night, reading, reading, reading.

5

The following evening, I go to Curzon Street without calling ahead. My mind's full of controllingmen.com, and I'm hoping to see what Felix is like towards Tilda when he's not hosting a planned event, because I now suspect that's what our meetings have been – the movie night, the river trip, the arrival of the Porsche – all set-ups for Felix to act the loving, romantic hero. A comment on the website is ringing in my head: *In public my husband acts like he's Prince Charming, so loving and caring. In private he's cold and he hits me, but never on the face. Only where the bruises won't show.*

Because I'm now playing the role of investigator and maybe rescuer, I'm nervous as I stand on the pavement outside the front door, pressing the buzzer. Twenty silent seconds elapse and as I turn to walk away, I'm actually relieved that I don't have to go through with this; I can go back home and have my sweet and sour chicken supper.

Then, through the crackling intercom, I hear Tilda's distorted voice – an uninviting 'Hello?'

'It's me. Callie… can I come up?'

'What? What are you doing here…?'

I'm about to make up an answer when she says, 'Oh, okay…' And she buzzes me in.

As I turn the corner at the top of the stairs I see that it's Felix standing at the open door to the flat, casually dressed in a grey t-shirt and dark jeans but still somehow smart and together – like those clean-cut Americans who give TED talks. He welcomes me with a flash of flawless teeth and a quick hug that I would normally describe as warm and friendly.

'Come on in… What's up, Callie? Why this unexpected pleasure?'

'Oh, I've brought a book for Tilda to read.' I fish in my bag for the novel I've put there as my cover. 'It's *American Psycho*,' I say.

He roars with laughter. Really roars. 'Crazy choice!' he says, good-heartedly, while I assess his demeanour. I'd say he's genuinely relaxed – I'd thought he might react with at least some element of suspicion or negativity.

'Just kidding… I got this.' I laugh with him and show him the book, which is a Scandinavian thriller I'm reading – *The Artist*.

'Where's Tilda?' It strikes me as odd that she answered the buzzer but isn't here to greet me.

'She's taking a shower,' says Felix, glancing at the shut

door. 'She won't be long, I'm sure… Would you like something? A glass of wine? I'll join you.'

'Okay.' I watch him open a kitchen cupboard, and see that Tilda's hotch-potch of mismatched glassware has been replaced by four tasteful, thin-stemmed glasses in a row; tiny ballerinas posing with their feet turned out. But it's not the neatness that alarms me, it's the fact that there are only four. Plainly Felix isn't planning any social gatherings at the flat.

We sit side by side. He's kind of spread out: one big foot resting on the other knee, one arm along the back of the sofa, and I'm kind of prim; upright in the corner, my wine glass juddering slightly in my hand. The momentary silence signals that my only option, until Tilda comes, is small talk – I don't want to challenge him when she's not there.

'Busy at work?' I ask.

'Horrendous…' He says it like he's amused rather than troubled. 'And you?'

'You know… The bookshop is never busy, as such. My boss spilled her coffee on a customer last week. That's as stressful as it gets.'

I hear sounds from the bedroom, or maybe the en-suite bathroom beyond, and I look over the back of the sofa to see if Tilda's coming. But she's not.

'What are your builders going to do to the flat?' My voice comes out a little fake and overly focussed and I realise I've changed the tone of the conversation.

'I guess they'll update it a little. Introduce a better

colour scheme, and some new furniture. It's not a bad space, good high ceilings, well proportioned.'

I've never really considered the proportions, and I say so. Then Tilda appears at the door to the bedroom, but doesn't come in to join us. She's wearing just a white knee-length robe and has wet hair and bare feet. Under her eyes her skin is stained watery black, her mascara I suppose, but it looks like black tears, like sadness and crying.

'What are you up to?' she says to me shakily. 'You never do this.'

Felix stands up and stares at her. I gawp over the back of the sofa. She seems weak like she might collapse, leaning against the door frame like it's the only thing holding her up. Her face is dead, as though she doesn't have the energy to form an expression and the word that comes into my head is *damaged*. A burning ball of anger forms in my stomach and rises to my throat, and in my head my sleepless night and nine solid hours of reading about sickening abuse makes my thoughts scrunch together into a surge of fury. I stand up too and face Felix.

'Look at her! This is your work... You're going to destroy her!'

He says nothing; he's stunned, and Tilda pulls herself upright, the life snapping back into her body and she shrieks at me, 'Un-fucking-believable! What's wrong with you, Callie? What the fuck are you on about? Lay off Felix and get out of here, right now!'

She comes at me, taking my elbow, marching me out of

the flat, closing the door on me. As I descend the stairs I'm beating myself up, thinking what an imbecile I've been, blaming my sleep deprivation for my outburst; thinking now that maybe she was just weary, like normal people get weary from time to time.

I make my way home on the bus, calling Tilda's phone five or six times as I travel, and texting her, saying sorry. But she doesn't reply.

*

A week later Tilda finally answers my call and accepts my apology. But she's short and business-like with me, not understanding at all and after she hangs up I feel even worse.

*

Everything changes between Tilda and Felix and me; it doesn't happen at once, but step by step. There's a retraction of Felix's energy. Or, more accurately, he excludes me from his force field and instead intensifies his focus on Tilda. I gather this because I'm no longer invited to spend evenings at Curzon Street, or to accompany the two of them on outings. And our phone calls change. Tilda and I used to chat on the phone fairly regularly and at the end of our conversations she would say 'Felix wants to talk to you,' and he'd ask how my week was going, or for my opinion on something they were discussing, like whether green olives were nicer than black olives, or whether some TV comedian was funny or just annoying. Small things. But Felix doesn't ask to talk to me any more, and Tilda seems happy for weeks to go by with no contact between us.

On the few occasions when she does actually answer the phone, Felix is her only topic of conversation – how he's taking her to a private view at an art gallery or a new restaurant or the opera (I've never known her go to the opera before). In May, she stays in his flat in Clerkenwell for a couple of weeks so that the builders can start their work in Curzon Street. Then in June the two of them drive to Provence in the Porsche for their holiday, and Tilda is out of touch altogether – not even a postcard – and she doesn't reply to my texts. When she returns, I phone and suggest that she comes round for a movie night, but she makes excuses, saying only 'sometime soon', and that she's busy at the minute because Felix is moving into her flat and 'we're rationalising our belongings'. I feel that I've been eliminated from her world, and that makes me scared. The controllingmen.com website has warned me about how predators try to isolate their prey, cutting them off from their friends and family.

In late June, Tilda and I meet briefly in a café in Regents Park and it's obvious that something's deeply wrong. My sister has always looked delicate, but now she seems undernourished, and is nervy. Just after we sit down, I knock my hot chocolate over and a river of froth snakes across the table, reaching her phone. It's an accident, a tiny mishap, but she makes it seem like the last straw, saying, 'I can't stand this,' and she walks right out of the café, leaving me scrabbling to clean up the mess – I'm on my hands and knees and a young waitress comes rushing over with kitchen paper. 'Here, have this,' she says. 'Was that Tilda Farrow with you? The actress?'

A few minutes later Tilda returns and apologises. 'Sorry, I'm feeling so edgy right now.' She slumps into her chair, wilted and limp. I want to say, 'What's wrong with you? You look so *ill*.' But I can't, because I'm frightened that she'll storm out again. So we discuss neutral subjects, like her latest outings with Felix and how wonderful the house in Provence had been. An ozone pool, she says, at the perfect temperature, and a cook who made extraordinary French meals. Not too much cream and fat, but using amazing fruit and vegetables fresh from the local market. French beans in France are nothing like the ones in Sainsbury's. There's no comparison; they have real beany flavour. She's talking like a travel brochure, and as she speaks there's an almost imperceptible shakiness in her voice. I take a risk. 'So the house and the cooking were perfect, but what about the company?'

'You mean Felix? He was perfect too. He'd planned everything, all our outings, food, everything.'

'You like that? It doesn't sound like you, not very free spirit.'

'It's fine, Callie.' Again that shakiness in her voice, a flicker in her eyes and I pause before speaking, aware that I'm about to steer the conversation into darker territory – but I have to do it.

'You should take a look at this website,' I say. 'It's called controllingmen.com and it tells you about the warning signs you should look out for with men like Felix. So you can be prepared... and safe.' I fumble with my phone, finding the site, while she drinks her coffee, looking around distantly, like she doesn't want to be here. She wants to be home with Felix. I find the site, and show her.

'For fuck's sake...' She's scrolling down, far too fast to read it properly. 'That's bloody crazy nut-job stuff, you're losing the plot, Callie!' Then she softens, which surprises me. 'I know you think you're helping... Now, eat that carrot cake, I need to get home.'

But I'm not ready to leave, and I say, 'How did you meet him?'

'God, you're even suspicious about that! Unbelievable... I met him through Jacob Thynne, the guy who played Max in *Rebecca*... It was perfectly normal... An evening out at the Groucho.' As she's speaking, though, her tone belies her words – her voice is weak and nervous, and I make one last effort.

'Please, Tilda, let me help... I want to help. Honestly, look at the controllingmen site!'

43

'You're ridiculous, Callie,' she says. 'You have to stop behaving like this!' She stands up, stares at me coldly, then hurries out of the café.

I take my laptop out of my bag and write: *Tilda seems fearful, unconfident, nervous. I told her about controlling men but she won't listen. When I talk to her, I make everything worse. I drive her closer to HIM.*

2000

6

The only time I feel that my sister and I are similar, from the inside out, is when we go swimming, which we do most Saturday mornings. Mum sits on the side of the pool, her legs dangling in the water, reading her book and looking up from time to time to check we haven't drowned, while Tilda and I dive under each other's legs, performing roly-polys, picking up coins from the bottom. Our weaving about and beneath each other feels harmonious and dreamlike, despite all the yelling and splashing going on around us, and it's a revelation to feel calm and confident inside. Usually my sister outshines me and I'm diminished by the force of her luminous energy. But as a swimmer I can keep up – even though I'm useless at other physical activities – and I suspect I have a champion pair of lungs. Underwater I can hold out for more than a minute, and I beat Tilda when we perform handstands. Also, our hair is scrunched up inside identical white swimming caps, so that her goldenness seems, for once, to be hidden. I look forward to Saturday morning swimming so much that often I start thinking about it around Wednesday.

School is another matter. There I aim at invisibility, which is the opposite of Tilda, who makes it her business to be noticed. When they cast the school play – *Peter Pan and Wendy* (with songs) – she pushes to the front of the auditions queue and acts her heart out like she's Mary-Kate Olsen auditioning for *It Takes Two*. She's not the best actor in the class, let alone the school, but she's the most insistent, her voice carries farthest and has a daring tone that frightens people. When she wins the role of Peter Pan she boasts about beating the hopeless boys, and practises her lines at full blast in the playground. *My dagger! Woe betide you Hook!* I watch in wonder. How can she brag like that with the obvious, massive assumption that everyone envies her? You'd think her boasting would make her unpopular, but it doesn't. Her friends offer to help her rehearse and to practise fighting with plastic rulers.

I generally watch from a distance, sitting on a brick wall by a privet hedge. But after a while I decide on a new routine for break-times, and start tracking the perimeter of the playground in pigeon steps, observing other children and stopping for any developments that seem worthy of my attention, like the secret tunnel being dug by the Year Threes and the insect zoo. I have a regular, clockwise route that takes me by the apple orchard, round the scrubby grass area with the climbing frames and the tunnel, and along by the iron fence and the road and the school gate.

For the final section, I edge through a forbidden gap between the corrugated iron canteen and the side of the school, picking my way over mangled crisp wrappers and shards of glass. It's cold and damp down there and smells of drains, and I'm accustomed to coming across small groups of children hiding, or girls sealing friendships by gossiping about other girls. So I'm not surprised when one day I go into the gap and become aware of people at the other end. I can't see them at first because I've gone suddenly from bright sunlight into dark, but I hear giggles, hushed and muffled, and the sound of Tilda, saying, 'Don't stop, it's only Callie.' I shuffle along towards her, and realise that she's wedged in the space between the walls with Wendy Darling and Captain Hook. Wendy has her face pushed into Hook's and Tilda is wrapped around both of them, her face up against the other two. Hook turns towards Tilda, and they push and kiss violently with Tilda's back against the bricks and her leg up on the opposite wall. She pulls her head away and looks at me, standing there, watching.

'What are you doing?' It comes out in an accusatory way, which I hadn't intended.

My sister opens her mouth up and slowly sticks her tongue out, a bunched up strawberry snake on it, the sort you can buy from the tuck shop.

'Pass the snake,' she says, carefully, so it won't fall out, and she's pulling down her sleeves and her skirt. 'Do you want it?'

I open wide, and Tilda pushes onto me and with our tongues we work the snake from her mouth to mine. I stand back, stunned that I've been allowed to take part.

Then we hear a screechy 'Out! Out of there this minute!' The teacher standing at the end of the passage is not Miss Parfitt, but scary Mrs Drummond. 'You know that alley-way is out of bounds,' she says, as we emerge in forlorn single file, and then, 'I'm surprised at *you*, Callie Farrow.' I stand with my mouth shut tight, full of snake, then I run into the girls' toilets instead of going to class, and stay in there looking in the rusty glass at the sweat on my face. I try to make the snake last. Not sucking.

That was the origin of my idea about eating things that belonged to Tilda. At night we would stand side by side in our pyjamas, cleaning our teeth before bed. But now I brush super-slowly, waiting for Tilda to leave the bathroom, then when I'm sure she's properly gone, I take her toothbrush from the cup and use it instead of my own, licking it and sucking on it like a lollipop to make sure I've taken some of her spit. Another time, after Mum cuts our hair, I pick a golden tuft from the kitchen floor, and take it up to the bathroom. It's hard to eat hair because you can't chew it and if you try to swallow it, you gag. So I use nail scissors to reduce it to tiny pieces and fetch a glass of milk from downstairs, then, looking in the bathroom mirror, I drink down the hair in the milk.

Tilda keeps a diary. One day I see it lying on our dressing table, alongside the glass animals that we collect, so I tear a piece from the corner of a page covered in her scrawly, chaotic script, and I eat that. Paper is easy to eat; you can make it dissolve in your mouth, but Tilda throws a mad fit when she sees the missing corner, accusing me of reading her diary and damaging it. 'I only read one page, but it was so boring I gave up,' I tell her. She hides her diary after that, but I know where it is – tucked in the corner of a pillow case.

Another time, I go into the kitchen pantry because I know that if I stand on a stool I'll be able to reach the shelf that holds the red tin that Mum uses for our baby teeth, the ones we put under our pillows for the tooth fairy. I'm standing on the stool, reaching up and touching the tin with my fingertips, and pulling it towards me, when I become aware of Mum watching me.

'What are you up to, Callie?'

'I just wanted to look at our teeth.'

Mum says, 'That's sweet,' and leaves me to it, so I take three teeth out of the tin and run upstairs to my bedroom, and hide them in my underwear drawer. I've decided to eat the teeth actually in Tilda's presence, but without her knowing, figuring that if I manage all three, there's a good chance that one or more will be Tilda's. My opportunity comes a week or so later when we arrive home from school one dark afternoon, and our house smells of baking. Mum's made a chocolate sachertorte cake; and as we come into the kitchen she says she has sold a painting. This is always a cause for great celebration in our house. We understand that Mum's work as an art teacher is a source of wholesomeness in our lives, that it pays the bills, but that her painting is something special. I dash to the bedroom to fetch a tooth; then join Tilda and Mum at the kitchen table for orange juice and cake. While the two of them are absorbed in a conversation about apricot jam, I pop a tooth into my mouth with some cake and swallow hard.

But the tooth doesn't go down with the cake, and is still in my mouth. So I try again with orange juice but this time I gag, choking up the juice; and the tooth shoots out and lies on the table. I slam my hand over it. Tilda and Mum don't see. They're still talking to each other and missed the critical moment, so I take the tooth and run out of the room coughing, with Mum calling after me, 'You okay? Did it go down the wrong way?'

After that, I decide not to swallow teeth in public. Instead I do it in the bathroom with the door locked. The first tooth of the three goes down with a massive gulp of water, and as I swallow, I notice that Tilda hasn't flushed the toilet and her pale greeny-yellow pee is sitting there, looking like apple juice.

I use my glass to scoop up a small amount of liquid, drinking it down so quickly that I can't really say what it tastes like – maybe sour like lemons. I feel a momentary rush of satisfaction and exhilaration, and then fear. What if I've poisoned myself? At night, I dream myself into a hospital bed being interrogated by male doctors in white coats saying, 'How did these germs get into you, little girl? What did you do?' And, as I'm slipping away in the grip of a terrible secret, Tilda appears at my side, tears in her faraway eyes, saying, 'Please, Callie, just tell them. It will save your life.' But I know I will stay silent unto death. In the morning I wake up traumatised, and make a resolution to stop eating Tilda's things.

7

After our disastrous meeting in Regent's Park, during the following days and weeks, I make calls to check that Tilda's okay, but her phone is switched permanently to voicemail and with the deepening silence I find myself sinking, constantly worrying about her emotional state. I suppose I'm becoming obsessed, because it's often the first thing I think about when I wake up in the morning. I'm now convinced that Felix is hurting Tilda, physically and psychologically, and while walking to work I invent ways of spiriting her away from him; then, after work, I regularly go online to the controllingmen website to join in the forums, to discuss emotional abuse and coercive behaviours. I even dream about Tilda, specifically about rescuing her, like mothers dream of rescuing their babies from raging fires or angry seas and I repeatedly find myself under water, grabbing her hair with one hand and using the other to swim against the downward force of an almighty current. It's exhausting.

Occasionally I take the bus into town and spend time at the Caffè Copernicus on Curzon Street, across the road from her flat. I'm not spying on her exactly, it's more that it feels good to be close. I fantasise that she might need me in some emergency that's more serious than a few bruises on her arms, and I sit in a favourite spot by the window, which has an uninterrupted view of Tilda's front door and of the sitting-room windows up on the second floor. Not that anything ever happens. The new blinds stay down, and there's no hint of what's going on behind them, so that I'm left with my thoughts drifting off in alarming directions. I find myself concocting bizarre plans for escaping from the flat – jumping out of the bedroom window at the back, for instance, with a glass roof to break the fall rather than risking the long drop from the sitting room to the concrete below.

I haven't seen Tilda at all and I'm hoping that the day will come when she'll confide in me and allow me to help her. In the meantime, I stay focussed by writing up my observations. I have to admit that the dossier has changed a lot. In past years it was like an occasional notebook, just recording this and that about Tilda and I'd return to it when I was feeling particularly overwhelmed by her, or she'd said something to upset me. But now I'm writing it almost every day on my laptop, and it's focussed as much on Felix as on her. I've found it useful to make an inventory of all his odd and sinister behaviour, writing more about the way he was tidying all her cupboards when I first met him, the vitamin jabs, that I accepted back then but now seem totally bizarre; the way he organised a holiday without consulting her at all and then had his builders do heaven-knows-what to her flat. And, even worse, the signs of violence – holding her under the water that day on the Thames, those bruises on her arms, and just the way she looks now. Sort of battered and gaunt. And that's what I'm doing today – re-working my files – and adding my thoughts on how he is isolating Tilda, keeping her from me.

I'm the only customer in the café, so I don't have any distractions, and I work quietly for half an hour or so, making my hot chocolate last a long time, and taking small bites from a banana that I've brought from home. Then I shut my laptop and pick up my book, the Scandinavian crime novel called *The Artist* that I took to Tilda's flat. It's about a serial killer who carves clues in his victims' torsos with a stencil knife and I'm immersed in it; but I glance up, as though prompted by something, a sound or a nudge, and see that, across the street, the front door is opening. I'm mesmerised, because in all the hours I've been spending at the Copernicus, that door has remained shut, like an impermeable barrier keeping me out and Tilda in.

I'm in luck and it's my sister standing on the pavement across the street, masked fleetingly by the passing traffic. I wait, wondering whether Felix will appear. But he doesn't. It's just Tilda, looking around her, up and down the street, and at one point it seems that she's peering through the café window, right at me. In that second I see that her face is kind of hollow, even thinner than when I saw her in the Regent's Park café; and her brow is furrowed. But I don't have time to draw any conclusions because she walks away.

I put three pound coins on the table, stuff the laptop and book into my plastic bag with my remaining half-a-banana, and rush for the exit, crashing my thigh painfully against the corner of a table. I stand in the doorway keeping my eyes on Tilda, who's heading along the pavement before turning towards Shepherd Market. Now I'm half-running, and I follow her down a narrow path and into a cobbled courtyard, filled with evening sun and packed with office people standing outside pubs, drinking and smoking. Tilda is ten metres in front of me, weaving through the crowd, keeping her head tucked down so that no one recognises her and I catch up just as she dodges into a newsagent's shop. I wait outside, beside the door so that she can't see me, and when she leaves I tap her on the shoulder. She jolts like she's been stung by a wasp.

'For god's sake, Callie, what the fuck are you doing?'

I'm not hurt by her reaction. In the circumstances, it's understandable.

'I just saw you. I happened to be on Curzon Street, and I saw you come out of the flat… Are you okay? You look worried… Shall we go to a pub and have a proper talk?'

'No, I can't. I mean, I'm in a hurry – I needed to buy some fags, but I've got to get back.'

I check her face and body for signs. She's wearing a

long-sleeved t-shirt, so I can't see her arms, and she has a thin, grey cotton scarf round her neck, so a lot's hidden, but I can see her bony knuckles and bitten nails. Her hair seems to me more straggly and unwashed than usual and I'm caught up in anxiety about her when she surprises me. 'Look, why don't I meet you for lunch tomorrow? I'll come to your bookshop at one, and we'll go to that pub you talk about, the one round the corner…'

'Really? You can do that?'

'Sure I can.'

'Shall I walk back with you?'

It sounds like an innocent offer, but really it's a test, and Tilda says, 'No. Don't do that.'

She leans forward and touches my cheek with her lips which, by the way, are dried up and chapped. I don't like the look of them and make a mental note to look up chapped lips later on, to see if they can be a symptom of stress.

'It's okay,' I insist. 'I can walk back with you.'

'Don't bother,' she says firmly. 'We'll talk tomorrow. I've lots to tell you.'

She stresses the word *lots* and I wonder whether she's planning to come clean about Felix.

'Okay. I'll go then.' I return her kiss, and set off through the crowds, turning down White Horse Street to Piccadilly, clamping the plastic bag to my chest.

8

I like getting home. My flat feels like a normal place after the mental onslaught of Central London. It's on the first floor, and has a small bedroom at the back of the building, overlooking a neglected garden that I'm not allowed to use. I don't mind. I can open my window to let the fresh air in, and I like the clatter of the trains on the railway track that runs behind the trees. Because of its connection with the outdoors, this is my favourite room and it's a good place for thinking.

The other part of the flat is the kitchen-sitting room, which is dark because of the bottle green walls that I want to repaint, but somehow never do. It has a breakfast bar and a two-seater sofa and a TV (with DVD player), and a little window facing the bricks in the wall of the next-door house. I cook in that room and watch reruns of *Miss Marple* and *Poirot* on television, and Scandinavian crime dramas. But I spend most of my time in the bedroom, sitting at a little table that I found in a skip and put under the window. I eat my meals there and use my laptop – which is what I do the minute I get home after my encounter with Tilda, because I'm eager to go online. I have made friends in the internet forum I told Tilda about – controllingmen.com. They are called Scarlet and Belle, and are both experienced with dealing with abusive relationships. Scarlet joined only a week or so ago – but seems to know a great deal. Belle has been around for ages.

I eat the remaining half of my banana, which is squished now, and I log on, seeing that Belle is online already, but not Scarlet. She notices me immediately.

Hey, Calliegirl. Welcome back.

Hey Belle. Interesting day. Need to talk.

Me 2!!!

I realise I'll have to hear her news before I can talk about Tilda; sure enough, in an instant, Belle is telling me all about meeting her friend Lavender at Starbucks that morning. They had ordered cappuccinos, she said, and granola bars, and had just put their tray down on a table when, before they had even sat down, Lavender's husband showed up 'to keep an eye on the conversation' so that Lavender couldn't discuss anything personal.

Classic controlling behavier, Belle writes.

Definitely.

Belle is a geriatrics hospital nurse in York and Lavender is her best friend from school. Belle has shared all the grisly details of Lavender's life and marriage. Her husband forced her to give up her job because he was worried she would meet another man and now he phones her at home five times a day 'just to say hello', and he's accusing her of loving the kids and not him. Belle thinks their relationship is reaching a crisis point.

Lavender cd not speak. But I no she is READY to leave!

She's really energised because she thinks Lavender might make a break for it with the children, and go to live in her mother's house.

All our conversations are anonymous, for obvious reasons. So Lavender is a made-up name and so is Belle. Like me, she is a Befriender – her job is to help a friend, support her in whatever way she can. And Lavender, like Tilda, is Prey – a woman in a relationship with a dangerous, controlling man. The Prey have onscreen names that are colours, and I gave Tilda the name Pink because I regard pink as optimistic. And we call all the men, the Predators in our language, X. So, online, Lavender's husband is called X, and I always refer to Felix as X. When Scarlet is around, she chats as though she is a Befriender like Belle and me, but actually she is Prey, trapped in a relationship with a control freak (although it's complicated – she enjoys the weird sex games they do). At first the system seems odd, but you soon get used to it. And I'm Calliegirl, because I got involved before I knew you were supposed to disguise your true identity, and I haven't told Scarlet and Belle that Callie is my real name.

I've been bombarding both of them with questions about Felix, about the way he has come between Tilda and me, about those bruised arms, and the day that he pushed her to the bottom of the Thames, so casually, like it was a normal thing to do. Sometimes I think I'm prey to sinister imaginings, that I'm getting carried away, but Scarlet is direct and analytical, and says that, taken together, the signs are clear – Felix is a danger to Tilda. Belle, also, has no doubts.

Eventually she says:

Whats ur news?

Saw Pink today and spoke to her.

!!???!!?? Is she ok?

Not so good. Very thin. Starey eyes, cut lips. Worried X is somehow starving her.

Xtreemly likely. Easy to do. Make sure NO food in the house. Withhold money. Typical Predator Tactics!!

She went out to buy cigarettes.

Easy 4 Prey to have skewed priorities. Maybe Pink has a few pence and craving nicoteen more than food!!

She will come to my workplace tomorrow and we will have lunch together.

!!! Without X????

Yes. At least, she didn't mention him. I'm hoping we'll be able to have a proper chat about the danger she is in. About an Exit Strategy. And how I can help.

It isn't long before I remember why it is I prefer chatting to Scarlet. Belle's spelling choices and random punctuation marks are distracting, and I can't help wondering what she's like at work in the hospital, on the old people's wards. 'Hey Dude!!! It's suppository time???!!!' or 'No WAY this is going to HURT Mr Rumbelow!!!?!!' Belle is a kind person, though, and she's always looking out for Lavender, being protective, and also telling us work stories like, *I sang the whole of the* 'Sound of Music' *to Mrs Prakash, because it was her favourite, but then she went and died!!!* Scarlet is the opposite – always serious, always holding something back, so that I never feel that I know her well. Just as I'm thinking this, she pops up on the screen.

Hello Belle. Hello Calliegirl. Can't stop, X about to appear – wanting x-rated attention – but can we meet in The Zone at 7.30pm tomorrow?

Off COURSE!!

Yes, fine with me. Seeing Pink tomorrow, so I can report back then.

Good. Watch the News tonight. It will be informative, S

It's typical of Scarlet to have that commanding tone – telling us what to do. And I've noticed that these days she often redirects us to The Zone, which is a separate message exchange for the three of us to use when we don't want strangers joining our conversation in the controllingmen forum. We use it when we have private information to share, like Belle's work anecdotes and Scarlet's sex life. I understand her concern, because it often happens – a man comes on the site to tell us that women can be controlling too, or to swear at us and become aggressive, although the Mediator deletes the worst abuse pretty promptly. But we have to be *so* vigilant – because it's easy for a Predator to infiltrate the forum as a spy. So we quiz new people hard, weighing them up. One time someone called Destini seemed genuine and for several weeks joined in our conversations, but then started to say that if the Prey were more 'feminine' and 'appreciative', their 'gripes' with Predators would disappear. Not subtle. And when he was challenged, he used horrific swear words at us.

Our topics can be specific, like giving advice to Prey and Befrienders in disastrous situations, and the same predictable old stories keep coming up, of Predators suspecting their wives and girlfriends of being unfaithful, or about to leave, or of disrespecting them. The surprising part is the Predators' creative ideas about punishments. Violet has to 'submit expenses' when she buys the household groceries, and keep receipts for a bag of tomatoes or a box of eggs. And Sienna told a story of saving up to buy a dress in a silky yellow fabric. When she put it on, and did a twirl, X told her she was mutton dressed as lamb, then he unzipped her and carefully cut up the dress into squares, for dusters. And we're all worried about Lilac because she's not allowed into her converted loft room. X has put a combination lock on the door and he spends most evenings in there, busy with some mystery hobby that requires hammering and moving furniture about. Belle's exclamation marks go crazy when she thinks about all the possibilities.

We also discuss news stories that are relevant for our forum, and there are so many of them, even in these past few months. Like Steve Chase, the Swindon cab driver with 'a winning smile', whose wife Sheree told him she wanted a divorce, so he chopped her up with an axe before he killed his children, four-year-old Lauren and two-year-old Bradley, and hanged himself in the garage. It's gruesome stuff, but it keeps happening, so often, in fact, that the Chase murders didn't even make the newspapers' front pages, and were item seven on the BBC News website. In controllingmen we realised that the signs were there all along. Sheree's sister told the press how, at first, Steve had been a romantic boyfriend, showering Sheree with gifts, whisking her off to Amsterdam, turning up at her workplace with white roses. After the wedding, he had stayed in command – buying Sheree's clothes for her, dictating when she could or couldn't see her friends, forbidding her from driving the car.

Then there was the Topeka kidnapping case. In the photos, Wez Tremaine looked horrible, with his demented hair and monumental beer gut, but so did all his mates, the regular guys whose eyes went blank and bewildered when they spoke to TV reporters. Wez had had a couple of run-ins with the police for beating up Jaynina, the wife who had run away in 2004 after he knocked out two teeth and cracked six ribs, and it was common knowledge that he had a dark side. But no one guessed that he had two teenagers chained up in the cellar. There was no back chat from Leeanne and Joelle, no sneaking-off for an x-ray when he showed them who was boss, no excuses when he wanted sex. Wez did make front-page news, of course, all over the world because, after three years in the Tremaine hell-hole, Leeanne and Joelle escaped, and everyone loves it when someone comes back from the dead.

I've had so much help from Scarlet and Belle, and others on the controllingmen forum, giving me advice about Felix, analysing his actions to see how closely he fits the typical Predator profile by being controlling and judge-mental. I'm not surprised by the general agreement with my view, which is that Felix is isolating Tilda and taking over her life. I have the impression that he's constantly monitoring her behaviour. Also, it seems suspicious that Tilda hasn't taken on any new work recently. Before Felix, she was always talking about the new roles she was con-sidering; since Felix, nothing.

Of course, I'm relieved that Felix hasn't persuaded Tilda to marry him, or made her pregnant. But when I mentioned to Scarlet that I hoped Tilda would find a way of leaving Felix, she pointed out that because my sister is famous, he will always have a good chance of finding her. Someone will post something on Instagram saying they spotted her in a café or lying on a beach. Scarlet's right, and sometimes I'm at my table under the window half the night, coming up with solutions. I wonder whether Tilda would be prepared to give up her acting career and take another identity – cut her hair short and dye it black, and move with me to Mexico or Australia. Or maybe take a French name and move to a big city like Marseilles or Bordeaux. Then I go online to check whether a change-of-name is a public document, wondering whether Felix would be able to track her down.

I'm busy with this sort of internet research when I remember that Scarlet has told Belle and me to watch the news, so I go to the BBC website and see that this morning a young woman named Chloey Percival was working in the perfume department in Debenhams in York, when a guy in a hoodie came in and commenced his attack, throwing bleach at her face then stabbing her in the stomach. A middle-aged couple, Sandra and Trevor Abbott, happened to be shopping and did their best to pull him off and hold on to him, but he broke free and ran out of the store into a crowded street. The police are now looking for a suspect named Travis Scott, and Chloey is in intensive care in York Hospital.

I can see why Scarlet wanted to alert us. Her boyfriend is paranoid about some other man taking her away from him because she's so pretty (she told us that in a matter-of-fact way, but I've never actually seen a picture of her). She could have been an actress or a model, she says, but X wouldn't allow it, and made her give up trying. Like Chloey Percival, Scarlet works in a public place, doing tanning, waxing and nails in Manchester. X often shows up at her work, unannounced, and Belle thought it was hysterical to ask: *Has X ever stormed in just as ur getting STUCK IN on a chalanging BIKINI WAX??!!*

But it's not funny at all, and I suspect that Scarlet is feeling spooked by the Chloey Percival case, terrified that she's next.

9

At school, I watch everything coming to life on the *Peter Pan* front. At break-times Tilda spends most of her time with Hook, whose real name is Liam Brookes. The two of them sit on the stony ground in a corner of the playground, hugging their knees and going over their lines. When I stand close by I hear Tilda say, *'First Impressions are Awfully Important,'* and the line she's in love with, she says it so often, *'To Die will be an Awfully Big Adventure.'* Then she notices me and says, 'Go away, Callie,' so I resume my tour of the edges of the playground.

At home, Liam keeps coming up in conversation. At first it's in the context of *Peter Pan*, which is now Tilda's main interest in life, and which allows her to speak in her Peter voice, a constantly rising lilt, so that she endlessly seems to be rallying her troops, *once more my friends!* We hear interminable stories of her scenes with Hook, and how their sword fight is so complicated, and requires terrifying jumps from rock to ship and back to rock. Then Liam's name starts coming up in everything else, so I hardly dare say anything for fear of prompting it, thinking that if I mention that I like peas, we'll be treated to a long description of how Liam absolutely adores peas. Over our beans on toast one time, Tilda, out of the blue, tells us that Liam can swim twenty-five metres under water and I slam my head down on the table and refuse to look up.

Mum ignores my protest, and picks up on Tilda's hint. In a nonchalant way like the thought has drifted into her head, she says, 'Well, Liam could come along to swimming on Saturday if he'd like.' Tilda practically shoots out of her chair. 'Can I phone him now and ask?'

I leave the table and stomp up the stairs, then I take Tilda's diary from its pillow case, and find little 'L's in the margins and kisses and hearts, and she has been practising the signature of the future Tilda Brookes. I can't help it – I tear off a corner and eat it.

On Saturday, when the doorbell rings, I run to answer it, and find Liam standing on the doorstep, his stripy towel rolled up under his bare brown arm, and serious-faced like a cub scout ready for inspection. I feel a surprising surge of warmth because of the undisguised element of expectation in his expression, as if he's waiting to be liked, or questioned, or teased. Also, I notice that his dark hair stands up on end. He just stands on the doorstep, looking at me, and I see that his towel is faded and rough and frayed at the edges, and his red swimming trunks are poking out from the middle, like the jam in a Swiss roll.

'You'd better come in,' I say.

On the bus, Tilda sits with Liam, and Mum and I sit in the seat behind, with all our bags. I lean my head on Mum and she puts her arm around me, saying, 'Chip chip,' because she knows that makes me smile. Then we both stay silent, trying to eavesdrop. But all they talk about is *Peter Pan*, and I realise that any other subject would be too much effort. And, in the pool, there's no conversation other than about swimming.

It turns out that Liam's a better swimmer than both Tilda and me, stronger and quicker and – as previously advertised – particularly good at holding his breath (*my* specialty!). 'Watch this!' he shouts, before he holds his nose, and sinks down to sit cross-legged on the bottom. We start counting – one, two, three. At thirty, bubbles come up, and at seventy-two we're still going. Then he bursts up in a great whoosh, looking like he'll explode. Afterwards, he swims a width under water, turns and comes halfway back, before coming up for air. On the way home, Liam asks Tilda if she knows how to roller-skate, and she says no but she wants to learn – so I expect a roller-skating invitation to come her way. After he leaves, Mum says, 'That boy has intelligent eyes.'

The days pass but the roller-skating invitation never

comes and, in its absence, Tilda becomes edgy if Liam's name comes up, no longer wanting him to be a feature of every meal-time conversation. It's in her character to be pushy and to ask Liam outright to teach her to skate, but either he puts her off or she keeps quiet. On my tours of the playground, I see that she and Liam still get together to prepare for *Peter Pan*, but I sense an awkwardness about their huddles that wasn't there before. And, at home, Tilda is scratchy and moody with Mum and me, and starts spending long hours in our bedroom with the door shut. One evening, though, she calls me up to help her practise her lines and when I arrive I find her curled up in her bed, bloodshot eyes, runny nose, the sheets pulled up to her neck. 'You look awful,' I say. 'What's the matter?'

She puts her finger in her mouth and bites on it so hard that I expect to see a trickle of blood. Then she sits up and starts bashing her head against the wall.

'Stop it!' I pull her away, thinking she's gone insane, and we both collapse back under the covers heaving with emotion. I stroke her hair and try to reassure her.

'Come on, it'll be all right. Really. Remember you have me to look after you... Remember that we're the loved ones.'

She manages a wet little smile. *The loved ones* is Mum's name for us – ever since we were tiny.

'And what about *Peter Pan*?' I say. 'Think about Friday, and how wonderful you'll be...'

'I know…' She sounds despairing. 'I *have* to be good on Friday… I have to…'

*

On Friday afternoon I keep an eye on her at school, fearing that she'll be in meltdown. When I ask if she's scared she just says, 'Oh no, I'm fine,' as if there's no cause for concern, but I carry on worrying right up to 5pm, when the audience arrives. By 5.30, the school hall is packed and buzzing and noisy, but the chat quietens down swiftly as the music starts and the curtains part to reveal the bedroom of the sleeping Darling children. A few minutes later, when Tilda appears, I feel sick.

She walks shakily to the centre of the stage, her face white, her eyes blank with fear, and I'm rooted to my spot by the wall, hardly able to breathe. But, from somewhere, my sister summons up her courage and starts to let rip with the Peter Pan voice, loud and clear. Soon she's dominating the stage, jumping around as though the floor were on fire, waving her sword about. And it becomes clear that it's Liam, not Tilda, who is shaken by the occasion. He was dynamic and swashbuckly in rehearsal, but is now somehow diminished by the spotlight. In every scene he's out-acted by Tilda. Sometimes she does little asides to the audience that have everyone laughing, and her performance causes several bursts of spontaneous applause. At the end, when the parents clap and whistle, she glows as she bows, with Liam glancing at her, half-admiring, half-puzzled. Afterwards, Mrs Brookes comes over to Mum, and I'm surprised to see that she's one of the obese mothers from the Nelson Mandela estate, and she has a row of fat metal hoops that go all the way up one earlobe.

'Right little actress, your Tilda,' she says, with a smile as wide and open as Liam's. 'I could see her going professional.'

She turns to me. 'What about you? Didn't you want to be in the play?'

I shrug. Liam joins us, and Mum says he gave Captain Hook a soulful side, and he must come to our house sometime. As she's speaking, Tilda arrives and we all go out to the car. 'See you Monday,' Liam says. And Tilda beams, as though he's mended everything between them.

Later, when we're back home, I go upstairs to our bedroom and rummage through the clothes in a drawer that is jam-packed full of my tops and t-shirts. There's an old red woollen jumper, too small for me now, that I keep right at the back, well hidden. I take out my dossier, which I keep wrapped inside the jumper. It's no longer in the Princess book I had when I was seven, but a smart notebook that I bought in W H Smith with my pocket money. I open it up and see that I haven't added anything for six whole months. But now I get writing, with the words coming into my head furiously and hard, like

I'm under a waterfall that's packed with words. I set out the details of how she fell in love with Liam and how it made her obsessed with him. Then I write about how she fell apart when she thought he didn't like her any more, crying herself to sleep at night and violently hurting herself, going nearly mad. Everything got better when she was acting, I add. She was an amazing Peter Pan and the whole audience loved her; I even think it made Liam want to be her friend again.

10

I wake up queasy, remembering that Tilda's meeting me for lunch today. Partly I'm nervous about screwing up, and scaring her off. Also, I'm angsting about Daphne, who sits by the shop doorway, watching everything. My boss has a habit of irritating people with her inquiring, nosy personality, so I suppress thoughts of work while I shower, and instead concentrate on the questions I'll ask Tilda. I tell myself, don't antagonise. Be subtle.

The bookshop is a five-minute walk away, on Walm Lane, just past the Samaritans charity shop. It's Daphne's baby – that's how she describes it – and is called Saskatchewan Books, which looks peculiar in the middle of Willesden Green, which is international but more in a Halal-meat way. But Saskatchewan is Daphne's birthplace, so that's a good reason, and she likes to say it's a suitable name because the shop is spacious and empty. Not empty of books, but of customers. I don't mind. I like the quiet. I work there three days a week: Tuesday, Wednesday and Thursday.

I tell Daphne that I'll be going out to lunch, instead of my normal routine of a cheese sandwich in the stockroom.

'Lunch out, sweetness? That's nice. Is it a special day…? It's not your birthday, is it?'

I get the truth out, and done with. 'No, I'm meeting my sister.'

'Tilda? Coming here?' Her tone has flipped from soft to sharp.

She gets up, walks around awkwardly, tidying the shelves, rearranging the non-fiction table. Then, 'What's happening with your sister? She was so successful, with all that TV, then *Rebecca* – but it's been ages, hasn't it, since she's been in anything? A year or something?'

The shop fills with silence. Eventually I reply with, 'She's fine.'

'It's absolutely right that you should be discreet. But I'm thinking an autobiography would sell well. I could see that being snapped up. And it would get her face back in front of the public.'

She carries on tidying, then settles at her desk near the window display, lining up her purple Moleskine notebook and Virginia Woolf coffee mug and opening her laptop. She looks like a giraffe-woman she's so long and thin, her legs stretched out under the desk, her feet poking out. It's always the same – she inhales on her electric cigarette with a little snorting sound, then starts bashing the keyboard for a novel called *The Lady Connoisseurs of Crime,* which is a sequel to *The Primrose Hill Murders* and *A Death Before Breakfast.* She calls the books her 'cosy murders' and they have quite a following, which subsidises the shop. Daphne says that other people have a business to support their vanity publishing – but she writes books in order to do vanity business. I'd say she spends half her time on her novels and the other half on internet-dating sites in her doomed quest to find a boyfriend.

My job is to look after any customers who come in – like Mr Ahmed, who buys one hardback P G Wodehouse a month for the collection he's building, and wants to put in his will for his son. Also Wilf, who works in the estate agent across the road and likes thrillers, especially Harlan Cobens. When Wilf comes into the shop he always looks out of place; he's big with ginger hair and he walks with a long untidy stride and he always looks like he wants to make a big announcement, but he's not sure what about. Daphne calls him 'the sack of potatoes' and a 'clutz', but I can tell she likes him. She always mentions it if he hasn't been in for a few days.

When the shop's empty I take care of orders and returns and bring Daphne cups of coffee, which she likes strong and black, no sugar. Sometimes, she gets up and paces around thinking about what she is going to write next, and I like the sounds she makes clacking her heels on the wooden floor. Then she'll stop suddenly and say something like, 'Hell's teeth, I haven't got a clue. Fancy an iced bun?'

And I'll go along to the baker's. This morning, though, she stays sitting, legs stretched out, gazing at her screen like she wishes the novel would write itself. Daphne is about fifty, and wears mini-skirts and a leather biker jacket, so I guess she really is mutton dressed as lamb. Which suits her, by the way.

Maybe it's because I know Tilda is visiting that time goes by so slowly. Only half a dozen customers come in and three of those don't buy anything, so they aren't technically customers at all, and one only buys a *Good Luck In Your New Job* card from the display-stand by the counter. Customers walk past Daphne like she isn't there which, given her length and her obviousness, makes me think they would walk past a baboon. Daphne's pleased, though, that she isn't interrupted. She likes the combination of activity and anonymity and feels that she has purchased her own personal coffee shop. Nicer than Starbucks, because of the books, and there are no crumbs on the floor.

Just before one, Wilf comes in to tell me he's finished *Tell No One* and to ask if I have any more recommendations. Daphne calls out, 'You again,' and he just shrugs and says he's a fast reader. Then he tells me that he'd like to branch out and asks if I've read John Grisham. He's kind of looking at me intensely and then inspecting my hair, then looking away unhappily. I feel myself blushing and looking at his chest rather than his face and I feel horribly embarrassed. But I try to act normal, saying he should try some Scandinavian writers. While I'm telling him about *The Artist*, our door bell jangles and Tilda comes in, wearing a long tweed coat, a man's coat I think because it's too big on the shoulders, and a man's trilby hat. She would have looked ludicrous in any circumstances, but in the summer heat she looks mad. Because Wilf and I are busy with our conversation, she starts browsing the books, picking up something in the self-help section, though she really isn't an *Eat, Pray, Love* sort of person. As I feared, Daphne stares at her intensely like a dog who's spotted a rabbit, then she gets up and says, 'Hi, I'm Daphne, I own the bookshop.'

Tilda doesn't smile, but she holds out her hand politely and says, 'Hello.' Daphne starts talking too much in a high voice, telling her how I'm such a great employee, always on time, committed to the book trade and she adds, 'I'm very *fond* of Callie, very serious about making sure she's okay and looked after.' I hate this effect Tilda has on people, making them fall over themselves to impress her or make themselves likeable, even someone like Daphne, who's a confident person. And it's typical to talk about me in a patronising voice, and to assume that Tilda is the older sister. But we are twins. And, if only they knew, I'm the one looking after *her*.

'Come on,' I say. 'Let's go.'

I'm aware that I've left Wilf without a decision on his next book, and I mutter a 'Sorry' as I pick up my bag, registering a forlorn look on his face that is somehow hound-like, like a big scruffy dog that's been told he's not going for a walk. 'Daphne can sort you out,' I tell him, thinking that, as soon as we leave, Daphne will start talking about Tilda, about how she was so fabulous in some TV drama and how she looks so strange now. And how she hasn't been in anything recently. I just know it.

I take Tilda's arm and steer her swiftly along the street to the Albany. It's only a couple of minutes away, and there's nothing fancy about it – a plain wooden floor, rickety tables that wobble until you put a beer mat under one of the legs. We find an empty table in a corner. 'This is on me,' I say. 'What would you like?'

She looks over at the bar. 'God, I don't know.' Her voice sounds weary, like the pub and its food has failed to meet her high standards. 'I'll have one of those blueberry muffins and a glass of white wine.'

An odd choice for lunch, but I don't question it and I order myself a cheese-and-Marmite toasted sandwich and a Coke, then walk back to the table, carefully balancing everything on a tray, while Tilda sits leaning on one elbow and looking around nervously. She has put her man's hat on a spare chair but she still has her coat on, and is shivering as she runs her hands through her hair to mush it up, and I notice how spindly her wrists are, how her skin is dull and pale. I want to force up the sleeves to see if she has marks on her arms. But I don't, and I can see that, despite everything, the thin face and cracked lips, she still looks starry. She has these wide-apart blue eyes that people like and high cheekbones. If you didn't know her like I do, you might think her paleness was sort of chic or romantic.

'So, Callie, how's everything?'

'It's been two months.'

'I know. I've just been so hunkered down. Reading crappy scripts. You've no idea the pile of shit that comes my way, and I have to wade through it all metaphorically barefoot. It's tiring.'

I give her a sceptical look.

'How's Felix?'

She stares at her muffin and when her answer comes it's in a rat-tat-tat way, like she's typing at me.

'He's fine. He got some humungous bonus at work, and we're thinking of going away to celebrate. I'm desperate for sunshine. We might go to Martinique... where no one knows me.'

I have no idea where Martinique even is, and I note that London is in the middle of a heat wave. But I don't want to be diverted, and I say, 'How come you never invite me to your flat any more? It's Felix, isn't it? He doesn't like you seeing me.' So much for subtle.

She looks at me now, and changes her voice into a kind of pleading.

'Really... Nothing personal. He's forgiven your crazy outburst – but he thinks it was damaging for him and me. Really, it's just that he works so fucking hard that he's got no energy left for socialising. We haven't done much lately – no parties or concerts or anything. Actually we've become really boring. Just work, sleep, work, sleep.'

Except in her case, she isn't working.

'Does he know you're seeing me today?'

Now she's pulling her muffin into small pieces, moving them round the plate with the tip of her finger.

'No, I didn't tell him I was going to see you... And, to be honest, why should I...? Don't look like that, Callie, I just prefer an easy life.'

Her phone is on the table, and at this moment – on cue – it rings. She presses a button to ignore the call but I know who it is, checking up on her. I want to come to the point but I'm nervous, thinking I've already gone too far, probing her on Felix. If I'm not careful, it'll be another two months before I see her again... But I can't stop myself.

'I'm worried... You're so isolated these days. And why aren't you working? Didn't the BBC want you for something in *My Cousin Rachel*?'

She laughs. 'Yes, Rachel. The lead role. But it's nothing sinister. I'm just taking my time over scripts, not accepting anything that isn't right. And with all these parts, there's often a lot of talk – oh, you'd be so perfect as this or that – and then it doesn't come to anything. And, yes, Felix helps me with scripts, and he's great...'

'Only, with Felix in charge, no script will ever be good enough...'

'Callie! This is why it's not so great seeing you... You

have to accept Felix, he's part of my life and will stay part of my life. For the long term. Understand?'

Now, despite the hot day, I feel as shivery as Tilda seems to be. *The long term* fills me with dread. I spend some time chewing on my toasted sandwich, considering how I might sound supportive and, importantly, reasonable.

'I realise you're not telling me everything,' I begin, in a measured, even tone, 'and I just want you to know that I understand men like Felix, and I know that they can be dangerous. So, if you ever need me, I'm here. I'll look after you...'

'Oh, I can't stand this! Felix is wonderful – adorable not dangerous. I don't need or want you to *look after me*. Can you get that into your tiny, pea-like brain? If you can't I won't spend time with you. You're way too toxic...' She's downing the last of her wine, grabbing her hat, and I panic.

'Please, please, Tilda. Face facts. Felix has poisoned you against me. And he's violent. You have to leave him!'

She looks right into my eyes and I think for a second that she's going to cry, then she shakes her head slightly before checking the time on her phone and saying that she doesn't want coffee and needs to go home. So we collect up our bags and leave. Tilda, I notice, has left her muffin in a state of devastation all over the plate. As she walks to the door, I gather up some crumbs and put them in my pocket.

At the Tube she puts her hat on and some big sunglasses,

and as we part she calms down and says, 'Please don't get carried away. It's all in your head, you know.'

I get back to the bookshop and Daphne says, 'That was short. Nice lunch?' Then we resume our normal day, except for me it's far from normal. I'm churned up inside, terrified that by arguing with Tilda I've driven home the wedge between us and made her situation a whole lot worse. In one of the many quiet moments, I eat the crumbs from her muffin.

*

When I get home I make supper, a microwave bacon risotto, and write up my meeting with Tilda for the dossier, letting out all my frustration and anxiety. I'm not ready to talk to Scarlet and Belle about this, but I'm looking forward to hearing their news when I log into The Zone at 7.30. To prepare myself I go online and check up on the Chloey Percival case, but nothing much has happened. She's still in intensive care because of the stabbing, and Travis Scott's still missing. The police say he mustn't be approached by members of the public and that he has a distinctive tattoo that criss-crosses his neck – in the picture it looks like his head is held up by barbed wire. The only new details are totally predictable. Travis Scott was identified as Chloey's ex-boyfriend, and she had dumped him when he became too 'possessive'. Travis had never had a girlfriend as pretty as Chloey, and his Facebook page had been plastered with couply pictures of the two of them – sharing a bag of chips, up to their waists in choppy English sea, screaming on the Nemesis Inferno roller coaster. The other development is that Travis's mother, who hasn't seen him in the past two years, is making 'an impassioned plea' for him to give himself up.

I log on to The Zone and find a message already posted from Scarlet. Just *click on this link*. It's an online rant by Travis Scott a month before he attacked Chloey, and posted on a website called RevengeBuddies, which allows its members to fantasise about pay-back plans for all sorts of behaviour, most of it trivial – leaving bags of dog poo on the pavement, wearing leaky headphones, putting a 'baby on board' sticker on your car – but one section is devoted to violent threats against feminists who post messages on Twitter. Travis's comments are in the romance section.

His spelling is worse than Belle's, but that isn't the main point. What sticks out is the force of his message – the pain he's been feeling, the desperation. All he could think about was Chloey. *My Chloey is prettyer than any model. Her beuty comes from the inside she is a PERFECT girl and our love is perfect and without her I wudnt want to live but I Know she is sometimes thinking of someone else, and who it is. Hes called Cameron and hes suposed to be my mate Im not going to take this believe me she is making a mistack.* He went on for ages like that, and added more a day later, when Chloey had dumped him. *Believe me I wud never harm Chloey she is a good girl but love is biger than a single persons feelings it gos deep like a knife and takes over so you have to do what you have to do it cant be helped. One day she will feel pain like I do, then she will understand.*

This puke is vile, writes Scarlet. *His language is so menacing. My X says the same things – he doesn't want to go on living without me, I am the only woman he could ever love, he thinks I want to leave him. He's right, I do want to leave – but you know why I can't. Blood will be shed unless we take control and do something.*

I didn't expect this. Scarlet's usually the one to calm us down, and tell us not to catastrophise. Also, I can't think what she might mean – because the whole point is that the Prey don't have any control, that they are in an impossible situation. So I write in the dossier that Scarlet is just expressing frustration, especially when she uses that ugly word – puke.

11

Wilf comes into the shop clutching his Jo Nesbo but then he doesn't mention the book, or say that he's looking for another one to read. Instead he just stands at the counter, focussing on the reserved-items shelf above my head. I study his arms. He has rolled up his shirt sleeves and I inspect the dark red hairs on white skin, the square tips to his fingers, the dirt under his nails. I'm about to do my 'Can I help you?' knowing I'm being way too formal – it's Wilf after all – but before the words come out, he says, 'I was wondering, Callie, would you like to meet for lunch today? At the Albany?' I'm not sure that I've heard right, and I mumble, something like, 'What? Did you say lunch?' But I *had* heard correctly, and we arrange to meet at one o'clock.

I glance at Daphne who's monitoring us from her viewing point at the front door, swinging back on her chair for a better view. I half expect a wink, or a thumbs up, and when Wilf leaves she says, 'Romance?'

'Of course not.'

I'm not an obvious love interest for someone like Wilf. For a start, I don't dress for it, and I don't wear make-up.

'Don't give me *of course not*,' says Daphne. 'You're perfectly matched. Both as shy as badgers; he just covers it up better than you. And look at you! All those curves, that luscious hair, no wonder that boy's always in here... I can't believe he reads as much as he says he does.'

'He's not a boy.'

We go back to our jobs. I feel humiliated by her intimation that the lusty rolling forms of my (too large) breasts and backside should act like a beacon to local menfolk. While she chews on her e-cigarette, staring at her keyboard, I decide to sort out the stationery section.

*

At one o'clock, the pub is packed and noisy, like lunchtime is an excuse for a party. Wilf and I inch through the crowd and squeeze onto high wooden chairs at the end of the bar, beside a group of shrieking young women who erupt every time a new girl joins them. On our other side, an older guy sits alone, not drinking his beer because he's playing a game on his phone. A builder, I guess, since he's covered with dust.

'I'm having the ploughman's,' Wilf says, unceremoniously. 'What do you want?' I order a cheese-and-Marmite toasted sandwich, the same as when I came with Tilda, but this time with cider. He has a pint of lager, which he gulps, smearing his mouth with the back of his hand, and he eats his food with huge, hungry bites. I watch, feeling uncertain about what to do or say, trying to figure out what's going on, not sure whether or not this is a date. I've not had a date with anyone for nearly a year, and I'm so nervous that I can't eat my sandwich. That, and it's too hot.

Shouting to make himself heard, Wilf says, 'Daphne seems okay. As a boss.'

'Yes. She's fine,' I yell back.

'What is she up to all day, writing…?'

'She's a novelist.'

'Oh yeah… I did know that. What sort of stuff does she write?'

'Crime.'

'Oh. Fine.'

We sit together for a bit, a vortex of silence in the commotion. Then, 'I was just trying to make conversation, Callie.'

I don't say anything, just sip the dregs of my cider and worry about my ability to communicate with people without alienating them. Wilf tries again. 'It would be nice to know something about you…'

'I don't see why… I'm very ordinary.' *Oh god!*

He looks almost angry, and I sense he might give up trying to talk to me. I can't blame him, and I feel like explaining – *I can't help it; I'm doing my best* – then he has another go.

'Just tell me something about your life. What's it like having a famous sister?'

'Not that again!' I'm screeching, over the din.

He puts down his lager and leans his head on his hand in a way that suggests *for fuck's sake*.

I think *this attempt at meeting up is going really badly*, and I want to say something to repair the situation, but I can't think what, so I gaze at my empty glass while Wilf examines the multi-coloured drinks bottles behind the bar, the whiskies and brandies and vodkas. Then he turns to me and I see that his eyes are dark blue, with green flecks.

'Shit. I didn't mean to pry. I guess everyone asks about her…'

'Yeah, they do… It does get annoying. Actually she's more than a sister. We're twins, and we're close. We look out for each other.'

'Good. Let's change the subject…'

But I've decided I'll make a superhuman effort to match his attempts to close the gap between us, and I say, 'It's okay. The problem is people always want to know about her career and her love life and what she's like; but for me she's my sister and "what she's like" is private. I don't want to tell any old stranger. In fact, she can seem mean and self-centred at times, but she's not really. She helps with my rent, and she practised my interview technique with me when I applied for the job at Saskatchewan Books, so she does nice things. And she used to buy brownies and bring them to my flat and we would watch old movies… *The Postman Always Rings Twice* and *Fatal Attraction* and *The Silence of the Lambs*. We like classics.'

'You make it sound like you don't do that any more?'

'No… it's different now. She has this rich boyfriend who comes between us and I don't trust him. He has a controlling personality and doesn't like her seeing me, and doesn't like her working. Actually, I'm worried that he's violent…'

'Bloody hell, that sounds ominous.'

'Yeah, it does, doesn't it? Sometimes I think she'll never work again. Sometimes it seems…'

One of the shrieking girls leans over and asks me to pass a menu. The interruption jolts me into thinking that I've gone from being the silent type to splurging and being indiscreet. Luckily, Wilf changes the subject and we start discussing books. I tell him about my favourite Scandinavian crime writers, like Henning Mankell and Camilla Lackberg, and he talks about Jo Nesbo. I learn, also, that he lives in Kensal Rise in a flat-share with two guys called Josh and Frank, and he doesn't see himself as an estate agent forever. He wants to start his own business designing gardens. I splutter into my cider. 'Gardens! If you're so interested in gardens, why aren't you working in a garden centre or something?'

'For a start, the pay's rubbish. And there aren't any garden centres near here anyway. Anyhow, the estate agent suits me for now – I'm on commission, and I'm saving my money.'

'Don't you miss gardens?'

'Oh, I have a couple of projects on the go. I do them on my days off and at weekends. I'm pretty professional about it. I studied landscape gardening at college. How about you?'

'Oh, I didn't go to college. I messed up my A Levels and I worked in a supermarket for a year, or maybe more, and then I got the job in the bookshop while I was figuring out what to do next. Whether to re-sit my exams, or not. But I've been working for Daphne for six years now. Six years! I don't know how that happened.'

After making such an effort, I retreat into profound embarrassment about myself, and my featureless life. I've never had a boyfriend that's lasted more than a few weeks. Boyfriends find me too intense, I think, and I'm sure my lack of a past must be obvious to Wilf, like a bad smell.

'Do you have a dream?' he says, 'Something that you secretly want to do, as a career?'

'No.' I look away at the builder guy, at the noisy girls, and I mumble. 'I mean, sometimes I think I'm better at observing things than doing them. I like watching… You're lucky. You have something you really care about.'

'It's one of the things I like about you,' he says. 'You notice small things that other people miss.'

'I think it would be good for me to notice less and *do* more…'

'There's plenty of time. Most people are doing stuff and giving it no thought at all. You're different, when you decide to start *doing* something, it will be special.'

We both grin and drink our drinks, totally self-conscious but maybe a little more confident.

*

When we leave the pub, I walk beside Wilf and point at trees and plants. 'What's that?'

'London Plane Tree.'

'What's that?'

'Beech hedge.'

'And that?'

'Have a guess.'

'Grass.'

He nudges me, and grins. And when we part we kiss each other on the cheek.

At the shop Daphne says, 'How was your date?' and I tell her I'd appreciate it if she didn't refer to Wilf in that way. But inside I feel surprised. I start thinking about him stomping about in gardens in Wellington boots, sleeves rolled up, dirt in his fingernails. I want Daphne's comments about him to stop, and I hope Wilf asks me to lunch again, but I'm confused – the lunch had been wonderful, but I worry that when he gets back to Willesden Estates he'll remember my lack of social grace, my verbal clumsiness, my vacant life.

At home in the evening, I see I've missed a call from Tilda. She hasn't phoned since our awful meeting at the Albany – or answered my calls for that matter. Feeling suddenly optimistic, I allow myself to imagine that she wants to mend things between us and maybe will suggest the sisterly gathering that I described to Wilf, offering to come to my flat to watch movies, like we used to do.

I listen to her message which is short and unrevealing. 'Tilda here. Don't call me back, I'll phone again.'

Hearing her voice and its severe tone changes my mood, making me worry that I was stupid when talking to Wilf at lunchtime. Tilda always warns me against gossiping because of the way private information ends up on the internet, twisted and exaggerated. It's happened to her several times, rumours that she was anorexic or was in a relationship with some famous actor, and I hope I haven't said anything too revealing. I need to distract myself, so I microwave my supper, a chicken korma and rice, and I sit at my table eating it, looking out at the bindweed in the jungle of a garden (in need of Wilf Baker to sort it out) and thinking that I'll log on to controllingmen.com. But then my mobile rings, and it's Tilda. She sounds whispery, like she doesn't want Felix to hear.

'I thought I'd let you know Felix and I are going away, and I wanted to check that you're okay. You were so bloody paranoid when we met up for lunch. Neurotic and aggressive – it worries me.'

'*I'm* fine. There's no need to worry about *me*. Where are you going?'

'Martinique. Remember, I told you? It looks divine there, all turquoise seas and white beaches.'

I think *and sharks and snakes and mosquitoes*, but I don't say so. Instead, I'm suddenly inspired to tell her that there's a problem with the water supply in our building. We'll be without water while the plumbers are in, I say, and it would be great if I could stay a night at the flat in Curzon Street while she's away.

She comes back quickly, in a harsh voice. 'No, Callie, that's out of the question… Felix has confidential business papers everywhere. Not possible…'

'I've nowhere else to go… I'm desperate.'

There's a pause and I feel dreadful inside because I'm lying. And if Tilda thinks about it, she'll realise that I could always get a bucket of water in, rather than move out. My argument is so obviously flawed that I find myself hanging on the line, waiting for her to tell me that I'm being an idiot. But she surprises me, saying that if I really am desperate and it's an emergency, I can collect a key from the cleaning lady, Eva, and she gives me a phone number.

'This is against my better judgement, Callie. Promise me that if you stay you won't go snooping on Felix and me. I know what you're like… especially in this bat-shit crazy mood you're in. And there must be no sign of you when we return. Nothing! No forgotten bras or knickers. Not even a crumb or a hair. Got it?'

'Got it.'

'But, really, don't come here to the flat. Not unless it's life or death…'

I promise, thinking maybe it *is* life or death. My voice sounds thin and strained, maybe because I'm worried about Tilda going so far away, out of my sphere of influence – I need to check where Martinique actually is. Before she hangs up she says, 'Chip chip,' like Mum used to and after she's gone I try to concentrate on the positives, like the fantastic fact-finding opportunity that has opened up.

12

Online later, all the talk is of Chloey Percival, the girl who was attacked in Debenhams. She's still in a critical condition in York Hospital, and most of the people chatting in the controllingmen forum think she'll die. Some say we should be praying for her. Belle, as usual, is online and discussing the new photos of Chloey that have been posted by her family – of her first day at school, and as a chubby teenage gymnast in a leotard, holding up a silver cup. Belle writes that Chloey was an innocent angel. I tell her to drop the *angel* and remind her that people are hardly going to point out shortcomings at a time like this. Then Belle says, *Let's go to The Zone.*

She has big news. Her friend Lavender will leave her abusive husband in two weeks' time, so the secrecy and planning is intense. Belle and Lavender are busy with practical things – making lists of what to take and what to leave behind. They're discussing the emotional side, too, like how to explain the situation to the children. Belle says that on the big day Lavender will pretend to take them to school, then return home once X has left for work. Belle will arrive with a hired Renault Espace and they'll load it up and drive to Lavender's mother's house five miles away. *X will figure out what's happened and turn up demanding 2 b let in, probably violent,* Belle writes. *So L will call police.* She pauses, then adds:

Back to Chloey – Did u c there will be a CANDLELIT vigil for her in York? Its near me and I might go. Would u like to come? We could ACTUALLY MEET UP!

From nowhere, Scarlet pops up:

No, meeting up NOT a good idea. We shouldn't be seen together. Don't do it.

Scarlet always assumes she's the boss, telling us what we can and can't do. On an impulse, I send an email addressed only to Belle.

Let's meet without telling Scarlet. I don't know why she thinks we should follow her orders – it's starting to irritate me. Also, I'd like to see York, and I could come by train on Friday, because I don't work then. What do you think?

Moments later, she replies, *I think DEFNATELY YES!!! I dont have 2 work Friday either – so I can litrally meet you at the station. AND we can still Keep our identities secret – like Scarlet says.*

*

I feel excited about the trip, but nervous too. I keep thinking about my meeting with Wilf, and how awkward I was. It's typical of me to be bad at socialising – and I'm worried that Belle will find me too difficult to be with.

On Friday, the anxiety returns, and on the train to York I keep going to the toilet to brush my hair and put on make-up. I've bought Fanomenal Lashes mascara and Miracle Touch blusher from Boots and I apply them, then worry that I've put on too much blusher, and smear it off again. I've tried to dress nicely and I'm wearing clean jeans and a new t-shirt, white with a smiley face. I told Belle about the t-shirt, so that she can recognise me at the station, and she said she'd wear a green dress and carry a jute bag with picture of a bee. I look for her through the window as the train draws into York Station.

At first I see nothing but crowds of tourists, and when I do spot a woman in a green dress, standing apart, I have to stare hard because she's nothing like I expected. I thought of Belle as a big flamboyant person because of her larger-than-life messages online, all the exclamation marks and capital letters, and I imagined a made-up round face and blonde frizzy hair, like a huge doll. In reality, she's tiny – her skin is brown and her hair sleek and black, and she looks like she's from somewhere like the Philippines or Indonesia. I walk towards her, cautiously, but then she spots me and holds up her bee bag, and I point at the smiley face on my t-shirt. When we meet, it's embarrassing because we both don't know what gesture to make – she leans forward to kiss my cheek, but she changes her mind and we shake hands instead.

As we walk out of the railway station I notice that Belle has a nervous habit of scratching her hands and arms. Also, she has a little chirrupy voice, as she tells me excitedly that the candlelit vigil had been at the hospital, but has now moved to a small park by York Minster. 'We can go there later,' she says. 'It's so lucky you came today, because Chloey's brother's going to speak. At least, that's what people are saying. Have you heard of The Flicks? They're a York band, and they're going to perform their new song… Oh, it's lovely to have you here! Perfect.'

She gives my arm a squeeze, then adds, 'And you can stay at my flat tonight. I have a spare bedroom, and I don't live far away. It's just a bus ride. Really short.'

I don't commit myself. Instead, I ask Belle about Lavender, and soon we're talking about her and Chloey Percival and Tilda (or Pink, as I continue to call her.)

It turns out that being with Belle isn't difficult at all, and we chat as we walk the streets. Then we stop for lunch at Pizza Express, which is by the river Ouse, and while we eat our dough balls she tells me that Lavender has changed her plans. Instead of escaping to her mother's house with the two children, they're going to Belle's flat in an area called Dringhouses. She's bought inflatable mattresses and bedding from Argos, and treats for the children – a Nerf gun for Alfie and a jewellery-making kit for Saskia. I think about telling Belle that she's gender-stereotyping, and also that she has revealed the children's real names, but I don't. I just nod and ask if she'll be able to cope with having them crowding out her flat. She says, 'It will be *fantastic* having them around, and there'll be masses to do – finding Lavender a new home, consulting lawyers to get a Non-Molestation Order to keep X away, and a Consent Order to get him to pay her maintenance money.'

'What if X shows up at your flat?'

She puts her head to the side, so that her long hair falls from behind her ear. 'Luckily he never sees me and doesn't even know my address, or my phone number, or anything. I'm not sure he even knows my surname. And Lavender will bring her laptop and her phone, so he can't go snooping there.'

'But still. He's violent.'

She leans in, and her little voice goes up a note. 'I know. And he's been making threats, literally about killing Lavender, and he puts his hands round her throat while he screams at her, and makes her choke.'

'Oh god... He'll go crazy.'

Our pizzas arrive, and Belle starts cutting her Margherita up rather intensely. I can tell she's mulling something over. Then she lowers her voice to a hush.

'Actually, Scarlet has been talking to me about that in The Zone. She has some radical ideas for a way to fight back. She's trying to figure out the details... She's asked me to help her, and I am. I want to play my part.'

This is a surprise. I didn't know that Scarlet and Belle

plotted together without including me. I raise my eyebrows, encouraging her to go on. But she retreats.

'Oh, I'm sorry, Callie, I shouldn't really have said that. Scarlet told me to keep everything a secret.'

'Fuck Scarlet!' Belle looks shocked. 'Sorry,' I say. 'It's just that there are so many examples of Scarlet being bossy.'

'It's because she's Prey, she's closer to the danger than us. Of course she has strong feelings.'

'I suppose.'

For a while we eat our pizzas in silence, looking out of the window. Six girls with ponytails row down the river, their oars slicing the water so that they are gliding along at speed and for a moment it seems like, on the other side of the glass, there's nothing wrong in the world. We carry on eating, not able to think of anything to say until Belle asks me about Pink's holiday in Martinique, and my opportunity to get into her flat.

My mouth's full of pizza, but I speak anyway. 'I'm not sure what I'll find. But I'm hoping that something there will unlock things. Make it clear what's going on.'

'You might find notes. Lavender's husband is always leaving her notes giving her instructions. Clean this, buy that. Wash the bed sheets…'

'I'm not sure that's Felix's style.'

'Felix! Callie, you shouldn't…' She blinks unnaturally, and scratches her left hand and her arm.

'Oh crap… It slipped out.'

'Oh well.'

After lunch she shows me around York; we visit several old churches and then the shops, stopping at Marks & Spencer to buy food for a picnic and a bottle of Frascati wine that's on special offer. As the sun goes down, we make our way to the vigil by York Minster. It's busy already, with people sitting in groups on the grass, some of them holding posters with Chloey's face on and the words *End Male Violence* and *Enough is Enough*. Most of the crowd is young and dressed for an indie music festival or an environmental protest. Beside us, an older, scrawny guy with a one-eyed dog and a guitar sits on a crate and sings 'Hey Jude', while a fair-haired girl with dreadlocks and piercings and a bare stomach, drifts about handing out cupcakes. A breeze sends scraps of debris, mainly food wrappings, swirling around the ground, causing a herby fragrance to come and go. I turn to Belle.

'What do they think this is – a party?'

She ignores me and says, 'Look, there's a lovely spot.'

Belle has a fleece blanket in her jute bag. We set it down, then lay out our picnic of prawn cocktail sandwiches with salt and vinegar crisps and apples, and we open the wine and pour it into plastic cups, while the scrawny guy jumps on to the stage and tries to make everyone sing 'We Will Overcome'. But the crowd isn't enthusiastic, apart from the cupcake girl, so he returns to his crate and the dog, which is barking now and straining to be free of its string. Belle has brought magazines to read, and we flip through *Grazia* and *Cosmopolitan*, until, just after seven, a vicar with straggly hair goes to the centre of the stage, with a microphone.

'Friends! Thank you for coming out on this glorious summer evening to express your support and your love for Chloey Percival and the Percival family. Our thoughts and prayers are with them all.'

Two young women in front of us hug each other.

'Let us welcome Chloey's loving brother, Brandon, who has kindly agreed to share some memories of Chloey.'

I whisper to Belle, 'She's not dead yet.'

Everyone claps, and a woman calls out, 'Bless you, Brandon!' We can see that he's a skinny teenager in jeans and trainers and a hoodie. His face is deathly pale, his eyes so tired he can barely open them. Brandon mumbles into the microphone, reading from a scrap of paper.

'My mum and dad and I would like to tell you some things about Chloey. My sister is a normal girl. She likes shopping, going out to clubs, buying make-up. Her favourite song is the Lumineers' Ho Hey song.' Here someone shouts out 'Ho! Hey!' 'She likes Taylor Swift and she doesn't rate Justin Bieber or One Direction.' We laugh politely. 'Her favourite film is *Bridesmaids* and her favourite James Bond is Daniel Craig.'

I feel like whispering 'Predictable'. But I don't because Belle might think I'm disrespectful, which I'm not.

'Chloey is brave. When Travis Scott made threats, she said she wouldn't hide like a scared animal, and she carried on going out with her friends and going to work. But now my sister is fighting for her life. We believe Travis is damaged and dangerous, and we would like to make a plea. Someone somewhere must know where he is. Please, tell the police....'

The vicar puts his arm round Brandon, and the vigil part of the evening begins with helpers handing out candles that we light, one from the next. Then, in a pompous voice, the vicar reads out a bunch of statistics which Belle and I are already familiar with. Two British women a week are murdered by their male partners, he tells us. In America three women and one man are murdered by their partners every single day.

When he's finished, The Flicks run onto the stage, and a guy with black eyeliner starts singing about death and rage, pouting his lips at the microphone in a way that Belle thinks is sexy. I don't like their music though, it's too loud, and I think about going back to London. But Belle says, '*Do* come and stay. I've bought food for breakfast, croissants and strawberry jam and real coffee.' She's so sweet and kind that I say okay, and we shuffle through the crowd and catch the bus to Dringhouses.

At Belle's flat, she shows me the bedroom I can use, which is prepared for Lavender and her children. The bed is made up with a shiny bedspread with sequin edges, and fluffy cushions, and folded up pink towels that look new. On the dressing table, she's placed plastic bottles of Boots rose-scented shampoo, bubble bath, face cream and eau-de-cologne, laid out in a crescent shape, and next to them the presents for Alfie and Saskia, wrapped in yellow paper and tied with ribbon. I tell Belle she's being a brilliant friend, and then we watch the BBC news, learning that, after we left York Minster, Travis Scott was arrested. A local news report shows a small crowd at the police station, yelling abuse. A woman with a baby in a buggy is screaming, 'Hang the filthy bastard!'

'They shouldn't behave like that,' I say. 'It's ugly.'

Belle makes hot chocolate and I'm impressed that she has a box of sprinkles in her cupboard to go on top. Belle says, 'Now I lay me down to sleep, I pray the Lord my soul to keep.'

In the morning she has to leave for work at 6.30, even though it's a Saturday, and she comes to my bedroom to say goodbye. I'm half-asleep, but I roll over to say thank you for everything, and I see her in her nurse's uniform all clean and pressed. 'You're the angel,' I say, and she laughs quietly and leaves me to go back to sleep. Later, I find the croissants and jam on the dining table, nicely set out on plates next to a small vase of tulips and some white cloth napkins. I eat breakfast then let myself out of the flat and catch the bus to the station.

13

I think about the way Belle is caring for Lavender, and it makes me realise that I should be more proactive on behalf of Tilda. So, as soon as I get home, I phone Tilda's cleaning lady.

Eva obviously isn't expecting my call because she keeps saying 'Huh? Huh?' in an irritated voice. It seems that Tilda forgot to tell her that I might need the spare key to the flat, and at first she doesn't believe that we are sisters because she doesn't even know that Tilda *has* a sister, and she wants to text Tilda to make sure. I tell her not to, that Tilda won't want to be disturbed while she's lying on a beach in Martinique. Eventually Eva agrees to meet me at the flat, and I offer to bring a photo of Tilda and me when we were children, to prove who I am. 'Don't bother,' she says grumpily. 'I remember something now about Callie.' (She pronounces my name *Collie*.) So she'd known all along about me and was being difficult. Even so, I copy

Belle and when I arrive I have a bottle of Lilac Bath Soak with me. Eva takes it without saying thank you, dropping it straight into her bag. 'It's not my cleaning day,' she says. Then she gives me the key and leaves me alone.

I haven't seen Tilda's flat since Felix's builders were there, doing their work. 'Nothing drastic,' Felix had said. But the place is transformed, hardly recognisable, and for an instant I'm disorientated, as though I've come to the wrong place. Before the builders, Tilda's main room had been in three distinct parts – kitchen and dining and sitting – all of them different colours, with cobbled-together makeshift furniture, acquired before she became successful. It was messy and cluttered. But now the place is a single minimalist shell in shades of white and pale grey. A nearly-white stone floor instead of painted boards. Two white leather sofas where the old sofa with the mangled springs had been. The squashy comfy chair is gone, along with the pine table and the kitchen units, all replaced by white furniture. I guess that the paint on the walls is called soft baby fawn or bare buff or something else equally anaemic. The brightest presences are the pale yellow blinds and a wan, lemon-coloured orchid.

I stretch out on one of the sofas and put my feet up on a glass coffee table, not minding that my trainers are filthy, and I'm overwhelmed by an urge to disturb the order of the place. A nosebleed would be very welcome, because I'm in a mood to protest; this vapid, sterile flat is all wrong. My sister isn't like this. She's always been a chaotic, messy person. You only have to remember our bedroom when we were young, her clothes in heaps all over the floor, her make-up scattered across the dressing table – clumped mascara going hard on brushes she hadn't bothered to put back in the tube, used tissues left for months on end. It's obvious that this newfound tidiness, all this order, comes from Felix.

I decide to make a cup of tea and look for mugs in the kitchen units, but I find that all you have to do is touch the drawers slightly and they slide out on their own, and then back in again with another tiny tap. I set them all going, in and out like a silent symphony of little white coffins, and I see that inside the drawers the cutlery is perfectly aligned – the forks on their sides all facing the same way, the spoons actually spooning each other. The crockery – all new – is creamy-white bone china and neatly stacked. I register the absurd neatness of everything, but what strikes me as totally, mind-blowingly insane is the fact that the crockery is wrapped in clingfilm, so that whenever you want to use a bowl or a plate, you have to unwrap it. I look in more drawers and find more clingfilm, around cups and glasses and pots and pans. It's obvious that Tilda was making an excuse when she told me not to come here. It was this mad stuff she didn't want me to see. Her clingfilmed life. As I make my tea it occurs to me that Felix might actually know how many tea bags are in the box, and know that I'd been here and taken one. Then again, Eva probably makes herself cups of tea.

My mug in my hand, I head for the bedroom. By now I'm ticking off the changes in my head. New cupboards, new blinds, new bed – king-sized and with a suede head-board the colour of rotted meat. Barely thinking about what I am doing, I start taking Tilda's clothes from the drawers and the wardrobe, piling them up on the bed, a strange mix of things – t-shirts in flimsy cotton, the same washed-out colours as the flat, jeans with nonsensi-cal brand names: *Paradise in the Park, XXOX, Lost and Found.* And long, sparkly dresses that I suppose she wears to movie premieres and awards ceremonies – not that she's been to any recently. I run my fingers over them, feeling the softness and lightness of the silk, the hard edge of tiny sequins, and then I take off my t-shirt and jeans and pull on a pale-gold, gossamer-thin dress with a network of thin straps that criss-cross down the back. It isn't easy to pull the dress down because I'm two sizes bigger than my emaciated sister, and when I do force it into place there's no question of being able to do up the zip – the dress just gapes open at the side. I pose in front of the mirror, looking preposterous: a lump of chicken tied up with tinsel. Also, I can hardly breathe. But I keep the dress on while I inspect the next cupboard, the one containing Felix's clothes.

Piles of white boxes, with shirts in. Twenty-five, in fact, all numbered – eight in blue ink, for blue shirts, eight in black ink, for white shirts, and four in red ink for shirts that are the palest pink. The remaining five boxes, numbers 21–25 (more black ink), are empty – so I suppose he's taken those shirts to Martinique. I imagine Felix checking that the boxes are perfectly aligned, and that the shirts are immaculately pressed and folded, and by now I'm finding the urge to ruffle things up unbearable.

Then I see, on the window ledge, a dead bluebottle on its back, its crunchy little legs in the air. Carefully, I pick it up and place it inside the collar of a pink shirt. Then I open a small white drawer, a tiny thing, and see a watch inside, and some cufflinks. I pick them out to inspect them, and find that they are all exquisite little pieces of jewellery, one silver set shaped like a star fish, another gold set like a four-leaf clover. I pick up a clover piece and turn it over and over in the palm of my hand, thinking about lucky Felix with all his perfect things. I pop the clover into my mouth, suck on it, then return it to its box.

I sit on the bed, amongst Tilda's clothes, and remember how I used to eat her things, and I become nostalgic for all the Tilda-sustenance that would lie around, the hair in her hairbrush, the paper from her diary, her teeth. There's nothing like that here. But, just in case, I get down on my knees to see if she's tried an old trick, and hidden something by attaching it to the underside of the bed. I crawl under, and feel around the empty space, and I'm crouched down like that when there's a knock on the front door – or rather, three loud knocks.

I pull myself up and survey the mess – clothes thrown on the bed and floor, drawers and cupboards open everywhere. I start to tidy up, but there's no time, so I sit on the edge of the bed, willing the intruder to go away. More loud, angry knocks. I stay perfectly still, until I hear the sound of a key in the lock, the door opening and footsteps on the stone floor, pacing about. I dash to the en-suite bathroom, grab a white bath towel, wrapping it round me, over the gold dress, then I run to the bedroom door and open it a tiny amount, so I can see out. Eva's standing there, hands on her hips.

'Hi,' I stick my head through the gap. 'What do you want?'

She looks at me with a distrustful expression. 'What you doing?'

'I was about to have a bath. What are you doing?'

'I come to tell you to bring key back to me when you leave.'

'But you don't need it. You've got another key. You just used it.'

'It's my responsibility. You must return it.' She's in the mood for a fight.

'Okay. Write your address down, and leave it on the table.'

I slam the bedroom door shut, and lean against it for a few seconds, listening to the sounds she's making, walking around; then I hear her leave. I come out, the towel still wrapped round me, and inspect the flat. I want to see the full extent of what Eva has seen, and realise that I left half the drawers in the kitchen wide open, bowls and plates out of their clingfilm, and my dirty trainers on the coffee table. It's messy, but not as bad as the chaos in the bedroom.

I return to the bathroom, to replace the towel and check the cabinet. Tilda always seems so spacey and I wonder about drugs. I even consider heroin and crack cocaine – not that I expect them to be on a shelf, neatly displayed and labelled. I find prescription medicines, though, that hadn't been there back in the spring, and I gather up bottles and packets and take them into the sitting room, where I left my plastic bag with a notebook inside, and my cup of tea. I write in the book: *Drugs that may be contributing to Tilda's decline* – and add Anafranil, Zolpidem and Ativan, thinking that I'll look them up when I go home.

Out of the corner of my eye I register a red light flashing on the phone, and I press the button to listen to the messages. Only three. The first is disappointing – just a reminder from the dry cleaners that the cleaning's ready, and would Tilda please pick it up at her earliest convenience. The second is a short, 'Hey Felix, it's Guy. Call me.' I have no idea who Guy is. But the third message is interesting – Tilda's agent, Felicity Shore, in a pleading voice asking Tilda to get in touch, 'Come to lunch or something, and let's go through your options.' It sounds like she's concerned. In the notebook I write: *Does Felicity Shore realise something is wrong? Have further information?*

I finish my tea, and put the mug in the sink. Then I remember how Tilda used to hide her diary in a pillowcase, and have the idea of looking through the linen cupboard in the bathroom. Like everything else, it's pristine – satiny cotton sheets folded in perfect piles. I take out the pillowcases and pat them one by one, checking, and when I reach the bottom of the pile I notice a lump in a corner. I reach in, and turn over in the palm of my hand something hard and smooth, like a small ingot, but lighter than solid metal. I pull it out, and find I have a shiny red computer memory stick.

I'm cross because I haven't brought my laptop to the flat, and I'm now in a rush to get out of there and home. Even unzipped, Tilda's dress is a nightmare to get off because it's so tight, and as I work it up my body and struggle to pull it over my head, I rip it along a seam. Taking a chance, I put it back on its hanger in the cupboard. Probably, she hardly ever wears it and won't notice for ages. Then I leave, ignoring the chaos, the crockery out of its clingfilm, dirty marks on the coffee table, clothes everywhere.

After Tilda's flat, mine seems like a disorganised jumble. Shaggy red rug, green walls, a thousand little things not put away – pens, notebooks, t-shirts and underwear, Cheerios box, cider bottles, and a sink full of dishes. It actually seems urgent to de-clutter the place, and I stop to pick up a dozen dirty socks from the bedroom floor before sitting at my table by the window and booting up my laptop. It takes an age to splutter into life, and as soon as it does I ram in the memory stick – only to see that I'm barred from entry. It needs a password. I try possible words and combinations, Felix, for instance, and Curzon and Callie and Faith, our mother's name. I even try Liam and Liam Brookes. But nothing works. Out loud I yell, 'Shit!' and it comes into my head to go back to Curzon Street to trash the place. The thought is overpowering and loud, like bird wings thumping on glass. It feels like a way of releasing Tilda, setting her free.

2006

14

Our family moves to Harcourt Road, a treeless street of Edwardian houses packed into long terraces, curving north towards the river. We agree that the new house is friendly – the vibes are good. Also, we like being closer to the Thames. At weekends Mum likes to say, 'Come on, let's have a blast of brown air,' and we walk along the old iron pier. My memories are of a penetrating damp wind, a river invariably choppy and grey, and hugging Mum's arm tightly, never letting go, because sometimes it seems she might actually blow away. I suppose this is because of her health – she's been diagnosed with breast cancer and has had chemotherapy. She tells us not to worry, that she'll be fine, but that doesn't stop her cancer becoming a pervasive heaviness in our lives. I imagine it with a voice, saying, *I am the nearly-death, I am the forerunner of death,* and I tell it to shut up.

Mostly it's just the two of us on these weekend walks,

because Tilda's busy with different interests like her new ambition for a singing career. She has set up a girl-band with the awful name The Whisper Sisters, and they practise in her bedroom, the move to Harcourt Road being all about our desire for separate rooms which, as happens with teenage girls, have become showcases for our personalities. It's as if the contents of our brains have been flushed out and plastered all over the walls and the furniture. Tilda's room is a gargantuan mess of piled-up clothes, make-up, music paraphernalia, posters and fashion magazines. She doesn't care if Tampax boxes are lying around, tampons spilling out, or if hairbrushes are evolving into puffballs of old hair. My room isn't exactly tidy but it has a solemn, organisational look to it, with my crime books lined up on a wooden shelf, and my note-books stacked on my desk. I regard it as a haven, whilst Tilda's bedroom is a centre of activity, somewhere to visit.

One Saturday morning I go there to while away the time until lunch, lying on her unmade bed reading an Agatha Christie, and Tilda is at her dressing table plucking her eyebrows. I look up to watch and she notices me in the reflection in the mirror, flinching as she says, 'Come here, and let's do something about you.'

'What d'you mean?'

She stands up and poses like a beauty queen. 'Let me be your stylist.'

'I don't want to be styled.'

'Come on. Sit on my chair.'

So I sigh, suggesting this is all very tedious, and put down my book, splayed open so I won't lose my page.

She stands behind me, legs apart, feet turned out like a dancer, and pulls my hair back from my face. Generally, I have a long fringe, and it's a shock to see an expanse of white forehead, sprinkled with acne craters. My exposed eyes are little black pebbles, and my eyebrows look thick and unruly.

'Erhh…!' I try to push the hair back down.

'No, let me have a go… trust me.' I capitulate, allowing her to set about my eyebrows with tweezers and cover up my spots with a concealer stick. She holds me by the chin, coming at me with blusher and eye liner and eyelash curlers, then stepping back to admire her work. There's quickness and lightness to her movements, but an intensity of purpose too. As she picks out a lipstick from the piles scattered over the dressing table, it seems she's taking an important decision, like a surgeon choosing the perfect scalpel. She dabs my lips with a tissue, adds another coat, and tells me to look in the mirror.

Usually I don't like my face because it's too big and kind of flat, like the man in the moon. But Tilda's attempt at a makeover has made it worse; now I have a child's garish drawing of a face. Arching black brows, black lines round my eyes, peachy patches on my cheeks. I mull over the possibility that she's been intentionally unkind. I check her face for clues – and see that she's suppressing giggles.

'You bitch!'

'What? You look a lot prettier. Honest.'

Still, I'm suspicious. She squeezes in beside me on the chair, gazes at her own face with distant, dreamy eyes and starts to sing one of her own compositions. *The girl in the mirror, so sad and so small, she knows who will kill her, she knows them all…* The words are nonsense, but the tune is sad and she sings in a wistful fashion, swishing her hair around. I interrupt.

'Do you think you're a special person?'

She stops in her tracks, as if she's been struck.

'What do you think?'

'Yes, you are.'

I say this because I do honestly believe that my sister is different. People are drawn to her because she's so pretty and committed to her talents, and she has that charming way of switching in an instant from dreamlike and ethereal to serious and focussed. But I realise that she cares too much about being special, and that the concept of ordinary is repugnant to her. Worse than that – if she thought she was ordinary, she'd self-harm, or take her own life. That's what I believe, anyhow, and that's what I intend to write in the dossier.

*

After lunch, Tilda disappears and I take my bike from the shed and cycle to the river, with my book in my rucksack.

As an experiment, I keep my hair pinned back and my make-up on. The journey's quick, about five minutes, and I find a bench and sit down. In front of me, the river is vast and grimy-grey and a dirty plastic tub of a boat is bobbing about on a slimy rope.

I pull up the hood of my jacket and read my Agatha Christie. In no time, I'm immersed and only vaguely aware of the shrieks and shouts coming from the bus stop at the pier, inane high-pitched comments blunted by the wind. *'That's insane...'* *'What?'* *'Fuck off fuckface...'* But a loud, *'Stop it, Robbie, you're hurting me!'* makes me look over. A group of teenagers is messing about on the bus-stop bench. I don't recognise the boys, but the girls are Tilda and Paige Mooney, her favourite Whisper Sister and loyal handmaiden. Paige is like Tilda reflected in a distorting glass, same pale features, same long blonde hair, but she's overweight – Tilda says morbidly obese – and there's an element of desperation about her. She endlessly tries to impress Tilda, who flips, soaking up the adoration one minute and brushing it off the next. They are kissing and touching with the boys, and I'm curious. I haven't seen Tilda so blatantly *in action* before. Then Paige runs away, hand in hand with her boyfriend, to hide behind the fish and chip shop, leaving Tilda writhing about with the other boy on the bench. I go over, wheeling my bike.

As I come close I say, 'Hello,' and she extricates herself with a look that makes it clear that I'm not welcome.

The boy's staring at me with an open face, curious and interested, and I know immediately that it's Liam Brookes, even though I haven't seen him in five years. His hair is darker, almost black now, but it still stands up away from his head and has the same woolly look. His face has elongated, and his body has changed – he has broad shoulders and is tall. 'Have you met my sister?' Tilda says.

'Hi, Callie,' says Liam.

'Her face isn't usually like that. A bit of a make-up malfunction before lunch.'

I ram the bench with my bike. Not dramatically, just enough for Tilda to know I'm angry with her. 'You said I looked pretty,' I hiss.

'You do, definitely. I just didn't have time to make it as perfect as I wanted.'

'What are you reading?' Liam is looking at the book sticking out of my pocket, then expectantly at my face, and I can tell he wants to reconnect with me.

'Oh, she's always reading murder stories,' Tilda snaps. 'Bye, Callie, we're leaving.'

'Where are you going?'

'To Liam's. His mum will be out this afternoon.'

I want to say, 'What? – I've seen you on that bench, in public, groping and snogging – what the hell will you do in private?' A futile question – I know the answer, and I suppress the urge to picture it in graphic detail. I ask Liam, 'Do you still live on the Nelson Mandela estate?'

He says he does, and I raise my plucked eyebrows at Tilda, because she's always disparaging about the estate, but she ignores me, stands up, grabs Liam's hands, pulls him upright and off they go. He has his arm wrapped round her, and she snuggles her shoulders into him, trip-tripping at his side, her skirt blowing against her legs. The air fills with swirling rain, and I cycle back to Harcourt Road, bringing the news that Liam is Tilda's boyfriend now.

Mum has lit a fire in the sitting room, and she's sitting in the comfy chair beside it, marking art work. I notice anew how small and fragile she is, swamped by the chair and its cushions. The chemo seemed to shrink her, and it made her hair fall out. It's now growing back in soft nut-brown curls, like a poodle coat, but you can see the contours of her skull and in a couple of places are little round bare patches, the size of a five pence piece. She makes her face cheer up at the sight of me, saying, 'You look damp and cold, darling. Would you like a cup of tea and toast and Marmite?' And soon we're drinking our tea by the fire, in a fug of smoky, charcoaly warmth, and I tell her about Tilda and Liam. She says, 'Doesn't he go to a different school now?'

'Yes, St Christopher's. I don't know how she found him again...'

'I think *you* rather liked Liam, didn't you? When he and Tilda used to practise for *Peter Pan*?'

I feel my face go red. 'Not really.'

I feel like adding that he's too nice for Tilda, because mostly she prefers the sort of boys who are trouble – disruptive in class and disobedient. Mum doesn't press me, but fetches the playing cards for gin rummy and we play for half an hour. Then I watch my favourite DVD – *Little Women* with Winona Ryder as Jo, while Mum makes supper.

*

A few days later, Tilda comes in from school, drenched by the rain. She's late, and flushed pink, and she thumps her rucksack on the kitchen table, wriggling out of her wet coat, saying, 'Paige is off school. Guess why?'

'Food poisoning?' I'm feigning boredom. Mum stirs something on the hob with a wooden spoon, making the kitchen smell of meat and gravy. She looks up. 'Paige Mooney?'

'Yeah. She's the only Paige. Anyhow – she's pregnant, thirteen weeks!'

Tilda looks at us with wide eyes. She's expecting a shocked 'Oh no!!!!' and 'What an idiot!' or a sorrowful 'Poor Paige.' But a sickly silence falls on the room. Mum wipes her hands on a tea towel. 'How do you know about this?'

'Everyone's talking about it... Her brother told his friends, and now it's all around the school.'

Nobody told me – but I'm not representative.

'It must be traumatic,' says Mum seriously. 'She's your friend, so be supportive and don't gossip.'

'I won't.' Tilda grabs some biscuits and pours herself a glass of milk, then goes upstairs. Mum follows her, telling me to guard the stew, and I assume she's going to ask Tilda about Liam, check that she's being careful. I wish I could listen to their conversation – I'm dying to know if my sister has a full-blown, proper sex life. I've read articles in teen magazines about sex being fun, about discovery and 'exploring your bodies', but it's obvious to me that these are half-truths; that there's a devastating emotional side.

Mum returns to the kitchen, briskly taking the wooden spoon from me, and I ask her outright whether Tilda is having sex. 'That's her business,' she says, with a loving smile so I won't be upset. I stare into the stew, thinking that Mum and Tilda now have some shared secret knowledge that excludes me and I sense that from now on my sister will drift further away from me, like she's sailing to the far side of an ocean while I'm stuck on land.

*

The next day the Whisper Sisters, minus Paige, are rehearsing in Tilda's bedroom and, for some reason, or maybe it's an oversight, she lets me sit on the floor in a corner and watch. The three of them sit on the bed, talking in a loud hush because of the seriousness of the subject – Paige's pregnancy.

'My god,' says Tilda, 'her life will be ruined – everyone will think she's a slag and brainless with it. Liam thinks she did it on purpose.'

She stands up on the bed and starts humming one of the Whisper Sister songs and doing the dance moves, shoving her hips out at angles and making the other girls bounce up and down. Then she flops down again, and in a confiding voice says, 'The thing about Paige is she has low self-esteem. You must have noticed. I think getting pregnant will make her feel important. But she doesn't realise how bad it all is... She's an attention-seeker and I think maybe she actually wants to keep the baby, like it would make her *someone*. But she'll never achieve anything, and she won't get famous. She won't even become a singer – which is a shame because she has a nice voice.'

She's high on the drama of the situation and her own role as best friend of the doomed protagonist, acting like she's steering Paige towards a tragic destiny – she *would* have the baby and then fall into an abyss of obscurity. By contrast, Tilda's own destiny is to involve fame, glamour and the recognition which is her right. I make a mental note, for later, when I'll write up my observations.

Eventually, Kimberley and Sasha go home, and I return to Tilda's bedroom. She's lying on the bed, texting, and she looks up. 'Stop lurking by the door and come in.' Then, 'Are you worried about Paige's baby?'

'I suppose.'

'Don't be. I know her, she won't have an abortion. She wants to be a mother. It's her calling.'

'What's *my* calling?'

'Come here.' She pats the pillow on the bed, and we lie side by side. 'Your calling is to be a nice person, looking out for other people, and protecting things.'

It sounds boring.

'There has to be more to me than that.'

'There's nothing more serious than your calling!' She looks at me crossly. 'You love where others don't. That's what the sheep skull day was about. And don't worry. I see your future as happy. You'll be a mother. You'll live in an old country house with a family that loves you. There'll be log fires and dogs, and fields of sheep all around, and I'll come and visit even when I'm famous.'

In my mind I start to cast Liam Brookes in the country-house husband role, but Tilda puts an end to that by saying, 'You know why I can't see Liam on Saturday? It's because he goes to the library to study. I think it's because he doesn't have a father, and he wants to look after his mother in the future. He says he'll be a doctor. Imagine! Liam, a doctor.'

'What about your calling? Will you be a doctor's wife?'

'Hmm. Maybe. I imagine Liam working for Medecins sans Frontieres. It's a French organisation he talks about that works in battle zones in Africa and places. I'll go with him, and write songs.'

'Wouldn't you be frightened in a battle zone?'

'I'd be concentrating on my songs. And I think the calling part makes the fear go away.'

'Really?'

Then she starts telling me about meeting Liam again, at a party three months ago. 'I hadn't seen him since we were at primary school,' she says. 'We fell out then, do you remember?'

'I never really knew what was going on with you two. I remember you had a row or something when you were rehearsing for *Peter Pan*. And you wouldn't come out of our bedroom, and then you did that maniac thing, hitting your head on the wall.' I lie on my side now, facing her, with my arm across her belly.

'I annoyed him by saying I was pleased I didn't live on the Nelson Mandela estate. Then we had an argument about whether the estate was scuzzy and dangerous. It made him hate me for being stuck-up and judgmental.'

'But you made up after that? After the concert.'

'Only for a while. Those things I said did too much damage.'

Then she kisses the top of my head and sings a song that goes: '*I'm in love, so in love with him…*'

I can't believe she's been seeing Liam for three whole months without telling me, and I realise that half her outings to rehearse with the Whisper Sisters were actually romantic assignations. I feel the old urge to eat something of hers – but I try to suppress it. Instead, when she gets up to go to the bathroom, I pull down her purple duvet and get right inside her bed, burying my face in her pillow. I breathe in her smell, which is thick and heady, and as I sit up again I notice one long blonde hair lying on the pillow, but I manage not to eat it and instead just take it to my room and tuck it inside my pillowcase. Then I write up my notes.

*

On Saturday I take my bike and go to the library. I find a seat by the window, spread my books out on the table and start reading, trying to ignore a mad-haired old lady in the chair opposite, snoring under a heap of dirty brown clothes. There's a stale dustbin smell coming from her too, which explains the empty chairs nearby. I open the window, and settle back into my reading.

Half an hour later Liam arrives, but he doesn't see me, walking right past my table, dangling his jacket over a shoulder and carrying a rucksack jammed with books. While he's walking he whispers into the ear of a girl, who also holds her coat over her shoulder – I note her bobbed dark hair and her straight back. She's tall, far taller than Tilda or me, so that her head and Liam's are side by side, tilting symmetrically into each other. She wears a short tartan skirt with black opaque tights and flat black ballerinas, and seems more elegant than Tilda and her friends. But I see Liam and the girl only for a moment, because they disappear to a table beyond a bookcase, not in my line of sight.

I stand up and pretend to be browsing the book shelves behind the bag lady, listening carefully, trying to hear Liam and the girl on the other side. But the only sounds are the scratching of chairs, and pages turning and books being moved about. So I peek round the edge of the stack, and see the two of them sitting together, their backs to me. I watch, and notice the girl's left hand, which is decorated with a henna tattoo of spiky flowers snaking from the end of her middle finger up her arm – she's pulled the sleeves of her sweater up to her elbows to display it. Her nails match the henna, being varnished a dark red that's almost black, and she seems mysterious to me. I do nothing for a while, just watch her and Liam reading their books, observing that they seem extremely aware of each other – they are so unnaturally still. Then the girl writes something on a piece of paper, and slides it across for Liam to read, he smiles and writes something and passes it back, then she briefly lays her head on his shoulder.

I pick a book at random from the shelf and take it to the seat opposite Liam, on the other side of the table. The book's called *Kitchen Cupboards: A Do-it-Yourself Guide*, and chapter one is *Designing your Cupboard*. I've hardly started reading when Liam says in a loud whisper, 'Hello, Callie. What are you doing here?' I don't answer.

'This is my friend Mary. We're revising together.'

'Hi.' Mary treats me to a vague, haughty expression. Like a camel.

'Callie is Tilda's sister.'

Mary nods, as if to say *Oh really…*

'Do you go to Liam's school?'

'Yes. We're in the same class.' Her tone is flat and dismissive, and she goes back to her *Madame Bovary*, making it plain that I'm of no interest. I shut my *Cupboards* book and stand up.

'That was quick,' says Liam.

'See you around.'

Cycling home seems to take forever. I'm practically on fire with excitement at being the bearer of bad news, breathless with the urgency of my mission. I drop my bike at the front door, and as I come in, I can hear singing upstairs, '*Tormented, lamented…demented on a Sunday.*' I thump up the stairs, and make an entrance into her bedroom. The Whisper Sisters (minus Paige) stop singing, and I say, 'Do you know Mary someone, who knows Liam?'

'Mary Strickland?'

'Tall, shortish dark hair, talks slowly, bit stuck-up?'

'Yeah, that's Mary Strickland,' says Sasha, looking at Tilda.

'What about her?' Tilda speaks in a strained voice, and runs her hands through her hair, to mush it up.

'She's in the library with Liam, and I saw them whispering to each other and passing notes…'

'So what?' says Sasha. 'They're friends, that's all. Are you trying to make trouble, Callie?'

'Go home! Both of you.' Tilda looks like she's about to hyperventilate. 'I mean it, go…! I need to think. And don't gossip. Really. Liam told me Mary was going to the library with him…'

Kimberley and Sasha skulk out, and Tilda sits on the bed, her head in her hands.

'Did he really tell you?'

She glares at me, her eyes ice-hard. 'Of course not. Tell me what you saw. Every little thing.'

I tell her about the head-thing, when she had leaned on his shoulder, and Tilda says Mary's a bitch and Liam's naive.

'Why didn't *you* go to the library with him?'

'He said he wanted to concentrate! He's so focussed on getting A-stars in his exams, that's all that matters to him. She must have tagged along, practically followed him there… Her father is a lawyer, like a judge or something, and she thinks that makes her a superior person. She's so up herself… She thinks she can just force herself on him when he wants to *concentrate*!'

'What are you going to do?'

She manages a small acid smile. 'I'm going to Liam's this evening and I'm going to be so nice to him, and not let him know at all what I think about Mary Strickland. Never complain, never explain… It's the best policy.'

I agree. I can't see how having a row with Liam would

improve anything, and later that day I watch Tilda get ready, removing all her make-up and starting again, changing her clothes several times, doing her hair with tongs and applying scent. I wish her luck, and she sets off.

15

I sit by my window for three hours or more, trying differ-ent passwords to unlock the memory stick, taking breaks to make tea, stretching my legs by walking around the sitting room. I try everything. I even type in Hook, and TildaandLiam and LiamandTilda and WhisperSisters and a thousand other possibilities, although it all feels rather straw-clutching and feeble and I want to give up, to go online to chat to Scarlet and Belle. Then, without thinking about it, I tap TheLovedOnes and, feeling weak and light-headed, I watch as the screen changes from a forbidding black to a welcoming, beautiful glowy orange. I'm reminded of those films of flower petals opening miraculously in the sunshine, and I think – of course! Of course she uses The Loved Ones, it makes perfect sense.

But then, a wave of disappointment, because there's only one file on the screen – a Word document with the dull name Script Notes. Not what I expected. But when

I click, I see immediately that the information inside has nothing to do with scripts; instead I'm looking at a letter, addressed to me:

Dear Callie,

God knows what's happened if you're reading this, because these are my secrets little one, and you will share them only if something fucking horrendous has happened. I should be more blunt – you're reading this because I'm dead and because I want you to know, at last, what happened between Felix and me.

Before I get stuck in, here are a few things you need to know about Felix – so pay attention!

I am intoxicated by him.

I am addicted to him.

He makes me feel *healed*. No longer wounded inside.

In short, Callie, he's the love of my life – and that's why I resisted your constant prying and snooping, why I refused to speak about him despite your whiny questions – *are you sure he's good for you Tilda? Will you let me help you Tilda?* I knew what you were up to, it was so bloody obvious. You were jealous of Felix and out to tear us apart, to destroy my relationship – did you ever admit it to yourself?

But you couldn't succeed because I adore him. I love that I can't boss him around like I'm the Queen of Sheba. So many of my exes have been obedient sycophants. I say sit, they sit. I say fetch, they fetch. But, from the start, Felix was different. He set the rules and I went along with them – he told me to wear my Oscar de la Renta dress, I wore it, he said he didn't like my scent, I chucked it in the bin. You couldn't stand that behaviour could you? It made you feel powerless and excluded. Then, darling sister, exclusion turned you paranoid and fuelled the controllingmen obsession that screwed up your mind.

I can see you there now, in your bedroom, reading this, and screaming *But I was right! You're dead Tilda!* Well, it's a whole lot more complicated than that, in ways beyond your imagination. It's hard to explain to you, because we are such different people, but let me try.

Think about this – you've spent your whole life trying to figure out how you belong. You want to put roots down deep into the earth, like a tree does, seeking water and nutrients – sustenance. I'm the opposite, I want to fly like a bird, escape, and move on. I feel exhilarated when something is new and dangerous. I love risk. See where I'm going with this? That's what Felix gives me – endless risk. With other men I have a sense of their limits, but not with him – what goes on behind those grey eyes is unknowable. I'd find myself just gazing at him, wondering whether he'll be my destroyer, or my saviour. At the minute, I'm believing that he's most likely my saviour. But – in case I'm wrong – I'm setting down in writing how my death came about. What you do with the information is up to you.

The first time he became violent was just a month or so after I met him. That night we were at a screening of *Rebecca* in a little private cinema in Soho, and as the film began I was practically orgasmic with fear – it was so important to me that he liked my performance, and I already knew that his standards were fucking high. He gripped my hand tightly throughout the film and every few scenes, he told me that I was gorgeous or sexy or beautiful… At first I was grateful and turned on, but after a while I noticed that his compliments were all about my appearance, not about my skill. So I fished for something deeper, asking, 'Did you like the beach scene?' or 'Do you think that final confrontation with Max worked? Did it have emotional integrity?' He'd do something affectionate like pull my hair away from my face or pretend-bite my fingers and come up with platitudes like, 'The camera adores you,' or 'That scene was yours.' Never anything specific about the hard graft of acting, and I sensed a cold undertone to his words.

Then, as the lights came up, a couple of young beardy hipsters came over to me and started telling me how wonderful my performance had been and this strange thing happened – Felix appeared to be enjoying the situation, saying 'Yes, she's amazing… I'm so proud of her.' But I could tell that, beneath the surface, he was angry. It was something about the tension in his body, and the way he was on auto-pilot with his oh-so-perfectly charming manner.

When we got back to my flat, he was moody, refusing to say what was wrong. Then he grabbed me and without speaking pushed me onto the bed and fucked me, forcing me into impossible excruciating positions, gripping my arms so hard that the pain was almost unbearable. Afterwards he fell asleep straight away while I lay awake stunned, trying to work out what had happened. I suppose that in a way I felt violated, but I also felt ecstatic, truly alive. And don't tell yourself it was rape, Callie, because it wasn't. I did not say 'no'. I did not try to push him away. I made my consent obvious. The fact was that I felt closer to Felix than ever because of the realisation that, like me, he's compelled to experience the extremes in life. In the days afterwards, I would look at the bruises he had made on my arms and cherish them, like they were emblems of our passion, badges of honour. I was sad when, after a few days, they went away.

About three weeks later Felix and I were having dinner at the Caprice, and one of his work colleagues happened to be dining there, an older guy called Julio who came over and asked to be introduced to me. I liked him straight away – he had this big crinkled face. Thick white hair. And he was tanned, like he spent half his life sitting on a terrace in Barcelona sipping fine wines. I laughed at his stories. Some of them were at Felix's expense, though in a very benign way. In a fabulous, almost camp, Spanish accent he called Felix's work desk 'his Bauhaus residence' and said he viewed 'good taste as a moral imperative'. Felix chuckled and I laughed too. When we parted, he man-thumped Julio on the arm in the friendliest way. But underneath he was seething, and when we were back at

Clerkenwell he was white with anger, stomping around, furious about Julio's jokes. It was 'that prick – pathetic has-been – he won't last long at the firm'. Then he began to attack me. How dare I flirt with Julio? Couldn't I see that I was an embarrassment to myself? I protested – 'I was *being friendly*.' I told him he was ridiculous, and I started to walk away. But Felix grabbed a glass vase, a heavy purple thing, and hurled it at me. Or perhaps he was aiming beside my head to give me a fright. Anyhow, it missed me and crashed into a mirror, which shattered, and the vase was all over the floor of his kitchen, a thousand tiny fragments.

He acted like nothing much had happened, ordering me out of the room 'while I clean up this mess'. His voice was aloof and weary; he seemed disgusted at me but – this is strange – as I went into the sitting room I was thinking that I *was* at fault, that I must have behaved badly with Julio, and I felt pleased that Felix cared so much. I liked the idea that his feelings for me were so strong that they'd forced him to lose control and smash something. The damage wasn't terrible, only a shattered mirror and a broken vase. I went back into the room, took him by his shaking hand and led him to the bed. He grabbed my arms, bruised me, hit me, fucked me. But I didn't think less of him, Callie – I loved him more.

So, this is the truth. He is dangerous, but I collude in and encourage that danger. He has never harmed me against my will. And in so many ways he is good for me.

He helps me go through the countless TV scripts that come my way. Most of the parts are lame, stale old clichés – sexy forensic pathologist, love interest for some ancient actor trying to resurrect his flagging career. I'm practically screaming, I'm desperate for something original. And Felix helps me sift through the dross. He's a genius with comments in the margins, the general theme being 'You can do better than this, Tilda'. He's right. I *should* wait until something outstanding or challenging comes along, something worth investing in. I had hoped to play Rachel in *My Cousin Rachel*, but Felix thought the script was mediocre.

He's generous too. Always buying me beautiful clothes and jewellery and he offered to pay for the therapy that you need. We discussed your pathologically suspicious mind and your obsession with us, and I told him how you used to be with Liam and me. How you used to sit on your bike outside Liam's house when I was in there, monitoring the bedroom window. Liam called you *our little stalker* – did you know that? I felt terrible back then because I knew you were unhappy and I couldn't help. And it's the same now, as I write this. I see you as pathetic, so lacking in a life of your own that you need to fixate on mine – and I want to help you, Callie. I really do.

16

Her letter leaves me breathless. I pace the flat, weak legs and spinning head; then I go into the kitchen searching for alcohol, wanting to get drunk. I had had no idea of Tilda's disdain for me, no suspicion that she saw me as a pitiful parasite, dependent on and captivated by her wonderfulness. Nor did I realise that she thinks of me as broken, and feels guilty because she can't fix me, that she pities me. I find a bottle of red wine at the back of a cupboard and, hand shaking, I unscrew the top, pouring it into a large tumbler, drinking it down, wishing that she were in my room right now, beside me, so that I could argue. I'd tell her she's wrong, that she has everything back-to-front. I'd say, 'You're the damaged one! Look at yourself, you need the spotlight so much, you're nothing without the adoration of others. And your behaviour with Felix isn't normal. You're sick – remember your past!'

I'd remind her of Liam and that day long ago when she

went off to the Nelson Mandela estate determined not to be angry about Mary Strickland. She left our house, all attitude, wearing her pink skinny jeans, saying, 'It's bloody nothing, I'm sure of it… they're just friends,' while I stayed behind in her bedroom, slipping under the purple duvet, feeling like I was under her skin. I was so comfortable that I fell asleep there, and when I woke it was to the phone ringing and Tilda snivelling down the line, 'Tell Mum to come and get me, *now*, I can't walk.' I waited while Mum took the car the three-minute journey to Liam's house and, anticipating trouble, I went downstairs to make hot chocolate for the three of us.

When they returned, Mum ushered her straight up the stairs, arm protectively around her shoulders, while Tilda seemed unable to hold herself straight. Once in bed, she curled up, clutching her stomach, black mascara-filled tears sticking to her cheeks. She couldn't even look at the hot chocolate, and it went cold on the bedside table.

This was the beginning of Tilda's breakdown. After that day, we became accustomed to hearing raw, hacking coughs emanating from the bathroom as she made herself vomit after meals; and in the following months she started cutting her arms, short untidy slashes made with Mum's kitchen knives or bathroom razors. At school she was the centre of attention, her friends huddling around while she displayed her wounds and they tried to console her with condemnation of that devious bitch Mary Strickland and the fuckwit Liam Brookes, reminding her of how beautiful she was, and how she'll soon find another boyfriend. But Tilda remained unconsoled and, in fact, deteriorated further, until her friends become bored by her self-pity, and dared to suggest that she was overreacting. Mum said that every teenager goes through it – being rejected – and that you just have to carry on and make the best of things. She even used the phrase 'plenty more fish in the sea', but I found the intensity of Tilda's feelings understandable. She had loved Liam and thought he would be part of her life forever.

Gradually, she became unable to manage the simplest tasks. She lost the ability to write, other than in big jerky infantile script, and she could no longer do maths; she could barely write out numbers, let alone compute them. Mum, Tilda and I dutifully attended 'family counselling' with an expert called Gary Moyse, who wore corduroy and occupied a squashy armchair which smelt of cigarettes. Tilda generally sat silently, and when she did manage to say something, it came out in a fierce whisper. 'It's no good, all this, you can't cure me.'

And Gary Moyse said, 'That's what we call black-and-white thinking, Tilda. Let's see if we can think of positive aspects. Those things that make us feel warm inside.'

'Kittens,' I said, as disgusted with him as Tilda was. Mum was the only one to make a proper effort, talking about the first magnolias of spring, her creative achievements with paint, a holiday we once had in Mallorca. But I felt like crying for her, trying so hard to make things better for Tilda when she had her own cancer to think about.

We saw Gary every fortnight, but Tilda refused to get any better. She clung to her grief and desolation, and her self-harming and bulimia became worse. While her school friends were taking their GCSEs, she became an inpatient at an addiction unit for teenagers at a Victorian hospital in South London, where the doctors medicalised her character, offering us no answers that made sense. There was talk of her co-dependency, of her addictive personality, of something called a borderline personality disorder; one doctor mentioned the word narcissism. It seemed like every specialist wanted to recruit Tilda for his own diseased community – and I was proud of her when she refused to cooperate. By the age of eighteen she'd been in hospital twice, and she'd acquired a permanent aura of fragility and frailty. But somehow she retained her old charm – that ability to switch in an instant from intensity to a beautiful, vague, other-worldliness, and back again. Also, she managed to build herself up from skeletal to merely thin.

Her life started to improve when, after an intense period of studying at home, she scraped three GCSEs and two A Levels, the minimum requirement to study acting at the Central School of Speech and Drama in London. She performed well at her audition, and when she was offered a place we celebrated with pink sparkling wine, which we drank in the back garden at Gravesend. We all felt so happy (nobody mentioned my mediocre exam performance a year earlier), all the flowers that

I had planted with Mum were in bloom, the roses and geraniums and sweet peas, and Tilda and I got drunk and danced together, barefoot on parched grass, sweet peas stuck in our hair, singing her most successful composition – 'Demented on a Sunday'. That September she left home, pulling a gigantic red suitcase onto the train. I said to Mum, 'She could live in that if she doesn't like the accommodation,' and we waved her off. I guess both Mum and I were nervous that she'd regress once she was out of our influence, but the opposite was true. At Central she became her old self again – the girl who'd been a dazzling Peter Pan, and who commanded the spotlight. We heard stories of her new friends – Henry, 'the star of our year', and Lottie, 'my girl-crush'. She told us that her teachers were inspirational, and said that acting was her passion.

At the end of the first year Mum and I saw her play Ophelia in *Hamlet*, and we realised that she'd matured; her performance was subtle and beguiling. By now, I was living in Willesden Green and Mum had moved to Wales, so merely being together made the occasion special, and afterwards Tilda introduced handsome Henry, who played Hamlet, and pointed, across a crowded bar, to a serious girl with dark plaits pinned up across her head – Lottie. She looked up, and waved to us. It seemed that Tilda had found her tribe and was somehow settled. But, because of her teenage breakdown, we can't ever take that for granted, we'll always have to look out for the signs. As I say, she is the damaged one.

I can't believe that her letter makes no acknowledgement of this, that it's so self-righteous and insulting, and I re-read it hoping that I've missed something; that I'm able to find some positive message buried in the words. But as I read I feel even worse: battered and miserable and disbelieving. I pour more wine, gulping it down like water and open up the dossier on the laptop in order to write down all my new worries. *Tilda is becoming delusional,* I type, *and has formed the ridiculous, perilous belief that she is in control of her relationship with Felix.* I note that her trust in him is misplaced, and I record the incident with the purple vase. What sort of person would do that? It's such an angry, hate-filled act. And then to make sure that sex is excruciatingly painful for her, leaving her with bruises. The emotional and physical brutality is horrendous. I write also about the increased isolation Felix is forcing on Tilda, separating her from me and Mum, and from her work, her acting. I feel like telling him, you can't do that! Acting is in her soul, you can't take it away. Then I note that Tilda's letter is so obviously and wilfully incomplete. She hasn't mentioned anything that truly explains her psychological state – the way she's so nervy and jumpy, always seeming on the edge. Possibly on the point of another breakdown – brought on by Felix, and exploited by him too. I decide to go online, to discuss the situation with Belle and Scarlet. This time, it's Scarlet who's already there.

Hello Calliegirl. Have you seen the latest news on Chloey Percival?

No. What?

Her condition has deteriorated. They say it's critical. Every day, another death, maybe Chloey, or Pink or me. I'm burned out, and tired of feeling frightened. And, Callie, I'm fed up with this stupid X stuff. I'm going to refer to my bf by his first name from now on – with you and Belle anyway – so let me introduce him, meet Luke. I've told you about the role-play sex games we like, but it's become too violent. He stuffed a tie down my throat last time, and tied my neck, pretending to hang me. And sometimes he locks me in the house, tied up, knowing I won't be able to get to the bathroom when I need to. He likes the mess when he gets home.

I've never known Scarlet be so revealing and I'm revolted. I stop her right there, and switch the conversation to Tilda.

Scarlet, I need your advice. There are some parallels between your relationship and Pink's. Not the role-play sex games exactly. I just mean that her situation with Felix (following your lead) is becoming deeper and dangerous. I stole a memory stick from P's flat, and on it I found a letter to me, saying that I'm right about Felix. He is isolating her, preventing her from working and sometimes being violent. He threw a vase at her head and her arms are bruised. But she won't listen to me. It's hard to stand by and do nothing.

I wait, but it takes Scarlet a long time to reply. Then this:

Calliegirl, you know I've been working on a proposal, something that might help me escape from Luke and also save your sister from Felix. We're both in life-threatening danger and we need to act before it's too late. I've already briefed Belle and she's helping me. I think now's the time for you to be involved also, but I can't give you all the details yet, and I don't want to do it online. I've reconsidered, and think we'll have to meet. Btw I know that you met Belle in York. She told me.

I knew Belle was incapable of keeping a secret. I write:

I loved seeing Belle, and would like to meet you too. But when? Do I have to come to Manchester?

No, I'll come down to London, maybe next month. We'll go somewhere anonymous – maybe a park, or a Starbucks. Luke about to come home – I have to go...

As soon as I log off, I go to Curzon Street to return the memory stick. I hope to steal it again in a week or two, to see if Tilda has added anything to her letter. Then I clean the place, wiping dirty marks off the coffee table, putting clothes back in the cupboards, re-clingfilming the crockery. Once I'm happy with my efforts, I leave, deciding not to take the bus to Eva's house to return the key.

17

I'm at home, tidying, and my phone rings. It's Felix, the soft tone of his voice meaning that I have to turn the radio off and concentrate on listening.

'We're home from Martinique,' he says. 'We should meet up for a drink. Champagne if you like, or cider. Or would you like dinner?'

'You, me and Tilda?'

'You and me.'

'What for?'

A quiet laugh. 'To re-establish good relations. Remember how we used to get along so well? Let's get that vibe back. I'd like to, and it would please Tilda. I'll take you somewhere special. How about dinner at the Wolseley?'

'You're joking…'

'No I'm not. Come.'

I feel suddenly light-headed, overcome by fear, but also weirdly exhilarated. I sense he has an agenda, that this isn't just a spontaneous show of friendship. But I don't think I'll manage to behave normally around him now I've read Tilda's letter, and I can't imagine us getting through the evening without it ending with me losing my temper and in some catastrophic confrontation. At the same time, the more information I can extract from him, the better I'll be able to protect Tilda. For ages I say nothing, then I agree to go, and the minute I put the phone down, I turn back to the dossier to make a list of questions to ask him.

*

The following day, in the bookshop, I'm packing up the returns and phoning customers to say their reserved books have arrived, but my mind is on Felix, and I find myself becoming absurdly fixated on the difficulty of fitting in at the Wolseley. I don't imagine it's a jeans and t-shirt sort of place, and before I know it, I'm seeking advice.

'Daphne, I'm going to the Wolseley, could you give me some advice on what to wear?'

She snorts in a way that Mum would call 'unbecoming', and puts her Virginia Woolf mug down.

'Bloody hell, sweetheart.' She's bellowing across the shop. 'How come?'

'My sister's boyfriend is taking me. The one I don't like… I think he's trying to win me round.'

'Well, make the most of it. I'm not sure I'm the right

person for style advice, but how about this? I'll buy you a dress. I'll close the shop for an afternoon and we'll go into town together and choose something.'

So that's what we do. She takes me to Fenwick's department store on Bond Street, and I try on several dresses that each cost hundreds of pounds, all of them picked out by Daphne 'to make the most of your shape'. She riffles through the rows of clothes, finger-walking through the hangers like an efficient filing clerk, saying, 'No, no, god no, that's frightful, yes, take this one…' And she follows me into the changing room, peeking round the curtain and commentating. 'No, it's squashing your bust,' or 'Too droopy, you need fitted.' I surrender to her wisdom, recognising that she's picking out classic designs for me, and is making me look stylish; although it's odd that her own way of dressing – leather mini-skirts and Cuban heels – is so different.

We settle on a royal blue dress. At first I don't think I can possibly wear it, I feel so exposed. Not that it's too low cut, or too short, but the fact that it follows my curves is embarrassing. When I protest, Daphne says, 'I'm not going to pressure you Callie, but you do look quite lovely. You have a fantastic figure… And you have no sense of how gorgeous you are, which makes you all the more alluring.' I feel my cheeks crimson, and I say, 'Okay then, I'll be brave.'

'Now for some shoes.'

'No. It's too much! You can't spend all this.'

'And you can't wear that dress with trainers.'

'I think it would be fun with trainers.'

'Not for the Wolseley. Come on.'

So she buys me shoes. At least, a pair of ankle boots in smoky grey suede with a thin little heel. 'I adore them,' I say. 'But I feel guilty.'

'View them as your summer bonus, a reward for persuading Mr Ahmed to buy all those P G Wodehouses, and selling so many Get Well Soon cards.'

I laugh, because we both know that I've sold only one Get Well Soon card in the past three months.

At work the next morning I wear the suede boots with my jeans, and Daphne says, 'Very nice. Dress them up, dress them down.' Wilf comes in, and I make a point of walking across the shop floor to put a cookery book back on its shelf. He doesn't notice the boots, but he looks at me with a bemused face, trying to work out what's different.

'Can I help you?' I say.

'Yes, I think you can.'

'How?'

'Are you free at the weekend? Do you want to come and do some gardening?'

'What? With you?'

'Of course with me… Do you have Wellington boots?'

'Yep.'

He leaves and I'm astounded by the turn of events, amazed that Wilf hasn't written me off. I look at Daphne and she looks at me. 'Don't get excited,' I say. And she starts whistling the tune of 'Love is in the Air'.

'I had no idea that you can whistle.'

'I had no idea you could garden.'

*

On Saturday Wilf drives to my flat, and picks me up. His car is a beaten-up Volkswagen, splattered with mud. He removes some old newspapers, cardboard coffee cups and other detritus from the passenger seat and tosses them into the back, where gardening equipment is piled up – spades, forks, trowels, and bags of compost and gravel – and I get into the passenger seat. It's a hot day, and I've dressed for gardening in an old cotton shirt with faded blue flowers on it, and shorts that used to be pink, but have faded in the wash so that they're kind of pig-coloured. And, as instructed, Wellington boots.

'I like the way the car smells of dirt.' I smile, so he knows I'm not being sarcastic.

'I love dirt.' He grins back, and glances down at my pale thighs which are very much on show in the passenger seat. I look at them too, and wonder whether they could conceivably be thought luscious, rather than just big.

*

We arrive at the gates of a whitewashed mansion on Bishop's Avenue, all pillars and portico. Wilf has to tap in a code for the ironwork gate, which opens electronically. 'I reckon the inside is made of marble and gold,' I say.

'You're not far wrong. Big marble floor.'

'Russian oligarch?'

'Nope… Middle Eastern diplomat.'

Wilf says the garden is in the 'preparation stage', which means that we should spend our time cutting and clearing and digging. It's heavy work, and I enjoy the physicality of pushing the spade in deep, and shovelling out great mounds of black earth which I sift with my fingers, pulling out weeds and bits of rubbish, and I'm reminded of the day, long ago, when I found the sheep skull buried under the bush. I want to tell Wilf about it, but can't find the words, and all I manage is, 'There's a whole world down here. Weeds and roots and snails – actually I've got a monster of a weed here, I'm not sure I can get it out.' Wilf comes over to help, and digs all around my horrendous weed, then together we pull on it as hard as we can until it comes loose. Wilf throws it onto our pile of debris, takes a deep breath and says, 'There's nothing more sexy than a gorgeous woman covered in dirt and sweat wrestling with the undergrowth.' I smile, and he goes back to his area of the garden while I watch a robin alight on a branch next to me, then dart down to snatch a worm.

Mostly, Wilf doesn't talk while he works, he just stomps up and down the garden with bundles of sticks and branches, clearing out a corner in preparation for planting, and I'm struck by how, in life, he resembles so closely my daydreams of him – long strides, rolled-up sleeves, beads of sweat on his forehead. When we stop for a break, we sit on a low wall, passing his flask of tea back and forth, and he's brought a packet of Hobnobs. He congratulates me on my digging, and talks about his plans for the garden, showing me a design sketched out in pencil on a creased piece of paper that he keeps in the back pocket of his khaki shorts. Somehow our conversation turns to Tilda.

'Are you still worried about her?'

I start to say no, but then spoil it. 'Do you know how many women are murdered by their partners? It's two a week. It's normal.'

'You can't seriously think Tilda's going to be murdered?'

'No… but…'

He gives me no chance to elaborate, saying, 'Grab your spade and get digging…'

Everything is fine in Wilf-world, and I go along with his positive mood, digging madly. I work up a rhythm for breaking up the soil, forking and raking and sifting, and become immersed – enjoying too the sideshow of the robin, endlessly looking for something to kill. But after an hour I'm exhausted, and Wilf tells me to rest while he finishes up. 'Let's adjourn to the pub,' he says. 'As a reward.' So we drive to the Albany.

It's less crowded this time, and we sit side by side

on a bench at a corner table, two manual workers with soil everywhere, under our nails, in our hair, all over our legs – it even feels gritty inside my mouth. 'Is that it until next weekend?' I ask. 'Or do you go back in the evenings?'

'I have a team.' He shrugs as if to say *It's no big deal*. But I'm amazed.

'A team! Like you're an employer? Already an entrepreneur...' I feel myself shrink inside. If he's this successful, why is he interested in *me*?

'Well, it's two Romanian guys who work on contract,' he says. 'And I go there most evenings to check that we're on schedule, and to set the programme for the next day. It's a competitive environment – too many people doing what I do, and too few customers. But if you're good, you can make it work.'

'How do you convince people to take you on?'

'Word of mouth, mainly... I'm bad at the admin side though, following up payments, sorting out the contracts...'

As he speaks, I'm aware that, because of our rolled-up sleeves, our bare arms are touching, lightly brushing each other. The sensation makes my chest feel tight, and my hands are shaking slightly. I hope he doesn't notice, and I say, almost under my breath, 'I could help... if you like, with the paperwork.'

His face contorts, like he finds that funny.

'What?' I ask.

'Who knew that the word *paperwork* could sound so… what's the word…? Alluring.'

He leans over, puts one hand round the back of my head, and pulls my face towards his. And we kiss, first of all little kisses on the lips, then a proper full-on kiss, me taking in his woody smell, the roughness of his lips. We pull apart, and Wilf says, 'Would you like to come and see my flat?'

'Oh no! I have to get home…' I pull away, stymied by a blast of fear.

'Oh, okay.'

He gulps down his beer, putting the glass down with a thump of finality, and I summon up my courage.

'I didn't mean to say that. What I meant was, I'd like to see your flat.' I try to smile at him, but my mouth is dry and the smile won't come.

'Good!'

He steers me out of the Albany and we walk to Kensal Rise, his arm around my waist, stopping twice to kiss, then speeding up, in a hurry to be inside.

18

I'm preparing for dinner at the Wolseley and reflect that I've become suddenly grown up. This dress, these boots, and the fact that I've acquired a boyfriend. I make up my face, taking Daphne's advice to go for smoky eyes, and follow a method I found on YouTube. I use a 'natural' shade lipstick, sort of creamy and glossy, and think it's possible that I actually look sexy and sophisticated. At one point, I skip around the flat singing the 'I Feel Pretty' song from *West Side Story*, but come to an abrupt stop when reality hits. An evening with Felix, just the two of us. Now I feel sick. Before I leave home I log on to controllingmen and have a quick chat with Belle.

I'm so nervous. How will I be able to talk naturally? My instinct will be to INSULT him and walk out!!!.

Stay focussed. It's important that u use your time well, to find out as much as possable. Be strong!!

I take the bus to the Wolseley and, although I'm five minutes early, I find that Felix is already there, sitting at the bar,
sharp shoulders, straight back, drinking something clear
– gin or vodka or, knowing him, fizzy water. He glances
up and stands up, surprise in his eyes. 'You look beautiful.'
He's kissing my cheek, placing his hand on my back as he
leads me to our table, making me think of those long cold
fingers. As we sit down he explains that he has already
ordered champagne, and I'm not surprised when he goes
through the menu, advising me what to order. The roasted
sea bass is 'excellent', the calf's liver 'very acceptable'.

'Do you like oysters? I recommend the oysters here.'

'Not really. I like Beluga caviar though.' I had read – 50g
for £255.

He laughs. 'If you like. This is my treat.'

'Just testing.' In fact, I order a lamb dish, reasonably
priced, and I look round the restaurant at the self-satisfied
men and wealthy women, jewels hanging in clusters from
their necks and ears, like fruit. I say, 'Do you come here
often?' I'm trying to sound natural. At the same time,
I'm examining Felix, his white wrists and knuckles, his
composure, his eyes. Scanning him for clues, but it's hard
to get beyond the veneer, the slight smile, the perfect teeth.

'Oh we only come here on special occasions... Tilda
likes it.'

'So why didn't she come today, why is it just us?'

'I wanted to mend fences… and to spend time getting to know you better.'

'Why? I'm very ordinary.' Thinking, *I have to stop saying that!*

'Ha! You're wrong – you're an unusually perceptive person… you're bright and you're funny. Those wry observations of yours – you have perfect timing…'

'Why all this flattery, Felix?' I'm too stressed, too nauseated, to pretend that I'm charmed.

He brushes an invisible crumb off the table. 'It's not about flattery. I'm trying to tell you that I like you, Callie. And I want to convince you that I'm right for Tilda. I'm in love with your sister, and I'm good for her… It pains me that you don't see me that way.'

His voice is practically a whisper, an articulated hush, and I lean in, not wanting to miss anything.

'Are you always like this with your girlfriends?'

'What do you mean?'

'I mean, taking a close interest in every aspect of her life. What dress she wears, what perfume she uses, who she sees, how she manages her work, how she decorates her flat…' I use a soft, aspirated voice, mirroring him, and I'm reminded of the quiet hissing that swans do, before they get angry.

He leans back in his chair, inhaling as though he's stifling a yawn then, looking into my eyes, he comes forward and places his hand on mine. It takes all my willpower not to pull away.

'You're wrong to be suspicious of me, you know. Those character traits of mine that you don't like – they're innocent... Don't smirk like that. It's not sinister to care about organisation and order... In a clean, uncluttered room, you can think, you can be your true self. It's the same with worries and anxieties, keep them under wraps, and you're free to excel in activity that *matters*, whether it's the strategic management of capital, or something creative, like acting.'

He pulls his hand away, and I'm relieved, at the same time registering some change in him. Something I can't quite place.

'Really?' It comes out hypercritical. 'You *like it* that Tilda's an actress?'

In a humouring voice, like he's trying to calm a dog, he says, 'Yes, Callie, I do. She's a very talented actress and I'm proud of her. And the more clarity and structure in her home life, the better she'll be able to focus on her acting.'

'Huh! I suppose you think that if I was more organised and *structured* at home I wouldn't be working in a bookshop... I'd be a brain surgeon or a high court judge or something.'

Still the pacifying voice. 'I'm saying that you might be doing something a little more exciting than working in a bookshop – yes.'

I want to tell him that he doesn't fool me. At the same time, I don't want to interrupt his flow, so I offer, 'Does Tilda agree?'

'We both know that your sister tends towards chaos and drama. You could say that we're opposites – but we complement each other. I help her take control of her life, and she prevents me from being obsessive about it. She's good for me.'

I note a soft tone when he talks about Tilda and it shakes me up because it sounds genuinely caring and affectionate. I'd become so focussed on his violent sex with my sister and his control over her, that I'd forgotten he might actually love her.

Elbow on the table, I lean my head on my hand. 'Okay, so let's assume that I'll let you sort me out… What do you suggest as a first move – to resign from the bookshop maybe?'

'No, resigning is never a first step. Much better to sit yourself down with a blank sheet of paper, and start writing down all the elements of life that are important to you, and those you could easily drop. That way you can begin to work out the journey you want to go on…'

'Going forward…?' I say, and we both laugh.

A waiter tops up the glasses and asks whether everything is all right. Felix says, 'Excellent, thank you.' And I nod my assent.

I'm sounding almost carefree now. 'Working with nice people is high-up… and not being stressed. I couldn't do your job – all that gambling with other people's money. But you're right about the bookshop, I guess, because, although I love Daphne, and books, I don't want to be

there forever. I should try and figure out what to do next.'
As I speak, I'm thinking about being in the garden with
Wilf, how the time flew because I was so into my digging,
and enjoying being outside.

'I like communing with nature…' I grin with embarrassment.

'Where did that come from?'

'Oh, I don't know… Felix, can I ask you something?'
I need to get back to the questions I had planned to ask.
Not to fall into the trap of liking him.

'Of course…'

'Do you have any family? I mean, you don't seem to
have any roots, or friends, or old flames or anything. It's
always just you and Tilda.'

'You're a funny one… Of course I have family – a
mother called Alana who writes children's books and a
dad, Erik, who lectures in economics in Boston. They're
still together, so no terrible break-up traumas to report…
and I call home every week, and always end the call with
a "love you"… How about that? That's not how you think
of me, Callie, is it? The good son.'

'What about siblings?'

'I have a brother, Lucas. We don't always get along –
we're very different and somewhat competitive. While
I trade strange, ungraspable financial instruments, he
works in bricks and mortar, solid materials…'

Somehow I know that Lucas isn't an estate agent, like
Wilf.

'Lucas is a talented architect…' he says drily. 'He lives and works in France, near Nice, and I took Tilda to meet him when we were on holiday there… He has an ex-girlfriend who lives nearby – Sophie. And Lucas is father to their baby. Lily.'

'She didn't tell me that… Uncle Felix… it's hard to imagine… What about your old girlfriends? Where are they – here, or in America?'

'I knew I was going to get a grilling.' He wipes his lips with a napkin. 'And it's fine. I realise that you have this obsessive thing going on, looking out for Tilda. And I know that I don't usually talk about myself. I'm a private person. Isn't that the term for those of us who find it difficult to share every little thing?'

'I'm a private person too.'

'So – yes Callie, I do have an important ex-girlfriend. She's American, like me, but lives in this country and her name's Francesca. We lived together for three years, and we broke up because she wanted to be married and I didn't want to marry her…'

At this point I look down at his hands. It's instinctive. I had half-noticed something before, but only now is it striking me properly.

'Shit, Felix! Why's that ring on your wedding finger? Do you always do that, or has something happened?'

'I wondered when you'd notice.' There's an element of nervousness in his voice. 'When we were in Martinique I asked Tilda to marry me, and we had a little ceremony on a beach. Nothing that's binding in law. But that *will* happen... pretty soon.'

For a second I'm totally numb.

'Oh god... I knew things were serious – but this... I didn't expect it.'

What I want to say is, 'This is awful.'

'Why didn't Tilda tell me?'

He smiles coyly, pleased to be imparting his news. 'We've been enjoying our secret. Not going public. But I thought that, since you want to know every little thing about me, I'd better tell you. It seems fair, in the circumstances. Now, sit up straight and breathe – have a sip of your wine.'

I realise now that this is the purpose of the dinner – that Tilda told Felix to bond with me, to become my friend, because he's about to be my brother-in-law. I feel like imploding, right there in the restaurant, crying and wailing and making a scene. But I go against my instincts, and do as Felix says, I sit up straight, draw my shoulders back and I raise my glass.

'To you and Tilda.'

'And to *you*, Callie.' He says it like he means it.

I drink my wine down, my head swimming from the champagne and I feel inclined to get totally wasted. Felix is drinking heavily too and as the evening goes on the alcohol has a palliative effect on me and a loosening effect on him, making him increasingly revealing. He tells me about Francesca, who's a journalist apparently and a workaholic, and she was critical of Felix's behaviour and didn't appreciate him, like Tilda does. I open up too, telling Felix about Wilf's gardening ambitions, and the way he comes into the bookshop all the time and how Daphne is like a hawk, watching everything that goes on.

We leave the restaurant after midnight, Felix's arm around me, and he gives me his usual hug as he puts me in a taxi, and then a tiny kiss on my cheek. He insists on paying my fare, and sends me off into the night. I slouch on the seat, utterly confused, traumatised. In the dossier I've noted that Felix fits the traditional controllingmen loner profile. Not the sort who sits alone in his bedroom contributing to internet conspiracy theories, or researching terrorism. More the type who has no real, meaningful friendships, but does have an easy charm, who plays people. And I wonder whether I've just succumbed to his power to manipulate. At the same time, I can't help thinking there's a tiny chance that I'm wrong about everything. Felix had seemed so nice this evening. Genuinely. And I have to admit that Tilda is a drama queen – she always has been. Maybe she hyped up the violent side of her relationship with Felix to fit her own glamorous, romantic self-image – *I love danger. I love risk. 'To be opened in the event of my death.'* Actually, it's more than possible. All our lives she's been prone to exaggeration.

As the cab climbs the hill towards Willesden Green I think maybe I could like Felix again; and it even seems possible that he could be an interesting, entertaining member of our family.

At home, I go online and say to Belle:

Help me! I think I might be mad. I just spent my evening with Felix and it made me think I might be mistaken, I might have read too much into his behaviour.

What do you mean???

He was nice to me... and interested. Maybe I'm wrong about him. Maybe I've been carried away, spending too much time on controllingmen. I've become paranoid.

Oh Calliegirl... don't be nieve. Remember he's a clever operater. And don't forget the important indicators – the violence, and the isolation.

Belle, I realise what you're saying. But I'm genuinely wondering whether I've got everything out of proportion. I'm going to stay off controllingmen for a while, to let things settle. And I don't want to be part of this plan that Scarlet is dreaming up.

Callie! Don't leave!!!! I will miss you too much. Xxxxxx

I have to, Belle. I need to sort myself out.

I can't talk about this right now, because Lavender and the children are here!!! They came yesterday, and I'm sooo busy. But please don't go. I'll email you when I get a chance, you HAVE to stay in touch, we are proper friends now.

I sign off with some kisses and a good luck message – but resolve to give myself a break.

The next morning I wake up with a bad head, and wander round the flat searching for paracetamol. Then

I make a cup of hot chocolate and phone Tilda – I want to challenge her over not telling me her marriage news directly, leaving it to Felix. And I want to quiz her about the wedding. But there's no answer, so I leave a message and phone Mum in Wales instead – she does her painting full-time now. I think the cancer she had years ago made her want to devote her life purely to her art.

'Mum,' I say. 'Have you heard from Tilda recently?'

'Not for a couple of weeks, darling, why?'

I don't want to tell her about the marriage plans, in case Tilda wants to do it herself, or have Felix do it. So I say, 'Oh, no reason. I was just wondering what you think about Felix. It seems to be pretty serious between the two of them.'

There's a long pause, and she says, 'I'm not so sure. He's a little strange. They came to stay a couple of weeks ago, I'm sure Tilda told you, and he kept tidying up the cottage. And he washed the kitchen floor. Maybe it's an American thing?'

'I don't think so. Do you think Tilda's happy with him?'

'Who knows? There's something in the air between them, I can feel it. Tilda didn't seem to be quite herself.'

'She's in love.'

'Yes, you're probably right.'

I leave it there, and we chat about Wales and Mum's walking group, and their drunken nights down the pub after a long day's rambling in the Brecon Beacons. And how she had a little exhibition of her art in a village hall,

166

and the big cheese in the fancy house, a 'proper chap' who wears maroon corduroy trousers, bought one of her red-and-orange abstract landscapes for £150. 'I actually think he might have been flirting with me!' she says. Then she tells me that she's thinking of getting a tattoo, a tiny tulip near her ankle – a symbol of life. Celebrating the years she has had free from cancer. 'Can't you celebrate some other way?' I say disdainfully.

Afterwards, I sit at my table under the window, and switch on the computer. While I'm waiting for it to boot up, I glance at my phone and see that I have a text from Tilda: *What the fuck is this crap in the Mail??? How could you? I despair.* I go to the *Daily Mail*'s website, and read the top headline in the sidebar of shame: *Tilda Farrow in love.* The article is filled with insinuation – Tilda Farrow apparently is so in love with her new man, wealthy banker Felix Nordberg, that she has given up acting to devote herself to the relationship. Felix is well known for his 'meticulous attention to detail, planning and strategy'.

I feel weak, my thoughts going immediately to Wilf. How could I have been so stupid, so careless? Or, to see it another way, so trusting of someone I hardly know? I pace the room, wondering what to do, and then I phone Tilda again. She answers this time, saying, 'You're the only person, Callie. The *only* one that this shit could have come from. Who the fuck have you been speaking to?' I don't want to tell her about Wilf, so I say, 'I'm so sorry, really I am. I don't know how it happened. I might have talked to a couple of people… maybe Daphne, maybe someone else.' I'm braced, ready for her to go ballistic at me and make threats, but instead she pauses, then changes her attitude completely, sounding upbeat and giggly. 'Oh well, fuck it. Let's ignore the bastards. What about my news? Isn't it totally wonderful! Aren't I the luckiest woman in the world?'

I've decided to go along with it all. To give Felix the benefit of the doubt, and in the most lively voice I can manage, I say, 'Congratulations! The future Mrs Nordberg… It sounds so grand! Can I be a bridesmaid?'

'No bridesmaids. None of that shit. Just a very small, simple, elegant wedding. It's so exciting!'

We talk about wedding venues and guest lists and other fripperies, then she's called away by Felix to 'enjoy my breakfast champagne!' and I imagine her skipping flirtatiously across the room to the kitchen area, then tiptoeing to kiss her fiancé's handsome face.

I sit down again at the table, weary from my attempt to be supportive and joyful, and I see on my phone that there's an email from Scarlet. So I turn to my laptop and read and as I do so, all my thoughts of Tilda and Felix's wedding and of Wilf's betrayal are obliterated. I re-read the message, and Scarlet's words sink slowly into my brain, and they are utterly devastating.

19

BELLE:

Her real name is Bea Santos. I know that now. Her mother, Patricia, came from the Philippines in the 1980s to work in the NHS as a nurse, and Belle carried on the family tradition. I know also that she could tap dance and sing, and liked to perform to 'These Boots Are Made For Walking' while wearing special white patent leather boots. I've learned that Belle was a proficient seamstress, excellent at blanket stitch and button holes and zips (she made her green dress). The other things I know are rather random – her fear of moths and of sticky labels, her poor exam record, her love for her childhood pet, a bulldog named Ed. I realise now that the sweet nervousness that I noticed in her was loved by her workmates and friends, and that a drawer in her bedroom contained more than a hundred thank-you cards and letters from her patients and their families.

I learn all this on a vile, rainy day in June, when I travel again to York – this time for her funeral. That email from Scarlet had plunged me into a bleak new world, leading me to a news story on the BBC website. A man had broken into a flat in the Dringhouses area of York, and had stabbed a woman named Tricia Mayhew along with her friend Bea Santos. Two small children were present, a girl aged seven and a boy aged four. Tricia had survived, and was well enough to attend Belle's funeral, and she sat at the back of the church, her face a mask, deadened by shock. According to the papers her husband, Joe, was in police custody.

The service is a Catholic mass, with Latin and incense, and a choir sings unfamiliar hymns. Mainly I look down at my hands, but occasionally I glance up, and see the coffin, and I think *Now I lay me down to sleep, I pray the Lord my soul to keep.* Two people speak about Belle, one her boss at work, Kevin Attwood, and the other someone who knew her from the church, a woman named Holly Gracie, who says she had known Bea since she was a little girl; I'm aware that her mother is sitting in the front pew, protected by large men on either side. Patricia Santos is a tiny figure, perfectly still, wearing a black veil over her black hair, not standing up when everyone else does, or kneeling, just sitting there. And she doesn't take communion.

At the end, the congregation shuffles into a neighbouring church hall, a modern building with a laminate floor and exposed bricks on the inside walls. I offer to help hand out sandwiches and refreshments, thinking that I'll be able to overhear conversations and learn more about Belle. I move from group to group, and offer mini quiches to a short, stocky young man, who manages to smile sadly. I ask him, 'How do you know Bea?' and he tells me that she had been his girlfriend in the years after they left St Xavier's School. His name is Charlie and he's a paramedic, and he seems perfect for Belle, since his voice is unmistakeably kind.

I move on, wandering about with my plates, and it occurs to me to look out for Scarlet. In our email exchanges, she said several times that *this changes everything*; that *we're entering a new phase* and, given the sense of urgency in her language, I was surprised when she said that she couldn't attend Belle's funeral. I suspect she's lying – that she's here, but that she doesn't want me to know it. So I try to establish who all the young women are, and I find myself ruling people out on the basis of the way they look – too garish to be Scarlet, too scruffy, or too many piercings or too loud a voice. All my observations based entirely on a concocted idea of her, probably wrong. I take a plate of cucumber sandwiches and sit down in a corner, next to a refreshments table. But I'm there hardly five minutes when Tricia comes and sits beside me.

'Hello,' I say. 'I'm Callie.'

She looks into my eyes, puzzled as though she doesn't understand, her raw exhaustion at odds with her formal

clothes and her neat chestnut bob. She says, 'Oh yes…
I remember. Bea described you to me… One of the last
conversations we had was about you. She loved it when
you came to York…'

I think I might cry and I sit still, brushing away crumbs
of cucumber sandwich that have fallen onto my lap. I
compose myself and ask Tricia what age she and Bea had
been when they met.

'We were eight… It's hard to believe that she was 34,
like me. She had a childlike quality didn't she? In her
appearance, and her personality.'

'I loved her bee bag,' I say. 'It was so sweet, like her.'

'It's my fault she died.' Her words come out flatly, like
she has no emotions left. 'I shouldn't have moved into
her flat… She discussed it with you, didn't she? How I
might escape?'

She sounds accusatory.

'She wanted to help.' I place my hand on her arm, just
for a second. 'Here…'

I reach into my bag, looking for a pen and a scrap of
paper. 'This is my address and phone number and email.
If you need anything, I'd like to help…'

It seemed unlikely that she would follow up – but I'm
trying to be more like Belle, kinder and helpful.

I realise also that Tricia is about to go through the
horror of Joe's trial, without her best friend beside her,
giving her support. I want to say something reassuring,
but nothing comes and instead I just look at her, noticing

that under her prim navy jacket her silk shirt is buttoned up on the wrong buttons. As she takes the paper from me, I notice too that her hands are bare, no rings or bracelets or varnish on her nails.

'Oh look,' she says. And we both watch as Bea's mother is led out of the room by a large man, sweaty in the face and wearing an ill-fitting suit.

'I didn't talk to her.'

'Don't worry…' Tricia is struggling to speak normally. 'She can't talk to anyone, or listen. She's not taking it in… Send her a card and write about a lovely moment that you spent with Bea, that's the thing to do. Here…' She takes the pen and writes down Mrs Santos's address and her own email. Handing it to me, she rises from her chair, picks up her bag and leaves – a ghost of a woman, weirdly dressed in executive clothes.

In the early evening I take the train back to London, miserably, in a carriage packed with shouty, drunk football supporters. At one point, they start singing, and it's a relief to get away when we arrive at King's Cross. At home, I run a hot bath hoping to wash away some of the awfulness of the day. I can't find the strength to hang up my clothes, which lie strewn across the bedroom floor. I don't care, and I'm about to step into the bath when my phone rings. It's Wilf.

'Hello, sexy girl,' he says, his voice drawling, and I can hear a commotion in the background.

'Are you in the pub?'

173

'Yep. Fancy coming down?' I haven't seen him since Belle died; he doesn't know.

'No… I've had a long day.'

'Fair enough… I've been thinking of you though… Just thought I'd tell you that… Shall we meet up soon?'

I feel weary. Now isn't the time to confront him about the story in the *Mail*. Belle's death means that I don't have the energy for it. Or the motivation.

'Let's speak tomorrow, when I'm not so tired. Goodnight.'

'Goodnight, Callie.' He sounds affectionate and unbothered.

*

We don't speak the next day, or the next. I don't answer his calls or reply to his texts as I'm still not ready to accuse him; instead I spend my time in the bookshop in a sort of daze. As I go about my routine tasks I'm able to move only in slow motion. I say to myself, 'One thing at a time,' replace books on shelves, empty the till, enter the new orders… Mr Ahmed comes in, and I say to him as clearly as I can, '*Thank you, Jeeves* is next, Mr Ahmed, shall I order that?' and he replies, 'What's the matter, Callie? Have you caught a cold?'

Most of the time, I'm not thinking of Belle, but I'm aware of a dead weight in me that signifies her presence, and when I do think specifically of her, images flash into my mind, of her standing at York Station and waving when she spots my smiley-face t-shirt, of her laying out her fleece on the ground so that we can have our picnic and then sitting down neatly, with her thin brown legs tucked under her, and her back perfectly straight as she reaches into her bag for our food and wine. I can't quite believe that she's gone and when, in the evenings, I log on to controllingmen.com, I half expect to find a message from her, full of enthusiasm for our mission as Befrienders.

Instead I find lots of chat *about* Bea Santos, specifically about her bravery. I learn that on the day of the attack Joe Mayhew had arrived at her house and hammered on the door, shouting up at the windows, and demanding to be let in. When he saw Tricia peek out of the window, he kicked the door and cursed, causing neighbours to come out of their houses and watch. When he still got nowhere, he retreated down the side passage where he sat on the ground next to the bins, and waited. It was bad luck that Belle was out while the rumpus was going on, at Tesco buying food. And when she returned home, and was putting her key in the lock, Joe reappeared, shoving a knife at her throat, demanding that she let him into the flat. Belle screamed for someone to call the police, while he forced her through the front door. He stabbed her several times and took her keys upstairs to the flat, and had just unlocked the door when the police did turn up, having been called by a concerned neighbour some time ago. They were in time to prevent anything but a flailing lunge at Tricia, but it was too late for Belle, who died in the ambulance that was taking her to York Hospital.

It's good to know these details. I owe it to her. It's strange, though, to see the fevered discussion on the website, page after page of it, by people who have no idea that she was actually a member, a proper Befriender. Scarlet doesn't let on, and neither do I. We don't want them to claim her, to manipulate her story, to make her their own martyr.

My private emails with Scarlet are intermittent and unsettling. We seem so at odds with each other because Scarlet is in a rage, a fury, constantly hoping that Joe will rot in hell or, at least, spend the rest of his life behind bars. But I'm too exhausted to care about Joe, too drained by sadness. And any anger that I waste on Joe seems to eat away at the loving thoughts I want to devote to Belle, as if my emotions are finite, and I have to think carefully about where to direct them. And when Scarlet keeps insisting that she and I meet up, I repeatedly ignore her, unable to summon the motivation to have the conversation. After a week, though, when she returns to the subject, I do at last engage.

Why is this so urgent?

Belle is dead. Can't you see how this affects us, you as a befriender, me as prey?

How are things with Luke?

I regret the question as soon as I write it. It comes not from curiosity, but more from a difficulty I have in assessing whether Scarlet's situation is like a chronic illness, just an ongoing dysfunctionality, or whether it's the relentless escalation of danger that she claims.

I told you before, she writes. *He ties me up around my neck, and one day he will strangle me. And he leaves me in the flat, abandoned, tied up. What if I had some emergency while he's gone? I could have an asthma attack and not be able to get to my inhaler.*

This is the first time that she's mentioned asthma.

What happens when you explain that to him? I write with trepidation, anxious that I'll receive a reply full of detail about depraved sex games.

It's simple – he says 'sure babe' and then completely ignores me. In fact I think I suffer later... I have cigarette burns on my back btw.

What! That's dreadful.

Yes, it's all dreadful. That's why we MUST meet. I'm not going to end up like Belle... I could come to London on Monday – could you meet me then?

Maybe...I'll let you know.

Please, let me know QUICKLY. I need to plan. Also I have to concoct a story for Luke, to explain my absence. Really, it's ESSENTIAL that we meet.

20

I call Wilf, and he answers with a note of laughter in his voice, as though I've caught him in the middle of a funny anecdote.

'Hey! Callie. At last… It's been ages, you know, since your impressive spade work in the garden… and afterwards… and everything. Can I persuade you to come out again?'

Raucous chatter in the background. 'You spend too much time in the pub,' I say.

'Not the pub – it's a going-away drinks in the office for Amy Fishwick – come and join us.' Then in a lower tone, 'Really, come over. I'd love to see you, and maybe we can go out later, for a meal or something… Or just go back to my flat.'

'Okay.' Even though I'm so low, I find myself applying make-up – eyeliner and mascara and lipstick – swapping trainers for my grey suede boots. And because I'm nervous about seeing Wilf, because of the leak to the *Mail*, I drink down a large glass of Strongbow.

At Willesden Estates it feels like the leaving party has passed its peak, is becoming stale. Drunk people in the street lean against the display window, and something unsavoury is splattered over the pavement. Inside, rock music is playing, and the small groups of people still there look tired. Wilf sees me by the door, and comes to collect me.

'It's been so long,' he says. 'Am I still okay for a kiss?'

'Maybe.' I give him my cheek, although it's obvious that he's expecting my lips.

'Come on in. I want to introduce you to people.'

'It's you I want to see.'

'And here I am. But please, Callie, I'd like you to meet my colleagues. I've told them about you, and they're curious.' He puts his arm round my shoulders and I flinch. He leads me into the office, picking up a glass of sparkling wine, and I take a gulp, feeling distant and detached – my new way of being.

He moves me this way and that, to introduce me to Bruce Oswald, whose handshake is clammy, and Tony Craig, the boss, who puts his face close to mine and slurs, 'You need to keep an eye on that fella.' And then, 'This is Amy, who's leaving.'

'Hello, Amy who's leaving.' I offer my hand, and as she takes it a flicker of a look between her blue eyes and Wilf's blue eyes makes my chest tighten, and my question comes out too directly. 'Are you going a long way away?'

She and Wilf laugh together, to the same beat.

'Oh,' she says. 'I'd never go too far from the Wonderwilf… The Maida Vale office.'

'The Wonderwilf?' I look at him, making a crazy face.

'She was headhunted,' says Wilf.

'I'm waiting to be headhunted… by a bookshop conglomerate.'

'Or a gardening multinational?' Wilf squeezes my waist, making me start.

I gulp more wine and whisper, 'Can we go outside?'

'Hey, Amy,' he says, 'catch up with you later… Urgent meeting…'

Again that flickering look, and Amy says, 'Run along.'

Outside, the evening has somehow become warmer and Bruce from the office has removed his shirt and is in the middle of a bare-chested rant about politics. 'Wilf agrees, don't you Wilf?' He's shouty, looking for a fight.

'Not now, mate.' Wilf steers me away.

'Let's walk,' I say. But he just stands there.

'Something's wrong. You've been avoiding me and now you're kinda jumpy… Am I being dumped, Callie?' He's nervous and for a second I want to tell him that everything is fine, and I want him to kiss me. But I check myself.

'Did you see that story in the *Mail* – about Tilda?'

'Yes… everyone saw it. It confirmed those worries of yours, don't you think? Talking about giving up her career… hinting at Felix's control problems.'

'Not many people knew about it. I know… and you knew. Maybe no one else…'

He's a bit slurry because of drinking, and his voice goes too loud. 'God… you don't think I had anything to do with it?'

'I know they pay hundreds for a story like that…'

'For fuck's sake – is that your opinion of me? Really? That's your fucking opinion?'

He throws his wine glass in the gutter, smashing it into tiny pieces.

'Why did you have to throw that…? Why!' I feel tears rising in my eyes, I'm reminded of Felix throwing the vase.

I walk away, Wilf shouting, 'Don't go… Come back Callie and let's talk about this…'

But I don't turn back, other than to glance round as I turn the corner, seeing Wilf going back into Willesden Estates, back to the dregs of the party. I pick up my pace, half-running home, to get away from him, to return to my flat and its reassuring solitude. I'm better off alone. It's simpler and less painful.

At home, my bedroom is impossibly hot and humid. I open up the window to let the air in and switch on my laptop to compose an email to Scarlet.

Yes, I write. *Monday will be fine. I don't work on Mondays, so I'm free all day – shall I suggest somewhere to meet?*

She comes back straight away.

This is the right thing to do, trust me. It's important

that we're not noticed together though, so we should meet somewhere anonymous, where no one will pay us any attention. Do you know Kenwood House on Hampstead Heath? We could meet outside, where the benches are – the ones that have views of the heath and the lake.

I'm surprised that Scarlet knows London – I assumed she was Manchester through and through.

Yes, I know Kenwood.

Good. You're going to think I'm being melodramatic – but I'm going to hide my identity, I'll wear a headscarf like the Muslim girls do, and sunglasses. I suggest you do the same.

Really? It sounds a bit idiotic.

You'll realise why... Let's say one o'clock. I'll have a red headscarf, and I'll be reading a book...

Okay. I have an orange scarf, so I'll wear that.

In bed later, Wilf's on my mind, and Belle, and my stomach is fizzing with too much alcohol. Also, it's hot, and I'm covered in a thin film of sweat. Twice I get out of bed to drink water, and I don't sleep properly, which means that I get up late, and panic about getting to work on time. I see in the mirror that my face is blotchy and my eyes puffy, so I splash cold water on myself, and head downstairs. The post has arrived – a small brown parcel addressed in a loose flowing script that I don't recognise, and a traumatising stiff white envelope with Tilda's handwriting on it. I suppress my thoughts and put both in my bag and leave for work, jogging half the way there.

Daphne says, 'What's the matter? You look like you need a strong coffee – sorry, a hot chocolate.'

'I'll make it.' I might sound a bit curt.

'There's been something wrong lately, hasn't there, sweetheart?' She rises from her position by the door, following me into the kitchen. 'Let me do the drinks today.' She reaches for the kettle, plugging it into the wall socket. 'And guess what I've bought – Jammie Dodgers! Guaranteed to cheer you up.'

Something gives way inside me, and I blurt out, 'I'm sorry I've been so useless recently... A friend of mine died...'

'Oh Jeez... I'm so sorry, Callie.' Her face collapses with concern. 'I'll put the closed sign on the door, and we'll sit down and you can tell me about it.'

So I do. I tell her all about Belle and the day we spent together in York, and the way in which she died, protecting Tricia. I cry a little, and Daphne finds paper towels in the kitchen cupboard for me and tells me how shocked she is that something so terrible could happen. Then she makes coffee, and I tell her everything I know about Belle's life, about her care for her patients, about the presents she bought for Saskia and Alfie, and the breakfast she left for me in the kitchen, with the white napkins and the tulips in a vase. I go on talking about her until I'm utterly drained, and then Daphne and I distract ourselves by chatting more generally, in a gentle, friendly way. I tell her that Tilda is marrying Felix and that I'm sort of in denial about it, not wanting to discuss things with her. I couldn't care less about her dress or the seating plan or the honeymoon. Then Daphne confides that she went on an internet date last night with 'another Mr Wrong. When I offered to go halves he hunched himself over the bill, like Uriah Heep, adding up the numbers… most unattractive.'

'Was there ever a Mr Nearly-Right?' I've never before asked her such a personal question, but an intimate space has opened up for us, because of my grief.

'Well, yes.' She's looking down at her coffee. 'A long time ago – but he's my publisher now, and married to the daughter of a lord; she has perfect taste, perfect teeth, perfect hair.'

'Grim.'

'How's it going with Wilf?'

I don't want an inquest, so I don't say I think we've broken up, just, 'Not so well… I don't think I trust him.'

'Really? That surprises me… I would say he's a trust-worthy boy.'

'Not a boy! Let's change the subject.'

'Ah,' says Daphne. 'I do have something I need to ask you about. I've been invited to a literary festival in Denmark. It's a last-minute thing, someone dropped out. Anyhow it's next week – can I leave you in charge of the shop?'

She leans forward and with her big, manly fingers, moves a strand of hair that's fallen across my face, and tucks it behind my ear.

'Of course – my pleasure.' It happens occasionally – that Daphne goes away, and I like being in charge – the ritual of 'opening up', turning the three locks on the door, the feeling of being in command when the customers come in. But then I remember – Monday.

'When are you going?'

'Tuesday. So you'd have to do Tuesday to Friday, is that okay?'

'I'll enjoy it.'

'I hate the bloody things,' she says, 'but my publisher – Mr Nearly-Right – likes me to do them, and I'll enjoy Denmark.'

'Scandinavia – crime capital of the literary world.'

'Yes, of course. At least I'll be with my people...'

Because we've been talking, I've forgotten the mail that I'd put into my bag, and when Daphne returns to her desk I take out the brown parcel and unwrap it, and as I realise what's inside, I almost start crying again. It's Belle's bee bag, with a note from Tricia saying *Her mother gave it to me, along with much else. I thought you might like to have it.*

The white envelope is still in my bag – and I know I'm avoiding it, the thought of it making me feel cold inside. Reluctantly, I reach down, but before I pick it up, I'm distracted by Wilf coming into the shop. He ignores Daphne, and the books, and makes no effort to pretend he's looking for something to read. Instead, he comes straight to the counter, where I am, and he's looking

185

ruffled and bleary as though he's just got out of bed. We're eye to eye.

'Three things,' he says. 'One – I can't stand all this moodiness. Something's going on, and you're not being straight with me. Two – I'm angry with you. Angry. Because you don't trust me. Three… No, I've changed my mind about three. I'm sticking with two.' Then he walks out, with a brief 'Hi, Daphne' as he reaches the door.

'Bloody hell,' she says. 'You'd better find out what three was, sweetness. If you don't, it will kill me.'

But I sense a horrible finality. 'I'm not sure I will…' I say. 'I think that was Wilf's way of saying he won't be coming back for another Jo Nesbo.'

'We'll see.'

I bite my lip, painfully, trying to suppress my emotions, and I pick the envelope out of my bag. I don't want to open it, and when I do, it's with a ghastly sick feeling in the pit of my stomach, partly reflecting my bad night, partly my row with Wilf, but mainly my anticipation of the contents. Tilda Farrow and Felix Nordberg, I read, will be married on 22nd July at a church in Berkshire. I'm invited to the ceremony and the celebration afterwards at a country-house hotel.

21

I'm folding my orange scarf around my head, trying to make it look authentically Islamic. It takes a few attempts, and I only get it right after watching a hijab how-to video on YouTube. I put on aviator sunglasses, and look at myself from all angles. Scarlet's a genius – it really works – I've become a different person, and I'm attracted to the idea of playing a role, walking down the street in disguise. I dress in a loose-fitting blue shirt, and jeans with trainers. And, as I leave the flat, I pick up the bee bag to take with me.

I feel self-conscious as I wait for the bus, even though nobody is giving me a second glance. And I'm worried that Wilf might come by – although the bus stop is several roads away from Willesden Estates and it's possible that, if I keep my head down, he wouldn't recognise me anyway. I'm nervous, too, about Muslim girls spotting that I'm a fake. Maybe I did something wrong when I folded the scarf, or there's some detail about my clothes that jars with them. On the bus a woman wearing the hijab sits next to me and I half expect that we'll exchange a look, a moment of recognition, but there's nothing and I sit perfectly still, my arm lightly touching hers, reading my book.

I walk the last part of the journey, and when I reach the heath, a path takes me through a wooded area, dappled with pools of shade, dry leaves and twigs crackling underfoot; and I pass people walking their dogs, couples arm-in-arm, mothers with young children; it almost feels as though I'm one of them – an innocent person taking an afternoon stroll. Then I emerge into the open and see Kenwood House, a white mansion on a hill, spread wide with an orangery to the west and a long, low library to the east. I've been here many times, coming with my book to sit and read, and as I walk up the hill, across the wide lawn, I look at the familiar benches in front of the house, hoping to see Scarlet's red headscarf.

I don't spot her until I'm pretty close. At the last bench before the café, her head bent down, reading – not looking out for me at all. She makes a tight shape, clenched in, focussed on her book, and I can't see her face. And yet, I know instinctively that it's her – and I think I would have known even if she wasn't wearing the scarf. I had always thought of Scarlet as intense, somehow electrically charged, and that's how she seems now. I draw near and she looks up, sternly saying my name. No hint of a question, just a matter of fact; no recognition that there's an element of absurdity in our encounter.

'Did you come down from Manchester today?' I'm trying to start a normal conversation. 'Was it easy to get away from Luke?'

'Yes, I came down this morning. Luke thinks I'm on a training course.' I look down at her hands, which she holds in her lap, resting on her book. Her nails are bitten down and there's a roughness to her skin; not what I expected from someone who works in a beauty salon.

'It's strange to see you in person,' I say. 'But you're just as I imagined.'

I thought my observation would prompt some reaction – maybe 'Really? What do you mean?' or some comment about me, how she had imagined I would be. But she doesn't seem curious at all, and while I observe her white, freckled face and stained red lips, she stares ahead at the lake and the heath, and the city in the distance.

'I thought you wouldn't come... You've been disengaged recently.'

She's right. Before Belle died, I was having doubts about controllingmen; since her death I've found it hard to connect with anything – even important things like the split with Wilf and Tilda's wedding.

'Look at this.' She pulls up her sleeve and shows me three burns on her skinny forearm, raised circles of mottled red.

'And you have more on your back?'

'That's right. Each week it gets worse – burns, kicks, punches. And if I run – what? I have to live in fear that he'll follow me, that he'll go mad like Joe Mayhew. And it's no good thinking the police can protect you – they can't.'

'I know…' Then, 'My sister's marrying Felix…' Scarlet's burns are stoking up my paranoia.

'Fuck.'

'What are we going to do?' I watch a man and his small son throwing sticks for a Golden Retriever dog. 'Really, Scarlet. You've been talking about taking control somehow… but I don't know what you mean. It seems so impossible.'

The dog bounds up to our bench and sniffles at some crumbs by our feet. I stroke its fur, but Scarlet shivers and moves away until the dog runs back to the lawn and the sticks.

'I have an idea,' she says, sounding tentative, like she hasn't made up her mind yet about revealing it to me.

'It's going to freak you out, Callie. But do listen. Have a cool head… and think of the alternatives.'

'Tell me…'

She leans forward, and a dark strand of hair falls out of her headscarf. She takes off her sunglasses and turns her face to mine, and I see how blue her eyes are. Deep set, with black lashes.

'I'll get rid of Felix,' she says, 'if you get rid of Luke. We'll make a pact.'

'I don't understand…'

'I think you do. I'm saying I'm prepared to destroy Felix,

to save your sister – but you must do the same for me. Nobody will find out because I'm unconnected to Felix, no motive, nothing – and you're the same with Luke.'

Her voice has changed – she sounds resolute, like she's telling me what to do, not asking me. And I fear her answer to my next question.

'What do you mean – destroy?'

'I mean kill in order to prevent a killing. Kill in order to save a life…'

I slump backwards, wanting to get my face away from hers.

'That's insane. It's a movie plot, not real life.'

'Think carefully… women die every week because they do nothing, because they let these fuckers take control. It doesn't need to be like that, not if people like you and I are strong.' She lays her rough hand on my arm and lowers her voice. 'You should know that Belle agreed with me, and look what she did for us.'

She doubles up to reach a leather bag that's under the bench, and pulls it up onto her lap.

'Here…' I look inside, and see several syringes and medical-looking boxes.

'I brought these to show you, so that you would know Belle was committed. She stole them from York Hospital so that we could use them.'

'I don't believe it… I don't believe that Belle would do that.'

'You have to – these drugs and these syringes are the

proof. I have diamorphine here – if it's injected in a vein, it will kill someone in minutes.'

I feel myself collapsing into the bench, battered by Scarlet's words. She's so extreme, so crazy – and yet, as I look at her hunched body, her cold gaze, I believe she's serious.

'That's not all, Callie… I know who Felix is. You've dropped enough hints and it's an unusual name – and I read the papers.' She's putting her book into her bag, preparing to leave, telling me that she'll take care of Felix, and she'll find a way of telling me about Luke, and how I can keep my part of the bargain.

She turns to leave, and I say, 'Wait, let me walk with you…'

'No. That's all I had to say – we don't need to talk further, not now. But take this, and look after it.' She pulls a plastic bag out of her leather bag, and passes it to me, then she walks off, along past the benches and right, taking the path that goes towards the car park.

I look inside the bag, and see that she has given me diamorphine and three syringes. I take off my orange scarf, and stuff it in the bee bag, feeling I'm discarding Scarlet along with it. She's evidently mad, and I wonder whether I should go to the police. I wish that Belle was here so that I could seek her advice. Maybe she'd tell me to lighten up; that she hadn't stolen drugs from York Hospital, that Scarlet is a fantasist and the best course of action is simply to cut myself off from her. As I walk back down the hill and through the woods I feel lonely suddenly – Belle dead, Scarlet insane, Wilf gone – even Daphne is going away, off to Denmark.

When I reach the bus stop, I throw the drugs and syringes into a bin.

22

I call Tilda. I'm suppressing thoughts of needles and diamorphine and murder pacts; I'm also ignoring her hysterical letter to me (that's how I'm thinking of it now).

For once, she answers her phone, but she sounds vague as though I don't have her full attention. As sincerely as I can manage, I ask her about her wedding preparations and say that I can't wait to have Felix as a brother-in-law. I ask whether Mum's attitude is softening (she'd been cold with Tilda, and asked her whether she 'was sure' about Felix, and about getting married). Tilda informs me that, yes, 'Mum's coming to terms with it.'

'She'll come round,' I say, 'like I did.'

'Hang on a second.' I can tell by the muffled silence that she's put her hand over the phone, and then she's back on the line, sounding almost friendly.

'Lucas is here… Felix's brother. He's visiting from

France. Would you like to come to Curzon Street for supper?'

'Absolutely!' The relief's bursting out of me; it's like Tilda's decided to play along with my new approach. A life more ordinary.

*

I dress up in new black jeans and an apple green silk top (I've been to a trendy shop in Hoxton and splashed out); I wear the suede boots again, and do smoky eyes and pale lipstick, and I set off. At Curzon Street it's Lucas who answers the door, with an easy handshake and a kiss on the cheek.

'Hey,' he says. 'How does it feel to be tying yourself to the Nordberg clan?'

His accent is broader, looser than Felix's – he sounds properly American, sounding the 'r' in Nordberg, whereas Felix always sounds a little Scandinavian, hard to place.

'You're the first member of the clan that I've met, apart from Felix, obviously.' I hand over my Strongbow (it seems like he's the host) and he says, 'Bold choice,' and pours me a glass. I watch, assessing him. His hair's blond, like Felix's, but thicker and wavy, and his eyes are the same shade of metal grey. Generally, though, he's unlike his brother, wearing artsy clothes, having a brash manner, and a brown hipster beard.

Felix and Tilda are out, buying wine, and they return

just as I'm saying to Lucas, 'So, you're an architect, and you work in France?'

Felix kisses me and says, 'You're so stylish these days,' making me feel like his special girl, just as he'd done at the Wolseley. Tilda does her usual thing – draping herself over the sofa, hugging a pink cushion (one of the few items that's survived Felix's makeover of the flat).

'Well?' she says.

'Well what?'

She sweeps her arm about in an actressy gesture. 'The flat of course – what do you think?'

I sit with her and she puts her legs and bare feet across my lap. 'I don't know… It's a little… psychiatric. Or like living in a fridge.'

'Trust you!' She glances at Felix, who raises his eyebrows at us genially. 'I think it's wonderful,' she says. 'It's so chic and well designed. The attention to detail is amazing.'

'I'm sure it is… Where's all your mess? Old biros and bits of string and magazines and old electrical cables, all that stuff.'

She flicks her wrist, like she's batting away a fly. 'Gone Callie… all gone.'

For a second I find myself identifying with the bits of string, feeling their pain.

In the kitchen area the Brothers Nordberg are making a dish with squid that's come from the market, and Lucas grabs a knife and lays the squid out on a chopping board.

'Can I make a suggestion,' Felix says, and starts

rearranging the squid, lining them up. 'If you put them this way, it'll be easier to remove the tentacles.'

'Here we go…'

'And then you cut just below the eyes, like this… and remove the quill…'

'Hey, Felix… I know, I know!' Lucas leaves the kitchen and comes to sit with us, saying, 'I'll let him play head chef… It's his kitchen after all.' Then, 'How do you deal with it, Tilda?'

'Oh, he's not so bad.' I detect a fragile tone in her voice.

'Really?'

'Well… he did give me a PowerPoint presentation of our trip to Martinique – before we went! What we'd do on each day…'

We laugh, and Felix shrugs and says, 'Okay, guys, laugh at me if you will – but it was an awesome vacation, wasn't it, darling?'

She purrs. 'Yes, darling. And beautifully planned… I adored your PowerPoint presentation.'

I squirm at the *darlings* and turn to Lucas. 'Tell me about your work.' Tilda asks him to fetch his architectural drawings from the bedroom.

Lucas returns with three rolls of heavy white paper that he opens up on the limestone floor, using books to hold down the corners, and I kneel next to him, immediately immersed in his confident fluid lines, delicate cross-hatchings, sweeps of watercolour. It's the design of a house which sits in a landscape of rolling hills, marked as *Provence*.

'It's beautiful.' I mean it.

'The wood cladding is perfect for the setting,' says Lucas. 'It will become silver-grey as it weathers – and I've stressed the relationship between the interior and exterior – this internal bridge crosses the double-height kitchen, and leads straight from the living room to the balcony. There's glass on two adjacent sides – to the south and west.'

'And who gets to live here? You?'

'Sadly not. I've designed it for a British couple.' He pronounces it 'Briddish'. 'It's a second home.'

'Another world,' I say. 'Have you seen these, Felix?'

'Oh yes.' He doesn't look up and I sense that he's being competitive – Felix's squid versus Lucas's drawings.

'It's my first house. Until now it's been all extensions and alterations, and supplementing my income with teaching… It's not built yet, though. We're laying foundations right now…'

'Drawings away,' says Felix. 'Supper's ready…' Lucas collects up the papers while Felix puts his dish in the centre of the dining table. 'Squid with chilli and mint…'

'That looks wonderful…' Tilda's being wifey, sending him a quick admiring grin. She circles the table, straightening the knives and forks, putting the wine glasses in exactly the right place.

'Oh look, you're turning into Felix,' I say, and she flashes me hostile eyes.

Over dinner, Lucas entertains us with stories of the

couple who'd commissioned the house. 'Corporate law-yers, more cash than they know what to do with. He's monosyllabic, keeps his verbal brilliance for the court-room, and she's one of those tiny, brittle women who has a session with her tennis coach before breakfast…'

'They have good taste though,' I say. 'If they've com-missioned you.'

'Yeah… That's what matters. But I worry that my beau-tiful house will stay empty most of the year; they both work all the hours… It's a building that's been designed to be *used, lived in.* Still, I'm grateful – creatively, I've never been so engaged, so fulfilled…'

Felix is sitting stiffly, gazing at his squid, as Lucas chat-ters on about France and architecture and his ambitions, and I actually feel sorry for my future brother-in-law – he can hardly effuse about the wonders of hedge-funding, or his personal ambitions to make more money. At one point he says, 'Who'd like chocolate mousse? I made it earlier.' And Tilda says, 'Yummy!' – making me wonder if is this the only sort of conversation they have when they're alone these days, baby talk, and banal comments about food and cooking, maybe occasionally talking about holidays? And then a riveting idea occurs to me – if I steal Tilda's memory stick again, I'll maybe get her version of this evening, of Felix's reaction to his brother's good-humoured boasting. Of her attitude towards me. And I say to myself, *that's what I'll do – and if Tilda's evening turns out to be benign, nothing sinister, I'll forget everything, all the controllingmen nonsense, and Scarlet's monstrous suggestion.* I feel that I'm conducting some sort of scientific experiment as I say, 'So, Lucas, what were you and Felix like as children? Were you always the creative one?'

'How can I put it? I was the one who, in all senses, was expressive – drawing, painting, playing baseball and soccer – generally noisy. My big brother was the observer in the family; always watching, keeping his thoughts to himself, making private plans.' Lucas's gaze flits lazily between Tilda and me, gently encouraging us to play along; only once glancing at Felix, but in that second his expression hardens, and Felix carefully moves the wine bottle three centimetres to the right.

'Callie's an observer,' says Tilda. 'You and Felix are alike that way.'

'What? I'm like Felix? No I'm not, not at all...'

'Thank you for sharing.' Felix's tone is wry and faintly comical.

'No – I only mean that, although we're both observers – you're a leader, a doer, you make things happen. I tend to follow, like a sheep.'

'You're not a sheep,' says Lucas. 'You're a beautiful little black pony...'

'What animal am I?' asks Tilda.

And together Lucas and I say, 'A white butterfly...'

'It must be true, then,' I add. 'But what about Felix? What is he?'

'A snake,' says Lucas in a voice that indicates he's joking. Felix pretends to laugh.

Then we turn to praising Felix's chocolate mousse, and Lucas returns to the subject of their childhood. Felix, we learn, never had leanings towards architecture but he was a remarkably capable builder, and had constructed a treehouse in their back garden. 'Do you remember?' says Lucas. 'All the planning you did. I think you spent nearly a year planning it in minute detail, then buying all the materials and tools with your saved-up pocket money…'

'That's what I meant,' I say. 'That's Felix…'

Felix says, 'Good thing too,' and returns to the kitchen, loading the dishwasher, wrapping clean bowls up in cling-film.

I watch him at his work, thinking, *It's okay to be odd, Felix. I'm not going to condemn you right now. At least, not until I've checked the memory stick again.*

23

It's Tuesday morning and I'm in charge of the bookshop while Daphne is promoting herself in Copenhagen. It's strange and quiet when she's away because, even when she isn't talking, she generally makes her presence felt – bashing her keyboard, drinking her coffee, tapping her feet on the floorboards. The unusual, slightly creepy, silence allows me to get a few tasks done – I sort out the new books, and I phone Mum, who's now up to date, and says, 'I'm not sure about this wedding… we don't really *know* him, not properly…' but she agrees to come to London to shop together for her wedding outfit. Then I go online and, despite my resolution to avoid controllingmen, I check out the site. The members are talking about Joe Mayhew and Bea Santos – several people reckoning that he'll try to have the murder charge reduced to manslaughter, pleading diminished responsibility.

He'll say he was depressed, that mental illness meant he

wasn't responsible for his actions, writes someone called Lemon-and-Lime. *He'll be on suicide watch now – the coward's way out.*

I agree. I want him to go to court, and I want him to be convicted of murder.

I'm scrolling down, reading, when our doorbell jangles, signalling the arrival of a customer, and I'm surprised to see Lucas. My nonchalant half-smile is supposed to suggest that I'm intrigued that someone as urbane as him has troubled himself to come to Willesden, and I'm leaning my chin on the back of my hand, hoping that my body language indicates that my work here is an amusing sideline, not a financial necessity. Possibly, though, I'm wasting my efforts. He says, 'I'm stopping by to inspect your architecture collection.'

'You could have gone to Central London. To Waterstones or Foyles or something.'

'But then I wouldn't have had a chance to see you. And look what I've brought.'

He has a paper carrier bag with two salads inside, in cardboard boxes, with little bamboo forks. 'Pea and mint with feta cheese,' he says. 'Tilda said that lunch might be a problem for you – with your boss away.'

'I'd brought a cheese-and-Marmite sandwich, but your salad looks nicer.'

I fetch him a chair from the back office, and we sit and eat, and he says, 'So, now you have a chance to ask me about my idiosyncratic brother – I could tell at dinner last night that you were dying to get the full story – all that digging you did, asking about our childhoods.'

I feel suddenly nervous – like he's been sent by Tilda or Felix to trick me. But he's eating his salad in a way that I'd call hearty, and looking at me with a straight, unbothered eye.

He's right, of course, I'm desperate for more information. All week my mind has been flipping between two extreme modes – one minute I'm filled with alarm at Tilda's letter, and the evidence that Felix really is a danger. Those bruises, that thrown vase. And then I think of good Felix, weird but nice Felix, in love Felix. Now I have Lucas to talk to. Clear-headed, easy-going Lucas.

'I just want to know that my sister is safe.' I've decided to be blunt. 'What is his relationship history like? He told me about Francesca, the journalist.'

'Why do you think Tilda may not be safe?' He doesn't look at me now, but at his food, moving it around with his fork, and I get the impression that he has, after all, had a pointed conversation with Tilda and Felix about me. That he's been sent by them.

'I don't know… Felix is a strong character. Everything has to be done his way.'

'You're right to think he's pretty dominating, I guess. And that's the reason that we don't always get along. You saw what he was like with a simple thing like squid – he just couldn't allow me to cook it my way – he had to take over.'

'And you let him…'

'That's the easiest way to deal with my brother – to let him take control.'

'I have to ask the obvious question…'

'What happens when you challenge him?'

'Yes… not that I see Tilda challenging him ever.'

He puts his salad box on the counter and faces me directly, like he's saying *Enough about food, now for the serious stuff.* 'Well, he can go into deep, black moods. A lot of anger… just below the surface, even over small things. When we were kids it could be anything – one time I went into the treehouse without his permission, and moved his things around… He was totally pissed, for weeks. Weeks! And he cut up my soccer kit with scissors, my favourite shirt.' He smiles, like it's a fond memory, not a horrible one.

'What happened with Francesca? How did she deal with the moods?'

He frowns. 'Poor Francesca. She was so in love… Which isn't unusual, by the way. Women do fall for him, repeatedly. He was always the better-looking brother – he has a certain charisma I guess.'

I'm in a difficult position. I can't say *Oh no Lucas, you're the attractive one!* because it isn't true. Even though Lucas is sophisticated and smiley and approachable, I can see that women are more drawn to Felix with his finer features, his enigmatic, unknowable quality. The mere fact that he speaks less than Lucas does.

'Felix is a bit like Max in *Rebecca*,' I say. 'I mean, sort of smouldering...'

'Francesca thought so. She always tried to please him, to be the person that he wanted her to be – perfectly dressed, well mannered, discreet. She was doomed to fail though. Her personality made her unguarded, opinionated. And she lacked something that Felix was looking for. It's hard to identify it exactly – I think Felix wants a woman to be a work of art, like a perfect painting... And your sister is definitely the closest he's come to finding that. She's extraordinarily beautiful. She's kinda... Venus rising...'

'We're the normal people, you and I – the civilians. They're from some other world...' I realise that we're talking about Felix as though he's an interesting character in a book, that we are being superficial, not truly exploring the sinister side of his psyche, and I want to ask *But is he physically dangerous? Did he harm Francesca? Is that the real reason that they split up?* But there's something so good-natured and affable about Lucas, that I find it hard to ask outright whether his brother is an abusive monster. I just hint at it, saying, 'If Francesca were with us now, what would she say about Felix?'

'She'd say he broke her heart... that he made her unhappy, and she's found it difficult to move on.' He picks up his salad and starts eating again. I'm not going to get anything stronger from him, and I take a different line. 'Do you ever see her?'

'No, sadly. She's an impressive woman. Very intelligent. I liked her.'

'Is she still in this country? Working here?'

'I think so. She's a correspondent at an American paper, in the London bureau. She's often travelling, though. She's covered Libya and Syria…'

I store the information, thinking that the time will come when I need to track her down, to find out the truth.

Lucas wipes his mouth with the back of his hand and says, 'And now you can tell me about Tilda. And, if we're going to quiz each other about our siblings, I may as well follow your probing style – what's her relationship history like?'

I'm taken aback. It hadn't occurred to me that he might have doubts about Tilda, and hearing my own words sent back to me gives me a little shock; they sound antagonistic.

'I'm sorry! I've been rude…'

'No need to apologise. It's fair enough. I mean – marriage is huge. Of course we want to know…'

'Well, Tilda has had lots of boyfriends, but they come and go. I never even met them… Nothing like Felix. He's the first that she's really included in her life – and it's amazing to see her behaviour with him, the way she's fallen into the adoring-wife role. I haven't seen her so in love since she had this huge crush when she was a teenager, on a boy called Liam Brookes… In fact, I know she's kept in touch with Liam over the years and I always expected her to get back with him. But now she's with Felix I can see that he's *the one*. He's her future, Liam's her past.'

I fold my arms in front of me, on the counter, let my head fall down into them and close my eyes. Out of the blue I'm overwhelmed – by the contrast between the violent undertone of Tilda's confessions on the memory stick and the blandness of the account I'm giving Lucas. Deep down I know I'm suppressing my worries about Felix and am blindly hoping for the best.

Lucas's hand touches my arm. 'Hey… What's the matter?'

I pull myself upright, recognising pity in his voice and realising that he thinks I'm jealous of Tilda! 'Oh, it's nothing. As you say – marriage is huge.'

'Yes. And that's why I need to ask you – all those boyfriends of your sister's – why did she fail to commit? Does she run away at the first sign of trouble? Or was she always in love with this Liam guy?'

'I don't think so, Lucas. I think it's more that she wanted someone other than Liam, but she's very picky. Maybe she has been waiting all her life for Felix. She needs his strength…'

'Well, I guess we should let Tilda and Felix live their lives – they're well matched and I've never seen Felix this committed to a girl. He loves her.'

I think *so you were sent by Felix after all, as part of his campaign to win me over.*

He stands up and stretches his chest. 'Now… show me your architecture books.'

At home later I google Francesca and Libya and Syria, and find out that her name is Francesca Moroni. She writes about British and European politics, and covers conflict and war sometimes. I think of the old days when Tilda used to talk about going with Liam when he joined Medecins sans Frontieres. I know now that she wouldn't have been brave enough, that she would never have had Francesca Moroni's guts.

I click Google Images, and find a page full of photos of a young woman with a mass of brown wavy hair that, when she's working in war zones, is pulled back into a messy ponytail, and at award ceremonies is allowed to fall around her face, flamboyantly. Her features are dramatic – big brown eyes, full lips – and her figure is large, but in my view, she's a beauty. Nothing about her suggests Lucas's image of 'poor Francesca'. One picture of a social event shows her in a red sparkly evening dress, in animated conversation with a man I recognise as a recent foreign secretary. Another, clipped from a TV news report, shows her in a flak jacket standing on a dusty dirt road, notebook in her hand while, behind her, three slouchy men in hoods are holding guns. When Lucas said 'poor Francesca' was nonetheless impressive, I hadn't grasped what he meant.

But I can see that, as he suggested, there's nothing discreet about her – that to fit into Felix's concept of the perfect woman she would have to change herself. It seems strange to me that such a strong character would have attempted to do that. If she did, it's further evidence of Felix's power. I can't help it – I open my laptop and go to the dossier, and I write about Francesca Moroni. I wish she was here, that I could talk to her right now, reassure myself that it's okay for Tilda to marry Felix. If only I could just go to Curzon Street and argue it out with Tilda – but she won't allow that. She'd defend Felix, and cut me out of her life. I write also: *I'd like to check the memory stick to see if Tilda has added anything to her letter. But I can't. She'll be at the flat until the wedding, and will know if I take it. I'll have to wait until she's away on honeymoon.*

24

St Gregory's Church in Berkshire is pretty. It's Norman, set centrally in a graveyard with old, leaning headstones, the names on them smoothed away by the wind or partially hidden by moss. Before the wedding, I walk around, trying to make them out, forming images of Emily Jane Goode who died in 1830 at the age of twenty-one, and Henry Watson who perished in a foreign field in 1809, at the age of twenty-nine. And those who lived to be old, Ernest Norwood Richardson, ninety-three, who is buried with a dozen or more of his descendants, perpetually guarded by a mournful stone angel. I sit on a rickety bench by a wall, and find that I'm missing Wilf. I wish he were here today, that the incident with the *Mail* had never happened. I would find his big earthy presence comforting, and I need comfort. I'm in a troubled daze, knocked almost senseless by the occasion, unable to work out whether I'm happy for my sister, or whether she's on a path that has nowhere to lead other than her own death.

Mum weaves her way through the graves towards me, unsteady in high heels, and I grin at her, feeling suddenly affectionate. I'd helped choose the floral chiffon dress she's wearing, with dangly bits at the bottom, and the shocking-pink fascinator. I'm a little unnerved by the ankle tattoo, but it's not as bad as I'd feared.

'You look lovely.' I notice that her complexion looks fresh and youthful. Sometimes it is infused with the high blush of too much alcohol, but not today.

'You too, darling.' I'm wearing the blue dress that Daphne bought me, and the suede ankle boots. I didn't want to buy anything new.

'The Nordberg parents have arrived, all the way from Boston, come and meet them. Erik and Alana. They seem jolly nice…'

She takes my hand, pulls me up from the bench, and we join Mr and Mrs Nordberg in the vestibule of the church. They each kiss me lightly on my cheek, and welcome me into their family. Erik comments on the beauty of the church, and Alana says, 'We're both so happy for Felix and Tilda,' in a light, vague voice that somehow sounds regal, like she is the Queen of Sweden. She's wearing a simple beige silk dress, no hat, and her husband looks chic in a well-cut, dark suit. They are both skinny and tall, and they make our curves and Mum's chiffon seem provincial, almost tacky. Lucas appears and ushers us into the church, and we are sent to the bride's side, whilst the Nordbergs sit behind Felix, who turns to chat to his parents, his arm draped languorously along the back of the pew, not reflecting the tension that he holds in his grey eyes, which dart around the church, checking everything is in place – the walls, the roof, the congregation.

It's the smallest of weddings, a cluster of a dozen people each side of the aisle. I recognise Paige Mooney (definitely obese now, dressed in ruched layers of green polyester) and Jacob Thynne (from his appearance in *Rebecca*), but no one else. Felix's guests look like they belong to a single tribe, financial people, slick and neat. I lean my head on Mum's shoulder, like I used to when I was a child, and she says, 'Chip chip.'

'Will Tilda be all right?' I say.

'Let's hope so…'

'I love the church.' It is simple and ancient, and the air inside is heavy, infused with the cold scent of rain and stone.

'You were christened here. My parents were married here…'

'Tilda told me… It's weird that I didn't know.'

The wedding march starts, and we stand and turn to look at the bride, and I'm confused by what I see. She's beautiful, of course, wearing a simple white satin dress with long sleeves, and she has small white flowers in her hair; there's a hint of *Midsummer Night's Dream* about her. My heart skips a beat at the sight of those long sleeves, covering up who-knows-what injuries to her arms. I am stung too by the sight of the man standing beside her, linking her arm, and I turn to Mum and say, 'Did she tell you?' and she shakes her head. Liam Brookes is leading my sister up the aisle, with the hint of a smile, and there is something so comfortable and easy about the two of them, it seems like they are from the same family. He looks just the same as when I last saw him ten years ago, his long, honest face and relaxed way of walking. After he leaves Tilda facing Felix, ready to take her vows, he slips into our pew, beside me, and whispers, 'Hello, Callie.'

'I didn't know you and Tilda were still so close,' I whisper back.

So quietly I can barely hear him, he says, 'I've always been her safety net...'

As the service begins, I think *This is the moment*, and she says, in a clear, confident voice, 'With this ring I thee wed,' and I try to go along with the spirit of the day, ignoring the side of me that is scared, is in freefall. I'll put my sister's wishes first. I think *I'll be friendly to Felix, give him the benefit of the doubt. At least until I've stolen back the memory stick after the wedding.* Tilda and Felix are off to Santorini for a week. It's a Greek island, apparently.

The vicar says, 'I now declare you husband and wife.' So that's it – there's no going back – and I conquer my nausea and smile as Tilda and Felix walk away from the altar, amongst us, their eyes sparkling, Tilda laughing out loud with happiness, doing a tiny skip with her feet,

Felix's arm squeezing her tight. It's just like any normal wedding. That is, until we leave the church, and find three press photographers hanging about outside – two scruffy middle-aged men and a young woman looking cool in black jeans and black t-shirt. Felix says, 'For fuck's sake,' and Lucas dashes over and tells them to take a couple of pictures and, 'Please leave, guys, allow Felix and Tilda to enjoy their day.' Nobody expects them to actually go, but they do, the young woman waving goodbye as she slings her camera over her shoulder and climbs into an old, open-top sports car.

'Assholes,' says Lucas. 'How did they know?'

'They always know.' I'm thinking about Wilf.

The reception is in a nearby country-house hotel, a grey stone Edwardian pile with vast bay windows and castellated walls, and freshly mown grass that stretches down to the Thames. The weather's overcast and breezy, but fine, and champagne is served on the lawn. I take a glass and find myself in a small group with Mum, the Nordberg parents and two friends of Felix's, expensive-looking men. They're talking not about the wedding, or how gorgeous Tilda looks, but about the international debt crisis, and the European outlook. Felix's friends are quizzing Erik, the eminent economist, whilst Alana smiles on softly, in a way that has obviously been honed and perfected over the years. Erik's glass of champagne is in one hand, and he's gesturing with it, with large swinging motions, as he pronounces on the failings of the Greek finance minister and the euro. His other hand is on the small of his wife's back, one finger moving back and forth. I wonder whether this is the model for Felix and Tilda's marriage, the one desired by Felix at least because, despite her recent attempts at wifeyness, I can't see Tilda being submissive in the long term. It's not in her nature.

I slip away, unnoticed, and am ambushed by Paige Mooney, a gigantic vision in lime, tottering on silver sandals with a six-inch heel. Her toenails are painted green, neatly and professionally, but they belong to lumpy uneven toes which have grown at strange angles to each other.

She gives me a big, damp kiss on one cheek. 'Callie! You're looking so lovely… so different!'

'Paige! You look just the same!' I don't add, *but even fatter.* 'How are the children?'

She tells me, at length, about Harrison, who's ten now and has taken up drumming, and Edie, eight, who wants to be an actress like Auntie Tilda, and Frankie, five, who has learning difficulties but is doing brilliantly in his new school. She prattles on and on, explaining that Robbie was sad he couldn't come to the wedding, but that it's his sister's thirtieth birthday today, and that she, Paige, was totally amazed that Tilda invited her to the wedding, but she was sad there were no bridesmaids, she would have loved to have been asked, and she was disappointed that she doesn't see much of Tilda these days, and she is so very, very pleased that Tilda is settling down; she had wondered whether she was the type, 'if you understand me…'

'Not sure…'

She makes her voice go breathy and excited. 'Well! I wouldn't have been surprised if she'd ended up with another girl…'

I glare at her, and splutter, realising that it's this sort of nonsense that made Tilda drop Paige.

'What in hell's name makes you think that?'

'Oh I don't know,' she looks up at the sky, for inspiration. 'Maybe just the way we used to be when we were in the Whisper Sisters, she was so touchy and strokey and kissy.'

'But she was in love with Liam back then…'

'I know! And he led her up the aisle too. What do you make of that? I thought – that just shows she wasn't *really* in love with him, that it was all a show, or maybe she was in love with the *idea* of him – the heroic doctor and all that.'

'It was real, Paige. You should have seen her after she was dumped. She went into psychological meltdown.'

'Oh, I'm probably wrong… I usually am. Probably it was just us adoring *her* that I'm remembering.'

I can't stand any more of her idiocy, and I make an excuse, saying I'm going to find Tilda now – but really I'm looking for Liam. There's so much I want to ask him – how are his dreams working out? Does he like being a doctor? I look around, but I can't see him amongst our group. I realise that I want him to be the person to tell me that Tilda is fine, that she's made a good choice in Felix. The

Liam I used to know had such good sense, good instincts. I think too that Tilda has probably confided in Liam, was straight in a way that she never is with me.

I spot him on the terrace, speaking to Tilda, and I'm struck once again by the way they seem so comfortable together. I go over, and Liam says, 'I'm afraid I have to leave, Callie, but it was so good to see you. I'm sorry I can't stay longer.'

'Liam has to work.'

'Do you work at a hospital? Is that why you have to work on a Saturday?'

'That's right.' He kisses us both before leaving.

'My God, Tilda, I haven't seen him in so long. Is he a surgeon or something?'

'He's a psychiatrist.' She widens her eyes in a silent *How about that!* 'He sections people.'

'I would have loved to have talked to him.'

And that's all I can think about for the rest of the day – at the dinner, and the dancing and the waving off of the bride and groom – I would love to talk to Liam Brookes.

25

Tilda and Felix are in Santorini and, for once, Tilda is in touch, sending me texts saying *blissfully, contentedly chilling*, or *F made us walk four miles today, to the lagoon*. She even emailed a photo – Felix and her sitting on the side of a turquoise infinity pool, their legs dangling in the water, a yellow shawl draped over Tilda's arms, her head resting on Felix's chest; it's a position that, for me, represents her submission, her unnatural placidity. Behind the happy couple, everything is beautiful: the cloudless sky, the azure blue of the Aegean sea.

The picture should look serene, but I find it unsettling. Maybe that's because, all the time now, Scarlet is bombarding me with horror stories: Grace and William Starling are found dead in their £3 million Surrey home; police are not looking for anyone else in connection with the case. I stare at a photograph of their wedding day. Can you tell that something's wrong? Grace looks into the camera lens, her eyes soft, her cheeks dimpled, and handsome William gazes at her – a gentle conscientious lover's gaze. Nothing to suggest the cocktail of hurt and resentment and suspicion that leads to a killing. Three days later and Jordan Freeman sends his nineteen-year-old girlfriend, Kelly Wallis, a text: *luv u babe and this is my promise – I aint going to hit u ever again. were the best babe.* But that night he breaks into Kelly's family home and strangles her with a length of wire cable. Two days after that Darren Lott texts his twenty-two-year-old girlfriend, Samantha McFadden, explaining that he's going to Scotland for the weekend, but he never leaves Liverpool. Instead on Saturday evening he waits outside Samantha's flat until she leaves for work at a local bar, and he stabs her seventeen times before dragging her body into the boot of his car, and driving off. It's practically every day, an endless narration of women killed by men they know.

I'm in the bookshop, reading up on all this, when the news comes in that, in York, Chloey Percival has died. For some reason I'd thought she would pull through, and even become a spokeswoman against domestic violence. But now I'm heavy inside, thinking that her death, after all, came with a sickening inevitability, and I feel brought down by the constant litany of hate – by Chloey's death and Belle's death. I switch off my laptop – I can't bear to read all the venom and outrage that will be on control-lingmen.

At the other end of the shop Daphne, who is back from

Denmark, is sprawled at her desk, and she calls across the empty space, 'So, I went on an internet date last night, nice guy – had a beard though, sixtyish, divorced, and he did all the talking, bit intense, but keen…'

'What does he do, like, for a job?' I'm doing my best to sound interested.

'He went on and on about it. Works in marketing at a pharmaceutical company…'

'With a beard…?'

'I know… But, get this, he had read two of my books in preparation for the date… and had googled me in massive detail, looking up stuff about Saskatchewan.'

'Be careful, he might be obsessive. Men like that can be dangerous…'

'Callie, stop worrying. You mustn't let your friend's death make you paranoid. Most people are decent and good, you know… the bad apples are rare exceptions. It's important to trust people, otherwise you turn cynical and unhappy.'

'Daphne! You need to listen to me… I know more about this than you do!'

Then, I can't help it, I start to cry, large heavy tears like raindrops sliding down my cheek, my nose running, my shoulders heaving, and I can't stop. Daphne sprints over, saying, 'Sweetness, sweetness – what is it? What's the matter? Here, let me find some tissues…'

'Oh god,' I sniffle. 'I'm so worried about Tilda, now that she's married. I was starting to feel better, but now it's all building up again…' That's all I can get out, because I'm wheezing and panting, as the tears start to dry up.

'Come on…' Daphne puts her arm round me, cleaving me to her puny chest. 'It's understandable that you're like this. Losing Belle was a major trauma…You're grieving.'

At that moment Wilf walks past the shop. Straight past, not pausing, not coming in – and he's deep in conversation with Amy Fishwick, the girl who left Willesden Estates. I notice for the first time that she has long blonde hair extensions, and is unusually pretty. It takes all my resolve not to cry again, but I don't – I tell Daphne that I'll be fine now.

At home, in the evening, I'm drawn back to controlling-men, and find that Scarlet has linked me into the details of dozens more female deaths, this time from around the world: America, Australia, Brazil, South Africa, Italy, France… I shut my laptop forcefully, pour myself a large glass of Strongbow, and lie on my bed, thinking about Tilda, and about the memory stick. I need to look at it again, urgently, before Tilda and Felix return.

26

I'm back at the desolate, sanitised flat on Curzon Street, heading straight for the linen cupboard, extracting the little red ingot. Before I examine its contents, though, I tour the flat – checking the medicine cupboard, inspecting Felix's boxed-up shirts, marvelling at the clingfilmed crockery. But there's nothing to arouse my interest apart from a pile of papers on a table. I'm shocked – I thought Felix *never* left papers lying around. I sift through them, finding an invitation to an art exhibition on Dover Street, another to a drinks party in Pimlico. Also, the paperwork for a conference called 'New York or London'? It will last two days, apparently, and take place at the Ashleigh House Hotel near Marlow in Buckinghamshire. I see that Felix has registered as a delegate, and I find myself noting down the name of the hotel and dates of the conference in the dossier. Then I insert the memory stick into my laptop, and scroll down. As I'd hoped, there's new material. Tilda has updated her letter:

Now we're about to be married there's a change in Felix. I'm sensing a shift away from passion towards violence for its own sake and, I admit it, Callie, I'm less turned on by his behaviour and more scared.

I wonder whether you noticed anything that time that Lucas came round for supper, a few days before the wedding. It was unbearable for Felix to listen to Lucas boasting about the French house he's designed because, for Felix, there's only one thing worse than Lucas throwing his life away on failed creative projects – and that's Lucas succeeding, proving himself as an architect. And then he started portraying himself as a sort of renaissance child – so talented at everything, while Felix was the 'observer', silently weighing up Lucas, endlessly watching him. I'm sure Lucas knew the effect he was having, and was relishing it; I was totally aware. It was only you, Callie, who didn't seem to realise what was going on. Then we were talking about 'which animal is Felix', and Lucas said 'snake' – and you let out the noisiest belly laugh (very unflattering, btw!). Of course, Felix was seething. When you all left he started cleaning the (already clean) kitchen, in the foulest mood, barely speaking to me. I tried to help, but he hissed at me, 'Get out! – I'll do this', pushing me away.

I was going to do as he said, and sat down on the sofa, opening the *Vogue* magazine, but then I had a brilliant idea – I wanted to provoke him, so that we'd end up in bed in our most passionate, frenzied state, and I said, 'Lucas is a fantastic guy – and so gifted. Those architectural drawings were beautiful.' I returned to the kitchen space. Felix was bending down, setting the dishwasher, ignoring me. And I softly stroked his hair, saying, 'Does he take after your mother? She's the creative one of the marriage isn't she – with her children's books?' Still he ignored me, and I said, 'Really, darling… I'm interested. What was it like growing up with him? Was he always doing beautiful drawings like that?'

He stood up, stared into my eyes with a fierce, wounded expression on his face, and using all his force he slammed me against the wall, one arm forcing my body backwards, the other across my throat, throttling me. I was in a state of complete surrender, my adrenalin pumping, suddenly light-headed, in a sort of blissful trance-like state, and I was expecting him to drag me to the bed. But then he was hissing into my ear, 'What the fuck are you playing at? Why would you do this?' putting greater pressure on my throat, so hard and painful that I couldn't even choke, although my chest was heaving uselessly. I thought I was going to die, but then he stopped and I slumped to the floor, while he stormed out of the house. He returned at some early hour of the morning – three or four o'clock – I was in bed, waiting, and he just got in with me, turned his back and went to sleep.

That night was horrible, but I'm sure I'll be able to suppress thoughts of it on my wedding day. Yes, Callie, I am going through with it – because I love Felix, and will never cease to be excited by him. I just need to be careful in how far I push him, and make an art of it. And my career? (I can practically hear you screaming the question at me.) I guess I'll have to take it very slowly if I'm to act again. A high-profile film role right now would be intolerable for Felix, I know it. So – we'll see.

Truth is, it's becoming more likely that I will be killed by him and that you will get to read this letter (what shall I do? Print it out and leave it in a sealed envelope with my solicitor – to be opened by Callie in the event of my death?).

I want you to know this, little one – that my only regret is that I will leave you alone; though sometimes I think you'll be better off without me stealing the limelight and dominating you. If I'm gone, please don't be sad. Remember that I've chosen this path, and I'm sure that, deep down, you were always aware that I've had a romantic relationship with the idea of death; that I'm fascinated by death, part of me longs for it. Think about it – all that self-harming and bulimia when I was a teenager. And maybe that was why I made such a convincing Peter Pan, *to die is an awfully big adventure!* These days, I don't see it like that exactly – the word adventure is too positive, too cheerful. I see death as terrifying and also mesmerising – I imagine the ecstasy of that total, ultimate release.

Doubtless you've gone through my medicine cupboard, noting all the drugs. Have you figured it out? I've enough in there to obliterate myself, and that's the important thing. I'm uneasy if I don't have the means, the freedom, to kill myself close to hand. But I'm not about to do it. I'd rather leave it to fate – or to put it another way, I'd rather leave it to Felix. Because he's becoming more violent, and he will kill me. I'm convinced of it now.

27

'He doesn't look like a brute… To the naked eye, I mean.'

Daphne's poring over pictures in *Grazia*, of Tilda and Felix on their honeymoon in Greece. On sun-loungers, in swimwear. I'm looking over Daphne's shoulder, studying Tilda's arms. I can't see marks – but the picture quality is poor. I'm looking at Tilda's face, too. From her serene expression you'd never know that she's contemplating her own death. And Felix is lying lazily, one hand behind his head, reading some fat paperback. As Daphne says, he doesn't look like a brute.

'The photos mean nothing…'

'Of course, sweetness. That was stupid of me.'

I return to my chair behind the shop counter, and am about to send Tilda yet another text asking whether she's okay. At least, on this holiday, she's still speaking to me – and my main aim is to keep our channel of communication open.

I'm pressing send when the bell jangles and an older guy comes into the shop. He has an unruly grey beard and a baggy checked shirt and, unlike most of the customers, he doesn't ignore Daphne – he raises his eyebrows at her and with a tentative grin says, 'Okay to disturb you while you're working – just for a minute?' At the same time, he produces from behind his back a bunch of flowers – pink roses, cosmos daisies, and a sprig of white lacy hydrangeas. 'From my garden,' he says. Daphne is blushing an unseemly blotchy red colour, and gets up from her chair, bashing her leg against the work table.

'Douglas, you're a darling!' She takes the flowers. 'I'll put them in a glass and have them on my table.'

He exits, with a cheery wave, saying, 'Not stopping. Just wanted to drop those by…'

Daphne says, 'You see, Callie, romance does happen. Life can be uncomplicated sometimes.'

'Uncomplicated! Are you sure? Don't you have complicated doubts about Douglas's beard, and your compatibility?'

She snorts. 'You know what, good sex can sort everything out – the complexity falls away.'

'You haven't!'

'Oh yes I have.'

'You're going to hate this… But what about all that research he did on you before he met you. It was practically cyberstalking. Don't you find that worrying?'

She leans her chin on her hand, is gazing at me in a

benign, smiley way. Sort of kind, sort of patronising. 'Actually no. Everyone does internet research on everyone these days and, you know what? He's rather lovely. A divorcé with three grown-up children, and a house in Somerset… I think I've done well.'

'Sometimes there's a fine line between romantic and sinister.'

'Sure. But this isn't one of those times.'

I realise that I'm projecting my fearful state onto Daphne, which is unfair. So I ask, 'Would you like an iced bun?'

She says yes, and I make tea for us to have with the buns. Just as I'm serving up, the bell clangs again. It's Amy Fishwick, the girl that Wilf likes. 'Hi. It's Callie, isn't it? We met at the Willesden Estates party…? I want to buy a book for Wilf – can you recommend something?'

I inspect her, up and down. Extravagant blonde hair extensions, styled into a wavy, tussled look (bed-head?), white pencil skirt, tight. Discernible cleavage. High-gloss magenta fingernails. Heels. She'd be a disaster in the Bishop's Avenue garden, digging and pulling out weeds.

'He likes psychological thrillers. Murder stories. He's read all of Harlan Coben, and has just started on Jo Nesbo.' In a grumpy way, I pick out a book called *Nemesis*, and give it to her. 'He'll like this.'

She flashes me a puzzled look, like she thinks I'm sending her a covert message, or the book is a trick.

'Really, he'll like it.'

'Thanks, Callie,' she says sweetly, tilting her head and widening her eyes, like she's speaking to a small child.

When she leaves, Daphne says, 'I don't believe it. She's not his type.'

'We don't know that. I mean, we don't know him that well.' I'm thinking that Daphne's wrong, that she hasn't witnessed the sharp little looks that Wilf and Amy exchange; hasn't taken into account Amy's spray-tanned legs or her come-hither smile.

I don't want to think about her, so I go online and log on to controllingmen. I want to discuss Tilda's letter and I write:

Pink has confided that she thinks X will kill her. And she actually wants him to do it. She tries to provoke him.

Within seconds I'm bombarded with advice. I'm told that the situation is 'critical', 'highly dangerous'. That it's not uncommon for women to become so psychologically broken that they become complicit in the violence. Lemon-and-Lime is back, and she writes about 'the gaslight effect', which is when an abuser manipulates situations so cleverly that his partner doubts her own sanity. 'This is often the modus operandi of a sociopath.'

Felix is screwed up, probably sadistic, but he isn't a sociopath, I know that – Lemon-and-Lime doesn't understand. Oh how I'd love to discuss this with Belle! I'm missing her so badly.

I log off and scroll through the dossier instead, looking at the write-ups I did after chatting to her online, and after meeting her in York. I'm looking for evidence that moral, kind Belle was actually cooperating with Scarlet, signing up to her insane murder plan. I don't want to believe that she was; but as I read through my notes, I realise that she was endlessly referring to Scarlet's superior status as Prey, being 'closer to the danger' than us. And in Pizza Express Belle had used the actual words, 'Scarlet has asked me to help her, and I am. I want to play my part.' Reluctantly, I write: *I do believe that Belle did it – that she stole diamorphine and syringes and needles from York Hospital.*

I research diamorphine, and discover that it's a cleaned up form of heroin that's given to cancer patients in agonising pain, and if you inject an overdose into a vein, death follows pretty quickly. It was how Dr Harold Shipman murdered more than two hundred of his patients. There was tons of it in Scarlet's bag – maybe enough to kill an entire village.

I return to controllingmen, looking for Scarlet. She's there, and we move to The Zone.

I want to ask you about the contents of your bag.

Don't do it. Some things can only be discussed in person.

I'm worrying about everything. You, Pink, Felix.

Stop… You need to know that the violence is getting worse here. I will give you more information about Luke soon.

Get out of there Scarlet. Go to a refuge.

Not possible. There's no funding for refuges these days.

No available spaces. We both know that. What's the latest on Pink and Felix? (We're going through the charade of calling her Pink still.)

They're away, back in a week. I don't want to go over Tilda's letter again. It's too exhausting.

Then they'll be around for a while? In London?

Yes, they'll be here for ages. I don't think they're going to travel anywhere – Felix is working too hard right now. Even when he goes away somewhere nice, it's for work.

Oh?

Yes, in October he's off to some flash country-house hotel for a conference.

Where?

Berkshire I think.

What's the hotel called.

Not sure. Ashleigh something; something like that. Why?

Might be important.

I have to go, I write. *I'm at work.*

Customers have come into the shop, and I sell a Napoleon Bonaparte book to an older man who looks a little like Daphne's Douglas, and a book on crochet and mindfulness to a young mother with two babies in a buggy. Then I write up my findings about diamorphine. And I note that I've told Scarlet about Felix's conference trip.

28

Tilda's been back from her honeymoon for two months and I haven't seen her. She phones and keeps me updated on how happy she is and how perfect Felix is, but makes excuses not to see me in person so that I can verify the authenticity of her gushy claims. Then, at last, I'm invited to Curzon Street for a movie night. She phones while I'm at home, online, gorging on controllingmen, and because I'm alert and in the mood to register every little inflection in her voice, every slight hint of fragility, I *do* notice. An element of woundedness, definitely, but something else also – maybe hope, or optimism.

'*Single White Female*,' she says. 'It's a film from the nineties about two young women, Hedy and Allie. Hedy's obsessed with Allie, insanely jealous of her and it all gets deliciously creepy. You'll love it.'

I hold the phone too hard against my ear, stuck for words. I suppose she's making a point about my obsession with her. I'm about to protest that I'm not jealous – that's not it at all, then, 'Callie? Are you still there?'

'Yes… I'll come. I'll bring brownies.'

'It's a special film,' she says. 'And I'm excited about you seeing it. I'll tell you why when I see you.'

'Tell me now.'

'No! You have to see it first.'

So I arrive at Curzon Street, clutching my bag of brownies (homemade!) and my Strongbow, and I'm reminded of that day in the spring when I met Felix for the first time. Now, as then, Tilda answers the door, and Felix is in the kitchen space, arranging things in cupboards.

I make my entrance as positively as I can manage, with a cheerful, 'Welcome home, Mr and Mrs Nordberg!'

Felix takes my cider and pours our drinks, while I notice the subtle glow he's gained from the Greek sun – just enough to emphasise sharp cheekbones, and the limpid paleness of his eyes. He hands me my glass, and as our hands touch I start, and realise how on edge I am. I mumble, 'Sorry,' and Felix mops up spilled cider. I try to start an uncontroversial conversation.

'Was your family home like this?' I say. 'I mean, shades of white, and spotless?'

'God, no. Growing up, my parents' place was all burnished oak panelling, dark furniture, rugs the colour of port wine. Pieces of impressive art – ceramics and paintings. Kinda like a gentleman's club.'

'Sounds formal.'

'I guess it was. More suited to decorous cocktail parties than to two small boys running around and jumping on the furniture.'

Although I fear Felix, and think he's deranged, it's hard to totally hate him. Maybe I even feel a little sorry for him – I'm imagining that he was screwed up by his boyhood, spent in a world designed and constructed by Alana with the primary purpose of making Erik feel important, a big beast. I imagine, too, that Erik might like to be called 'sir' by his children and that, even when the boys were young, he was endlessly pontificating on interest rates and productivity statistics, spouting his views on the global economy.

We move to the sofa and I want to ask Felix what it was like to be the son of a renowned 'thinker'. But Tilda says I must see the honeymoon photos, and then we'll watch the film. She opens her laptop, and I admire pictures of her in neon-coloured cotton kaftans, lounging about at their villa. Eventually there are a couple of photos of her in a bikini, but she's turning to one side, looking flirtatiously over her shoulder at the camera. It's useless. I can't tell anything.

'It's hard to be back in London,' Felix says. 'Work and everything.'

'Did you manage to switch off while you were away?' I'm still trying to do normal, not wanting to be thrown out of the flat.

Tilda laughs. 'Of course he didn't. Zillions of calls to the office, and constant checking online.'

'Hey! I wasn't so bad. What I mean is, I'm back to long hours away from you, and I have this wretched conference on Friday.'

'How long will you be away?' Tilda asks.

'Two days.'

'I'll miss you.'

'I'll miss you too, babe.'

The 'babe' makes me get up from the sofa, unable to stomach being close to him, and I sit by myself. Tilda presses the remote.

She's right. The movie's atmospheric and brilliant. Jennifer Jason Leigh as Hedy is a dark-haired, quiet observer (like me), and Bridget Fonda is fair-haired and successful (like Tilda). You might think that is just coincidence, but there's another element that gives me the creeps – it turns out that Hedy is a twin, her sister having died years ago. So at first it seems like she's tormented, looking for a lost soul. Everything gets darker and darker, because it's that sort of film, and by the end I feel winded – and still suspect that Tilda's making a point about me.

'It was amazing,' I say. 'The character of Hedy is so intense, she was riveting.'

Tilda and Felix are lying together on the sofa, she cradled in his arm. She eases herself away, sits up straight, mushing up her hair. 'Well, guess what, Callie? Guess fucking what?!'

'Yeah?'

'They're making a new film – same themes as *Single White Female* – a close study of two young women, one of them slightly unhinged, always observing the other. One of them envious, the other glamorous and successful.'

A stab of pain in my chest.

'Sort of like *Rebecca*, too, then?'

'Absolutely. The working title is *Envy*. Two main characters, Evie and Helen. And – amazing fact – it looks like I'm going to be cast as Helen!'

I'm looking nervously back and forth, at Felix and Tilda. 'The glamorous one?'

She gulps her wine. 'Yes, the glamorous one. I auditioned the week before the wedding – and I've got the job!'

Felix is sitting there looking stunned. Cold eyes, stiff body. And I snap, becoming high-pitched and shrill. 'Don't you dare stop her! I know you hate her being successful – but if you do anything to harm her – anything – I'm going to the police!'

Felix gets up from the sofa, and says angrily, 'This is too much. I'm going out. I need wine.'

'We have wine,' says Tilda nervously.

But he's gathering up his keys and his jacket, and leaves, slamming the door.

In an instant, everything has changed. I know this sudden exit is a prelude to violence later on and I imagine gripping and punching and suffocating. For an instant, I imagine her death.

'Oh god,' she says shakily, struggling to articulate the words. 'I didn't tell him that I'd gone to the audition… I thought that when he saw *Single White Female*, he'd realise what a fabulous film it is, and be pleased that I'm doing something similar. Something that could be totally brilliant for me…' She curls up into a foetal position, making herself tiny, and I make a mental note – *she's being honest*. For the first time, to my face, she's blaming *him* and not me! I think she's sobbing now, silently, her face hidden and it's hard to believe that the evening has fallen into this state; it's gone so suddenly from pretended conviviality to utterly broken.

I kneel beside her, placing my face so that it touches the back of her head. Softly, I say, 'He can't do this to you. You can still leave him…' I'm about to tell her that I've read her letter, that I know Felix might kill her at any moment. But she turns, leaps up and screams at me; a frenzied, piercing screech. 'I will not leave him! I will not! Just shut your fucking mouth!'

She stumbles towards the bedroom and even in this moment of crisis, I'm heartbroken by her beauty, her physical fragility. Those thin white legs, thin hips.

Now she's locked in the bathroom and I feel that we're re-living the scene from early in the summer, when Felix stormed out in search of fizzy water. Except then he was faking it – this time it's all too real. I'm in a heap at the foot of the bathroom door, and I call out, 'I'm staying here. I'm not leaving you alone with him…' Then I haul myself up, pacing the bedroom, desperately searching for something of Tilda's to eat. My shaking hand grabs a red lipstick in a gold case, and I chew off the end and swallow. I see in the mirror that I've made a ghastly crimson mess of my teeth.

29

Two hours later, Tilda and I are lying in her bed. She's sleeping gently, and I'm listening to the even tones of her breath, wondering how she can sound so peaceful when her life is being torn apart. Like me, she's wearing just her underwear, and I carefully pull down the duvet, trying to check her skin, though it's hard to see by the feeble light of the bedside lamp. I think her shoulders are fine, devoid of blemishes – her skin is milky white, her bones making smooth contours, like soft stone. Like the contours of the lamb's skull, years ago. Her back, too, is clear, apart from the mole on her left shoulder. I want to inspect her arms and thighs. But I don't want to wake her, so I inch the duvet down gradually, and she doesn't stir. I see maybe one little ink-spot bruise and I think I can make out scratch marks too, on her forearm, which is thin and speckled with freckles and fine blonde hairs. I wish I could see the other side, her inner arm.

I pull the duvet up, so that she isn't cold, and I stroke the golden hair that is lying across the pillow, and try to bury my face in it without disturbing her. I breathe in her smell, which is thick and heady, and I think of childhood, of eating her hair and her teeth. Carefully, I shape my body so that it is like a protective shell, following the outline of her back and her legs, and for a while I close my eyes, and allow my breaths to follow hers, in and out, in and out. Then I roll over, away from her, because I need to check, and I feel under my pillow, or rather, Felix's pillow, and I'm reassured as my fingers slide along the cold hard blade. I've placed a kitchen knife there.

I glance up and see the clock. It's 2.15. I suppose Felix isn't coming back tonight, and I turn to face Tilda again, feeling calm and sleepy. On the memory stick, Tilda wrote that Felix made her feel lit up inside, like some dreadful wound had gone away – and that's the way I feel now. Or rather, I don't feel healed exactly. It's more that I feel complete. Just Tilda and me together. Felix safely out of the house.

I'm drifting off to sleep, wanting to stay like this forever. But I'm jolted out of my complacency by a noise. The door to the flat being opened, Felix returning after all, and I sit bolt upright, my hand under the pillow. My sharp movement wakes up Tilda, just as Felix enters the bedroom. He looks pale and wasted, and he steadies himself with his hand on the wall. He's been drinking.

'Get out, Callie.'

'I'm not leaving.'

'Fucking get out! Leave Tilda and me alone!'

He lunges at me, grabbing me by the arm, yanking me out of the bed. I pull the knife with me, and it brushes against his side, swiftly and lightly, like I'm an artist tracing a line with a red-inked pen. Seeing the blood seeping through his shirt, he grips my arms, holding them up above my head, slamming me against the wall, repeatedly, so that my head thumps on the edge of the window frame.

'Drop the knife!'

I don't, I grip it even harder – but he wrenches it from me, with one clean wrench, and throws it clear, onto the floor. He puts his head close to mine, eye to eye, against the wall, and hisses, 'You're insane. What the fuck? Get out of here now.'

Tilda is watching, with horrified pale eyes.

'For god's sake, Callie. Why the knife? What are you doing?'

'I need to protect you. Look at him! He's mad with anger… You're not safe.'

The room is filled with a dreadful, painful silence – the three of us frozen in our space, looking at each other, unable to articulate our fury. Felix starts heaving, loud desperate breaths, and he forces his words out. 'We all need to be calm, and to talk… Something terrible and strange has happened here, and we need to work out what it is.'

'Tilda?' I'm wanting more from her. I want her to come clean.

'Felix is right.' She gets out of bed, wrapping herself in a woollen throw, stumbling across the room in flamboyant distress, like she's playing Medea or Lady Macbeth. She inspects Felix's wound, licking her finger, smearing it along the thread of blood.

'You're okay, thank heaven... It only needs a plaster. Callie, you've crossed a line... We need to talk about it, let's go into the other room.'

I grab the duvet, pull it around myself, and the three of us go and sit on the sofas. Felix is slumped forward, his head in his hands. He's failing to get his emotions under control, and there's no way I'm going to leave Tilda alone with him. I'm in the corner of a sofa, cocooned in the duvet, hugging my folded-up legs, thinking about how to explain the knife. Tilda's looking at me like she's amazed by my behaviour, and I'm once again on the point of saying that I've read her letter. But I stop myself, realising that if I confess, she'll evict me in disgust, not caring what the consequences will be for her. So I fake a confused face, and say, 'I don't know what happened... I don't know why I did it...'

'Fuck it... you had a knife!' She's overwhelmed with disbelief.

'I know... I know. When Felix went off in that angry mood, I got a knife and put it under the pillow. Just in case... in case I needed to defend you... I knew it was

244

crazy. Really. I didn't mean to use it…' Even to myself, I sound weak.

'You're unhinged – you know that right?' Felix is sounding like he might hyperventilate. 'I thought we might be able to talk this out, but we can't. It's too extreme, Callie, too bizarre. You've got to get out of here. I don't want to see you – not for a long time. You have to leave Tilda and me alone. You realise I could get a restraining order? God knows what you might have done! You need psychological help. I'll pay for it – so you can sort yourself out. And, honestly, stay away and get your own fucking life. It's about time… I'm calling you a cab…'

I look to Tilda for support, but she says, 'Felix is right. You have to sort yourself out.'

He starts pacing, working himself up into an increasingly angry state. I can see fear in Tilda's eyes. But she refuses to be disloyal, and instead she says, '*I'll* call the cab,' and she does. I'm sent out into the night, and she is left with him.

30

I didn't hear anything from Tilda or Felix. No phone call to say they'd fixed me up with a psychiatrist, no offer to make amends. It was a pity, because I wanted to say that I'd dreamed up a solution to our problems in the form of group therapy – maybe under Liam's guiding hand! In that sort of safe environment we could, maybe, slowly, gently address Felix's anger and violence and Tilda's complicity, her twisted, perverted death wish. We could work out protocols for the three of us to get along, maybe try out some kind of role play. But as the days went by, my family therapy ideas dissipated, and Tilda's silence became ominous. I was so frightened about her safety that I'd wake in the middle of the night, finding myself in a cold sweat. I couldn't even be sure that she was still alive, and I kept thinking of the words she had written – *he will kill me. I'm convinced of it now.*

At the bookshop, I was distracted, finding it difficult to concentrate, and I kept wandering back to controllingmen, checking the latest news, hoping to see that Joe Mayhew would stand trial for murder rather than manslaughter. Then, two days ago, towards the end of a rare working Friday, as I was half-dozing at the payment counter and Daphne was deep into her novel-writing, my phone rang and I saw Tilda's name on the screen. I answered nervously, but could barely comprehend her whispered words. In an agonised, jagged voice she was saying, '*Come here, Callie. Come here now.*'

'Tilda… what is it? What's happened?'

'Just come here. I need you.' Then she hung up.

A sharp chill ran through me. I blurted something out to Daphne, talking too loud, grabbing my bee bag, running out of the shop on weak legs, turning left towards the minicab company.

At Curzon Street, I buzzed repeatedly until I was let in and I ran up the stairs, finding the door to the flat wide open, entering in a frantic, fearful state, expecting catastrophe – but all I found was Tilda lying on her sofa, looking slightly drained and sleepy. In the middle of the afternoon, she was wearing a flimsy grey silk nightdress and her hair was messy and unwashed, but other than that, she seemed unchanged from when I last saw her. But then she spoke, and it was obvious that she was afraid.

'Oh, come here… I can't get up.'

I knelt beside her, put my cheek against hers. 'What's happened? What did he do to you?'

'It's not that Callie, not this time…'

She pulled herself upright, so that we could be face-to-face. 'Oh god, I'm so worried. I've been calling Felix all morning and he hasn't answered his phone. He's away in the country, at some conference in a hotel somewhere, so in the end I phoned the hotel, and they were so weird… they told me that they "weren't in a position to comment about Mr Nordberg", so I practically screamed at them to tell me now whatever it was they had to tell me, but they said that I should stay at home and wait and that "someone will inform you of the situation in due course". Doesn't that sound dreadful? Like something awful has happened?'

'It doesn't sound good… How long ago did you speak to them?'

'Ages ago, about two hours. It's been bloody horrible, just lying here imagining ghastly things.'

I was about to suggest that I make a cup of tea, but at that second the buzzer sounded. Tilda and I looked at each other, simultaneously clasping our hands to our chests, and I went to answer.

'Hello, is that Tilda Farrow?' A woman's voice, kind of croaky.

'It's her sister… who is this?'

'Is Miss Farrow at home?'

'Yes she is… who is this?'

'It's the Metropolitan Police, may we come in?'

Sergeant Dawn Nokes had a bad cold and painful throat, but she did the talking anyway, while a young constable, Lyron Wright, stood in the background with a contrived look of concern on his face. Sergeant Nokes made sure that Tilda was Tilda, and asked us both to sit down, and we were side by side on the sofa, as stony and stiff as two statues, while she sat in the white leather armchair, dragging it across the floor to be closer, leaning forward to an unnatural degree. I was focussing on her red nose, raw under her nostrils.

'I'm afraid I have bad news,' she said softly. 'This morning, when he was staying at the Ashleigh House Hotel, your husband... Felix... went for a run. Afterwards he was found in his hotel room. He had died, I'm afraid, and it looks like he had had some sort of attack or fit.'

Tilda snapped back, angrily, 'No. No. That can't be right. Felix is extremely fit, exceptionally healthy... Peak fitness... You've made a mistake!'

'I'm so very sorry.' Sergeant Nokes put her hand on Tilda's arm, but she swiped it away just as Constable Wright stepped towards us and said, 'Yes, me too.'

Something about his casual manner made Tilda leap up and she threw herself at him, shrieking, 'No! No! How dare you – get out of here!' She was thumping him with her fists, aiming at his face, so that Constable Wright had to bring his arms up to defend his head. Sergeant Nokes and I pulled her off, and she staggered back to the sofa, and put her head in her hands. We couldn't see her face for her falling hair. Constable Wright looked uneasy.

'I'm sorry,' I said.

'No worries.' He shrugged. 'It's what people do.'

I sat by Tilda, and tried to make the news sink in, but I couldn't anchor it to any imagined context, any understandable chain of events. 'What do you mean, an attack or fit? It's not possible. He's thirty-two, way too young for a heart attack. It doesn't make sense.'

'We don't know the full details yet,' said Sergeant Nokes. Then, through a hacking cough, 'There will have to be a postmortem.'

'That's right… there will,' said Constable Wright.

Tilda looked up, her anger giving way to despair. 'I won't believe it until I see him,' she said. Then she flopped down again into my lap, and I held her to me, while Sergeant Nokes told us that the American police would inform Felix's parents. Then she made us all tea.

The police left at about the same time as the reporters arrived. I'd gone out to buy bread and milk, and on my return found three scruffy male photographers leaning against the wall by the front door, and I overheard snatches of their conversation.

'Her career's pretty fucked, isn't it…?'

'The desk is only interested because she'll look like shit…'

'Celebrity meltdown…'

I pressed the buzzer, calling out, 'Have some respect! Leave her alone!' which prompted them to grab their cameras and take pictures of me. I felt like shouting abuse, but Tilda buzzed me in, and I escaped before I could do any harm.

She wasn't in the sitting room or the kitchen space, so I looked in the bedroom, and found her lying face down on the bed, covered with piles of Felix's clothes – random white, pink and blue shirts, dark suits and cashmere sweaters. I dropped the shopping and crawled under, to be with her, and she turned to me, her skin mottled and red, her eyes bloodshot. 'I'm trying to find his smell, and I can't! Everything smells of fucking washing powder... I can't bear it.'

Like her, I couldn't smell anything of Felix, I could smell only Tilda, and as she rolled away from me I buried my face in her back, and we breathed together. I wanted to fall asleep, and I had to resist sinking into unconsciousness.

'Oh... I'm so sorry...' I said. 'I'm so sorry about everything.'

And in that moment, I was truly, deeply sorry that I had spied on Tilda, had been paranoid about Felix, had become so obsessed with controllingmen. It seemed like I had made this happen, had caused Felix's death.

But then Tilda got out of bed to go to the bathroom and I saw fresh bruises, yellow-purple stains next to each other, bleeding into each other, on her upper left arm – and I was jolted into remembering the reality of Felix. And although I was sad for my distraught sister, I also felt profound relief.

She said, 'Callie... will you come to the hospital with me, to see Felix's body?'

'Of course I will...'

She came out of the bathroom and sat on the side of the bed, picking up a white shirt and holding it to her face. Then she pulled off her t-shirt, and put on Felix's shirt, struggling with the buttons because of her trembling hands. 'I want to go tomorrow,' she said. 'I phoned Sergeant Nokes while you were out – and she said we need to go to Reading. He's at the hospital – she's arranging for us to be there at eleven.'

'I'll stay here tonight,' I said, 'so you're not alone.'

She was at the dressing table, and she said, 'That's sweet of you,' as she looked at herself in the mirror. 'I need to speak to the reporters downstairs… I was going to make my face look respectable, but I don't think I will. It's better that they see my distress. It's the truth after all.'

I went with her to the front door. As she opened it, the photographers scrambled away from their position by the wall, and took pictures. Tilda stood silently, then said, 'As you know, my husband Felix Nordberg died today. We had been married only a few weeks and I'm not sure I will ever come to terms with this tragedy. I ask you please to respect my privacy.' Then she came back inside and shut the door, and as she did so, she slid down against it, and became a little ball of grief on the wooden floor.

'Let me help you,' I said, feeling suddenly happier inside than I had been for months. It was so good to be of use to my troubled sister, so reassuring. And as I guided her up the stairs, I scarcely noticed the guilt that I felt.

31

I'd thought Felix would be in a refrigerated drawer, in a stack of cavities filled with the recently dead. But he wasn't. Instead, he'd been wheeled into a small white room in the basement, and covered with thick sheets. A policewoman introduced herself as Melody Sykes, asked Tilda if she was ready, and pulled the sheet down so that we could see his face. His eyes were closed so that we would never again see their greyness, or that aloof gaze; his desiccated lips were dark, and parted, as though he was about to say something as he died, words that were now lost for all eternity. I felt nothing other than repulsion as I looked at him – a ghastly, yellowing waxwork. Tilda was practically hysterical. She laid her face on his chest, stroked his hair, kissed his forehead, then turned into me, nestling her face into my shoulder, saying, 'I can't bear it… I can't bear it.'

Afterwards, in the car park, Melody Sykes said she

belonged to Reading Police Station, and explained that there would most likely be no more police involvement. The postmortem would take place, and then we'd be free to have the funeral. She had a strong, rich voice and an accent from somewhere north of Newcastle; after she drove off in her red Peugeot I said to Tilda, 'If she were a tree, it would be an oak tree.' But she wasn't really listening, and said, 'I want to see where he died.' She had cleaned up her face and was looking presentable, and as she spoke it seemed like a reasonable thing to do. So we phoned for a minicab to take us to the Ashleigh House Hotel.

In the taxi, I had my arm through hers and, looking out of the window, she said, 'When people see a dead body they say, "Oh, it wasn't him," that it's obvious the spirit has left. But it wasn't like that. To me, that *was* Felix, it's what he's become… Forever alone.'

The car took us along a wooded lane, then turned into the driveway of the hotel, a straight gravel path cutting through long lawns, arriving at a white building with a Georgian-style façade. The reception area was large with leather comfy chairs arranged on one side, the reception desk on the other, and straight ahead a wide staircase up to the bedrooms. *Felix's last steps would have taken him up that staircase*, I thought. Behind the desk, a young woman was working at her computer; she looked up and asked if she could help. Her name badge said Agnes, and her accent suggested she was Eastern European, maybe Polish.

'My name is Callie Farrow, and this is my sister, Tilda. Her husband was staying here, for the London–New York conference. And he died here. Just yesterday.'

'Oh, I'm very sorry. Yes, it was terrible. I was here, and I saw him go for his run. He looked so well! I'm really very sorry.'

Tilda turned away, like the words were hurting her.

'We were wondering if we might look around,' I said. 'Maybe see the room where he died. We think it might help…'

'Of course. I'll call the manager.'

Within a minute, the manager arrived and introduced himself as Otto, and he explained that he had been one of the people to find Felix in his room. Tilda gripped my arm as she asked, 'Where was he, exactly? I have an image of him lying on the floor, and nobody knowing he was down there, nobody coming.'

'Oh no… It wasn't like that. He was on the bed. It was as though he was lying in some comfort. If you'll forgive me, I'd say that he looked peaceful, like someone in a painting. It was a strange thought of mine, but I thought it might reassure you to know this…'

'Yes,' said Tilda. 'In a way it does.'

'I went to the room because I was summoned by Mr Julio Montero, a colleague of Mr Nordberg, I understand.'

'Yes… yes he is,' said Tilda. 'Is he still here, in the hotel?'

'No, I'm afraid not. But, excuse me, what is it that we can do for you?'

'I'd like to see his room. The room where he died.'

It was decided that Agnes should show us, and as she led us up the stairs, she kept turning around as if about to say something, before changing her mind.

My first impression was that the room was so light and white and uncluttered that Felix would have been happy here. Tilda and I looked at the bed, as though it could tell us something about his last moments, but it had been re-made into a state of pristine neatness, as though his death was a minor event, easily erased with the changing of sheets and the puffing of pillows. I went to the window to see Felix's view, which was of a garden and a golf course, and silvery woods in the distance. At the same time, Tilda walked round the room skimming the surfaces with her fingertips, touching where she thought Felix had touched.

'Everything's gone,' she said, 'but I can feel his presence. I can see him in this room doing ordinary things, having a shower, changing into his running gear.'

Her eyes were wet again, and Agnes said, 'I took some photos yesterday morning. Of him, and of the room. Just in case they might be important… I didn't know whether you, or others in his family, might like to see them…'

Tilda looked at her harshly, her voice a strained whisper. 'What? What are you saying? That you photographed his dead body? Why would you do that?'

'I don't know. For some reason, I thought it important to make a record. I don't really understand why.'

Tilda sat on the bed, her head drooping as though she were too tired to think, but she rallied herself and said, 'I'd like to see them. Come here and show me.'

Agnes sat beside Tilda, and I sat beside Agnes, and she showed us pictures of the bathroom, his shaving gear and used soap, of the bedroom, the untouched hospitality tray, the view of the golf course, and finally of Felix, lying on his back on the bed, his eyes open then, staring vacantly at the ceiling, bathrobe gaping open, and left arm hanging down the side of the bed, fingers suspended above the floor.

Tilda stared at it, her face white, her expression frozen. 'I want you to email these to me, then delete them.' She looked in her bag for a paper and pen, writing down her email address.

'And where are his things? His clothes and toiletries, his wedding ring and watch and cufflinks? I should have them.'

'Yes, of course. We've packed them up... You can take them when you leave.'

As we left the room and descended the stairs, we saw Otto waiting in the reception area, his arm resting on a black suitcase on wheels.

'These are your husband's effects... Please take them, and if there's anything else I can help with, don't hesitate to ask. I've put my card in the bag.'

So we took the suitcase and ordered a minicab to the station, heading back to London. Tilda said she'd rather be alone in her flat, and I returned to Willesden Green. Even though I was shattered, utterly spent, I turned on my laptop – it was a reflex action, I didn't consciously want to do it. I gazed at the screen, and saw that I had received a dozen messages from Scarlet.

32

Her emails all said the same thing. *I've done everything that we agreed. Now it's your turn.* Or, *Callie, you have to keep your side of the bargain. We must meet to discuss logistics.* Or, *Don't ignore me. You must act now... remember, it's what Belle wanted.*

I *must* do this, I *must* do that. She suggested nothing that would incriminate her, or me, and yet her words were all too easy to understand, and I felt so ill that I thought I'd throw up. Her claims were horrific – and yet I realised that I'd been expecting them from the moment I heard of Felix's death, that I'd been carrying around my poisonous knowledge like a disease, knowing that Scarlet would take advantage of a horrendous tragedy. Right now, I desperately wanted to shut her up and shut her out, to distance myself from her.

For fuck's sake, I wrote. *I don't believe you. You're sick. I don't want to hear from you again. Stay out of my life.*

She replied straight away: *You're funny, Callie. The evidence couldn't be any stronger. By the way, please pass on my sympathies to your poor sister. I'm sorry for her loss. At the same time, let's hope that her life and yours can return to a peaceful state now.*

Don't even mention my sister! You're a toxic bitch.

The whole country is mentioning your sister, whether you like it or not. Have you seen the internet? The papers tomorrow will be full of her.

You're a leech – sucking my blood at a terrible time. As I said, I don't believe a word of what you write, so piss off and die.

Don't get into a temper! Give me your address – I have something to send you.

No!

I slammed down the lid of the laptop, disgusted with Scarlet, disgusted with myself for having had anything to do with her. I felt like this terrible situation had only happened because my weak character had been taken in, and taken over, by Scarlet's forceful, overbearing personality. Trying to calm down, I went into my kitchen and microwaved a chicken tikka masala and as I returned to the bedroom, and ate it, I tried to feel normal. Like an ordinary person having an ordinary supper. I gazed at the garden, a massive tangled mess of weeds, and at the train track beyond, thinking of the trains that ran so swiftly past my house, packed with commuters going to fluorescent-lit offices and home again. They seemed so remote, those thousands of travelling workers, and I envied them. As happened so often, my thoughts drifted to Wilf, and I wished I could tell him everything about Belle and Scarlet and controllingmen and Felix's death. I imagined, too, having him in my bed so that I could get totally lost in him, could forget about being me, and the horrors in my life. I was thinking of him warmly and regretfully as I finished the chicken, as I ate a banana, and then I did something I hadn't intended – I turned the laptop on again, and typed Tilda's name into the search engine.

An immediate bombardment. Pictures of *tragic Tilda Farrow* grieving for her husband of a few weeks, the American banker Felix Nordberg. Mainly of Tilda standing at the front door on Curzon Street, wearing Felix's white shirt, her long hair falling half over her face, her pose weak and yet somehow beautiful, like the emaciated girls you see in fashion shoots. Some websites had found a photo of Felix, that didn't properly look like him – it was a headshot taken in a studio, and seemed too glossy, his smile too broad, like an advertisement for white teeth. The reports all said that he had died of a suspected heart attack, and some drew attention to the phenomenon of sudden death from heart disease in athletic young men. Others mentioned that Tilda hadn't worked since *Rebecca*, that she had been considered for the role of Rachel in *My Cousin Rachel*. The *Mail* reported that 'friends say that Tilda Farrow has her eyes on Hollywood'. And the *A List* website said, 'Nobody would be surprised if she fled Britain for the States to make a fresh start after such a tragedy.'

I yelled at the screen, 'Leave her alone! What on earth makes you write this crap!'

I returned to thinking about Scarlet, remembering the bent-up figure on the bench at Kenwood House. If I believed in auras, like Mum does, I would say her aura that day was an intense, burning red, signifying danger. I opened up the dossier and wrote: *Scarlet claims she killed Felix. I don't believe her. I think she's telling a preposterous lie. To kill Felix she would have somehow had to get access to his room at the Ashleigh House Hotel; would somehow have to have jabbed him in a vein with the syringe that Belle stole. It's too outrageous. And yet, Scarlet is deadly serious. I know that. I can only hope that she is playing mind-games, because I'm certain that she isn't joking. She's not the joking kind. I think she's hoping to make Felix's heart disease a means of making me murder Luke. If she thinks I'll do such a thing, she must be deranged. For now, I'm trying to stay calm until we get the results of the postmortem.*

The more I thought about it, the more I wanted immediate reassurance. So, when I was still up at three in the morning, tired and wired, I sent Scarlet my address. It was my way of challenging her, of saying *Prove yourself, or go away forever.*

At work the next day, I was ragged, on edge, and I kept doing things wrong. I was late, for a start, then

I broke a coffee mug, and I snapped at Daphne even though she was trying to be nice. I was irritated that, while she was acting sorrowful and concerned, she found it impossible to disguise the fact that she was so happy about Douglas. She kept checking her phone for texts from him, and whenever she received one she smiled to herself, and typed really fast at her novel. I couldn't stand it, and I told her I needed to go for a walk, to get some fresh air.

When I returned, she said, 'You missed Wilf. He came in.' It was the first time since he'd come to tell me how angry he was, and I was pleased I'd been out. I didn't want him seeing me like this, so low and helpless. I settled back behind the payments counter, and Daphne said, 'Are you sure you don't want to talk about things? Everything is so hard for you right now. Is Tilda desperately sad?'

'I've no idea,' I said, surprised at myself, because I knew she was distraught.

I was about to change the subject and make tea, when Wilf returned to the shop, striding in like he wanted to hack down a giant bramble. I braced myself. 'Did you like that book that Amy bought you? *Nemesis*.'

'Haven't read it. I guess it was chosen by you, right?'

'Yeah. How is she – Amy, I mean?'

'Amy's fine… I keep calling, but you never pick up… I wanted to see if you're okay. I heard the news about Felix.'

'Yeah. Everything's been bloody awful. There's a

postmortem today, they're probably doing it right now. It's too weird…'

I wanted to tell Wilf how I was feeling, so scared about Scarlet, and the results of the postmortem. But I didn't. Instead I mumbled, 'Have you been seeing a lot of Amy? Have you come in here to buy her a present?'

'No, Callie. I came in here to see how you are. Try and believe in me will you?' And then he turned and left.

He was scarcely out of the shop when my phone rang. Tilda, shaken and tearful. It took a while to realise that she was trying to tell me that the postmortem was over, and while the results weren't yet official, Melody Sykes had called. 'They said heart disease was the reason he died… Something called hypertrophic cardiomyopathy. It could have killed him at any time. Imagine – since birth, he'd been living with a deadly weakness that he didn't know was there. It's so awful. It struck out of the blue… The small things they found are so sad. Raisins in his stomach from breakfast. So he'd had his favourite, pain au raisin, that morning. And, guess what, there was some damage to his lungs from smoking. Felix, smoking! He never told me. He was always so disapproving about smokers… There's so much about him that I don't know, that I'll never know.'

'Would you like me to come round?' I was so relieved as I spoke. It *was* heart disease, hyper-something cardio-something, and Scarlet could go to hell.

'No. I'll be okay. I have things to organise. His parents

are coming back… and Lucas. I have to prepare for the funeral.'

'Have you spoken to Erik and Alana?'

Tilda paused. Then in a tight voice, 'Briefly to Erik; Alana refused to come to the phone. It's upsetting.'

'But understandable I suppose.'

'I'll be in touch.'

Her parting words made me feel happy, and for the rest of the afternoon I was able to function better, to deal with the customers, even the woman who wanted her money back because the storyline in her book was 'just sex with a bit of murder'. I had to explain that the publishing business didn't work like that. 'Books are always a risk,' I said. 'That's part of the excitement.' I was amazed when she saw my point of view, and on my advice she purchased a Harlan Coben. When she left, Daphne said, 'Go to the top of the class, young Callie.'

That night in bed my thoughts kept returning to Wilf. He was right – I did need to believe in him. I needed to fight against the permanently paranoid frame of mind that I'd been in, maybe because I'm so often lonely, and loneliness breeds paranoia. Tomorrow, I thought, I'll go to Willesden Estates and find out whether or not he's actually seeing Amy. If not, I'd see if I could get him back.

In the morning, I felt optimistic. I wore my suede boots with my best grey jeans and a new rose-coloured top that went well with my dark hair. I admired myself in the mirror, skipped downstairs, and saw that the post had arrived, lying untidily all over the mat, most of it junk. I sifted through the ads for Indian takeaways and local handymen, and found a brown padded envelope with my name on. I could feel something small and hard inside, and I inspected the address – written out in a heavy-handed black script that I knew, instinctively, belonged to Scarlet.

33

A gold cufflink in the shape of a four-leaf clover. I recognised it immediately and turned it over in the palm
of my hand, feeling its weight and its smoothness, like
I did before, that time at Curzon Street when I'd gone
through Felix's clothes, found his cufflinks, put the dead
fly inside his shirt collar. For a while I stayed by the front
door, just standing in our shabby hallway, turning the
four-leaf clover over in my hand, thinking about what
it represented, thinking in a vague, floaty way, unable to
come down to earth. Then I ascended the stairs, went back
into my flat, dropping the bee bag on the floor, crawling
into bed, deep under the duvet, not even bothering to
take off my boots. I popped the cufflink inside my mouth,
and sucked on it, tempted to swallow. But I didn't. I spat
it out, placed it on my bedside table and, because I was
overwhelmed, I closed my eyes and fell into an uneasy,
troubled sleep.

It was midday when I came round with a pounding head and saw I'd missed two calls from Daphne, doubtless wondering where I was. But I couldn't phone her right now. I wouldn't be able to handle her comforting voice; instead I did the last thing I wanted to do and made myself dial Tilda's number. She picked up straight away, and I asked if she had looked through the bag she'd been given by the manager of the Ashleigh House Hotel.

'Yes, I did that this morning. It was so dreadful seeing Felix's things, his shaving gear, his shampoo for fuck's sake – but at least there was a shirt that he'd worn which hadn't been washed, and if I hold it close, I think I can smell him.'

'Was everything there, which you expected to be there…'

'Why? Why do you ask?'

'Oh, no reason,' I lied. 'I mean, sometimes hotel staff aren't honest – they steal things.'

'Callie! The hotel staff were so nice to us… I wouldn't expect anything like that. Though, something was missing. I'm sure it's a mistake.'

'What?'

'A gold cufflink – one of a set that I gave him as a present. They're lovely – in the shape of a four-leaf clover. But, it turns out that Felix was the unluckiest person I've ever known.'

'Oh.' That's all I could say.

'Callie?'

'I have to go now. I'm supposed to be at work.'

I phoned Daphne. 'I've been unwell with a bad head, but I'm coming in now.'

I'd decided to be strong, to take charge of my relationship with Scarlet, and discover her identity.

34

Instead of paying attention to the customers, I was email-ing. *I received the four-leaf clover and I'm trying to come to terms with what it signifies. I don't understand everything. I can't think how you did it, Scarlet. I can't explain what has happened since.*

By *I can't explain what has happened since* I meant the postmortem. If I were able to speak plainly I'd say, 'There's an inconsistency here – you want me to believe that you killed Felix, but the postmortem says he died naturally. How do you explain that?' I couldn't be explicit as I needed to abide by Scarlet's rules, make her think I was on her side.

I'm confused about what to think, I wrote. *I'm impressed by you, and grateful to you – grateful that my sister is safe. At the same time, I'm overwhelmed by the burden of knowing that I must now play my part. But I am ready, Scarlet. As you suggested, we should meet up again to discuss it. As a start, why don't you send me Predator details?*

I read and re-read the email. Did it sound too unnatural? Was it too incriminating? I dreamed up a scenario in which I was on trial for conspiracy to murder – wondering if I could be condemned by my own words. The word Predator jumped out at me as problematic and, sticking with the controllingmen terminology, I changed it to X. With luck, Scarlet would believe in me, and would send me Luke's full name. Once I knew who he was, I figured, I would be able to identify *her*.

I was about to write more, but was interrupted by Daphne saying, 'Is now a good moment to discuss stocktaking?' I could hardly say, 'No, it's an awful moment,' so we spent the next half hour making a schedule for our annual stocktaking and analysis of our sales to see which genres have sold best, and which worst. In truth, I already knew that crime books are our bestsellers. But Daphne thought romance was doing pretty well too, and there's a good solid following for military history in our part of Willesden. When we finished it was lunchtime, and instead of going back to my email, I made my excuses and walked round to Willesden Estates. The two young women behind the desks looked at me pointedly, like they were expecting an embarrassing scene. One of them swished her hair. 'Is Wilf in?' I stammered, just as he came through from the back room. I felt self-conscious as I asked him if he'd like to go to the Albany for lunch.

'Sure.'

We walked in silence, each of us not wanting to risk saying the wrong thing.

We'd beaten the lunchtime rush, and picked a corner table – the same one that Tilda and I had chosen at the start of the summer. I had a cheese-and-Marmite sandwich and a cider, and Wilf had his usual, a ploughman's and a pint of lager.

The food arrived, and Wilf started eating, turning to me with his mouth full, saying, 'What's been the matter, Callie? Why have you been ignoring me?' He was trying, but failing, to sound nonchalant, which gave me the confidence to make my confession.

'I owe you an apology… I suspected you of selling a story to the *Mail*. When we were here, at the pub, I confided that Tilda was having trouble with Felix… then, within days, a nasty, insinuating story was in the paper. It seemed too much of a coincidence. But I realise I was wrong, and I'm sorry… I've been thinking about it, and I had to speak in a loud voice that day, because the pub was so crowded, and the builder guy who was also at the bar, the one who was covered in dust – he could have overheard everything. And one of those shrieking girls on the other side of us – she leant across and asked for a menu, but really she might have been listening…'

'Come here.' His hand was under my chin, pulling me in, and he kissed me. But then he said, 'There's one thing wrong with your apology. It's based on you thinking you were overheard in the pub. Not based on your assessment of me, your belief in me. You need to accept that I'm not that sort of person – I'd never do anything like that. Can't you see?'

'Yes, I can see. I'm sorry about that too… There's something else, Wilf; that day when I helped out in the garden in Bishop's Avenue. I want to tell you how that was the best day for me. I'm always living inside my head. Spending my whole life in the indoor world of the bookshop, or reading crime books, or staring at my laptop, or observing others. It was amazing to be outside, cool air on my face, digging earth, and being with you.'

'Hey… Any time… I loved seeing you concentrating so seriously on your weeding, getting your hands dirty. And your muddy thighs of course… I still dream of those pink shorts.'

'And another apology… I've been suspicious about you and Amy Fishwick…'

'Ah! Amy Fishwick.'

'Yes. I was getting the impression that something's going on with the two of you. And it's been driving me mad, turning it over. Not knowing the truth… then she came in, all kind of pert and perky, and bought you the *Nemesis* book.'

'Well – the *Nemesis* book, as good as it was, couldn't buy my affections, you'll be happy to know. All that's happened with Amy is that I fixed a problem on her computer, and she bought me a book. We're work colleagues who get along pretty well. That's all.'

'But she's keener than that, isn't she?'

'Maybe…' His grin told me that he was happy to leave some uncertainty in my mind.

His hand reached across, and held mine, not fingers between fingers, but firmly wrapped around, so my hand was squeezed inside his. I wanted to stay in that moment, with everything it promised. And I so wanted to be back in Wilf's bed… but I had to take a risk…

'Wilf, I've got some pretty bizarre stuff I need to tell you about…'

'Okay…'

'It's about Felix and the way he died.'

'Yeah?'

'Well – it might be more complicated than the post-mortem suggests… I've been on the internet, on a forum about dangerous men who are violent to their partners, it's a support group. Anyhow, I've been on this forum, this website, for months now. It's called controllingmen… have you heard of it?'

'No… no I haven't.' He sounded wary, but I had to keep going, I had no option…

'Well, I've made a friend on this site, called Scarlet. And I had another friend, called Belle, but she was killed… by a violent man. He stabbed her, and he's on trial. Anyhow, Scarlet's been telling me that she killed Felix. That it wasn't heart disease at all… As I said, it's weird stuff.'

'Callie, you're sounding crazy.' He pulled his hand away from mine, and took a sip of his beer.

'I know I am… I'm in so deep in this mad world. And I'm worried about Scarlet, I think she is seriously danger-ous…'

'Okay… So do you have any actual evidence?'

'Sort of… She has these syringes that Belle stole from a hospital… and lethal doses of diamorphine… She showed them to me.' I didn't want to freak him out any more, by explaining that she had given some to me, that she wanted me to kill Luke, that I was pretending to go along with her plan.

'And why haven't you gone to the police, if this is true?' He sounded cold now, stilted in the way he voiced his words. And he'd shifted away from me, so that our legs were no longer touching.

'I can't. It sounds too unbelievable, like *I'm* the lunatic. Especially as I don't even know her true identity. Scarlet is a made-up name. I need to discover who she really is – then I can go to the police. They'll be able to raid her flat, maybe find diamorphine and syringes… maybe other evidence.'

He was staring at me now, right into my eyes, looking almost frightened of me. I examined his face, revelling in its rough beauty, desperately hoping he would be sym-pathetic.

'Callie, you're right. It does sound unbelievable. It does sound like you're the lunatic… I'm sorry, I need to get back to the office.'

Then he pushed the table away roughly, got up and

left, muttering, 'I'll call you,' in a stony voice. I watched him barge through a group of young men in suits, and disappear through the swing door.

I was so disappointed – I'd thought he might be my wing-man, at my side while I tried to get to the truth about Felix's death and Scarlet's involvement. But he was gone, and I was still on my own. I made my way back to Saskatchewan books.

Daphne said, 'Nice lunch, lovebird? I saw you and Wilf heading off to the Albany.'

'Stop it, Daphne! I've had enough.'

She pulled a long face, and returned to her writing while I switched on my laptop. Nothing from Scarlet, so I wrote to her again.

Send me Luke's details! If I'm going to do this thing, I need to get on with it. I don't want to waste time.

After five minutes: *I have to be sure you are committed to the project.*

I'm a hundred per cent fucking committed. How can I make you believe me?

Okay. I'll meet up with you to tell you his name and what you must do. Same place as last time. Be there at 1pm tomorrow.

35

I did the headscarf thing again, because that's what Scarlet wanted, using the same orange scarf. And, as I made my way to Kenwood, I wondered how it was that she was so at ease with giving instructions to other people. Maybe she had been raised like that – a little princess led to believe that her own wishes were paramount. I wondered too, how it was that she could travel from Manchester to London so easily on a weekday when she should be at work. Maybe she was part-time, like me.

I took the same route as last time, walking uphill through the woods and across the grass and, as before, Scarlet was already there – sitting on the last bench, head covered in the red scarf, her bag beneath her feet. The same bag – the one that had contained syringes and drugs. As I approached, I reminded myself to learn as much about her as possible, to study her appearance, and ask her questions that might elicit useful information.

She glanced up. Pale blue eyes, shaped thick black eyebrows, thin lips, long skinny face. Not unattractive, but also not the stunning beauty that she had pretended to be. And no hint of a smile. 'Hi, Callie, come and sit down.'

'Did you come from Manchester this morning?' I tried to keep my voice natural, not too inquisitive.

'Yeah. My train got in at eleven. Check it if you like.'

'Oh, that's not what I meant,' I lied. 'I was just thinking that you've had to take time off work.'

'Yes I have. But it doesn't matter.'

She was looking straight ahead, at the woods and the lake at the bottom of the hill, at the grey city in the distance, at the haze of tower blocks grabbing at the sky; and I was looking at her, thinking, *Is this what a murderer looks like? So ordinary…*

'Scarlet… I'm so amazed by what you've done. I'm struggling to comprehend it… How did you kill Felix? Without him struggling at all? Or there being any sign?'

'I can't tell you right now. But I will eventually – maybe after the funeral… The important thing is for you to keep your side of the bargain… with Luke. Listen carefully because I don't want to repeat myself – his name is Luke Stone. Got that? He works for a TV production company in Manchester. It's called Hollybank. He's a researcher there…'

'Are you sure you want me to do this? Really sure?'

'Absolutely. Remember Belle, and what happened to

her. She'd still be alive today if someone had got to Joe Mayhew first – and there are hundreds of women like her, *hundreds*. And if I leave him, he'll come after me. You know this, Callie… You're not having doubts?'

'No. I'll go through with it – to save you, and in honour of Belle.'

'Good. I hope you have the syringes and the diamorphine in a safe place…'

'Yes, of course.' It was true. The bin was as safe a place as anywhere.

'Okay – this is what you should do. Go to my flat in Manchester, it's only a ten-minute walk from the station. When you arrive you'll find Luke in a deep sleep. You'll need to find a vein in his left arm, the inside of the elbow is a good place, I'm sure you've seen it done often enough, and there are videos on YouTube. Anyhow, you'll inject him with sixty milligrams of diamorphine – that's twice the lethal dose. Have you got that?'

'Yes – sixty milligrams. In his left arm. Will I need to do more than one injection?'

'Probably… While you're doing it wear those thin latex gloves that medics use – you can buy them at a pharmacy – do that in London, somewhere busy, like Oxford Street. Anyhow, when you've finished, make sure his fingerprints are all over the syringe, then drop the syringe by his right hand. Got it?'

I was impressed by her ruthlessness. Doubtless, she'd be at work when Luke died, giving her an alibi – and I was supposed to scamper on back to London. It was perfect *Strangers on a Train*.

'How come he'll be sleeping? Won't he wake up?'

'Don't worry about that. I'll have given him something that ensures that he won't wake.'

'What – rohypnol?'

'That's my business. But take it from me, he'll be knocked out…'

Then she told me to stand by and wait for her to send me an address, a date and a time. 'I'll post them to you. Read them, and destroy them, then act.' She gave me two keys, one to the front door of her building, the other to the flat.

'I'm going now, Callie. You must stay focussed. Obviously, don't tell anyone about this – not a soul.'

'Scarlet… Before you go… Can I know your real name? It would make me feel better.'

'No. Of course not.'

She left and I noticed that she walked elegantly, with poise – walking slightly hips-first like models do. Maybe she hadn't been lying about that after all. I sat on the bench, figuring out what to do next. A light rain filled the air, and walkers on the heath put up umbrellas, pulled up hoods, and I drew my parka around me. Then I walked back down to the bus stop thinking I must track down Luke Stone. It was critical now.

At home, I ignored the dirty dishes and mugs in my sink, and microwaved myself a hot chocolate. Then I put 'Luke Stone Manchester' into my search engine and came up with an eleven-year-old school boy who'd received a bravery award for rescuing a dog from a canal, and a retired soldier who'd served in Afghanistan. Obviously the wrong Lukes, so I looked at the Hollybank website – and found profiles of several senior members of staff – but nothing for Luke Stone. Facebook was also a dead end – the Luke Stones were all the wrong sort. It occurred to me then that maybe Scarlet had given me a false name – after all, my instructions were clear, I was supposed to go to her flat and inject the sleeping man. I didn't need to know his name.

36

Felix's funeral was on a cold Friday in October, the air sharp and fresh, even though the sun was casting a gentle light on St Gregory's Church, on the graveyard of crooked headstones and the ground swell of copper-coloured leaves. I arrived early and to pass the time I revisited the graves of Emily Jane Goode and Henry Watson and Ernest Norwood Richardson, then sat on the broken bench by the stone wall, thinking that I'd slip into the back of the church later, hoping that nobody would notice me.

Felix's international colleagues arrived in small solemn groups: women in black coats, thin, stockinged legs, heels; men in dark suits. I saw Paige Mooney, this time with Robbie on her arm, and Kimberley Dwyer, and Mum (who didn't spot me). No sign, yet, of Lucas or Alana or Erik, and no sign of Tilda. But I saw Liam enter the church, and hoped that I might speak to him after the service. I thought about how calming it would be, how soothing, to confess everything, and to follow his advice. I was so adrift, and he was a psychiatrist now.

I found myself following him into the church, but not to the pew. Instead I stood at the back, leaning against the wall, sinking into the shadow. The coffin was already in place, centrally in the aisle, with a huge arrangement of white lilies on the top, like a ridiculous, frothy hat; and at the side of the altar, on a wooden stand, a massive photograph of Felix was smiling inanely at the congregation, the same glossy photograph that had appeared in the press and on websites when he died. Dazed, I looked at the backs of people's heads, and realised that I was looking for Scarlet. I half-thought that she'd be unable to stay away, that she'd want to engage with the death she caused. But I couldn't see her, and I closed my eyes, actually praying for Felix to rest in peace, to be forgiven his sins. When I opened them again, I saw Francesca Moroni coming into the church, crouching slightly as she slipped into a pew. She was exceptionally beautiful, her mass of brown hair falling across her shoulders, dark eyes gazing at the coffin as she knelt down, clasping her hands together in front of her face and I wished I could examine her thoughts and emotions. Was she grieving the love of her life? Or was escape from Felix her salvation?

I thought about moving from my position at the back wall, towards Francesca. But then I was distracted because Tilda arrived, walking slowly up the aisle, acknowledging no one, taking her place at the front, between the coffin and the photo. She was holding herself still, reverentially – and I struggled to know what was going on inside her head. I couldn't tell whether she was as distressed as she'd been on the day Felix died, or whether her true feeling was one of relief that she could now abandon her terrible flirtation with death, her sick game – goading and taunting Felix until he snapped. I looked at the back of her head, her fair hair falling from a tasteful black hat that Felix would have approved of, and I saw only her exterior – the actress playing her part.

Erik and Alana arrived next, Alana clutching Erik's arm, almost falling into him, her steps weak and faltering. Behind them, Lucas walked sedately like a guard, ready to catch his mother if she fell. They sat next to Tilda, and I wondered if they'd reach out to her. But they didn't; they simply nodded, very slightly. My heart burned in my chest. My sister and her suffering deserved recognition, not cruel disdain. Lucas was different, though – he reached across his parents to squeeze her hand.

We sang 'The Lord is my Shepherd', and all the time I was deeply aware of the way Erik and Alana held themselves, resolutely angled away from Tilda, and towards their dead son. I suppose they blamed her. Maybe they blamed England too, and hedge funds in Mayfair – all the people and places that had taken Felix away. At one point Lucas went up on to the altar to read from the Bible, and it was hard not to cry as we heard his voice wavering and recovering and wavering again, while Alana buried her face in Erik's unconsoling arm. The service wasn't long, and afterwards the immediate family went to the crematorium. I'd asked Tilda whether she wanted me to come, and she said no, so I didn't get to see the final moments before Felix went up in flames.

Instead I shared a car with Paige and Robbie to a hired room at a small local hotel where we were supplied with triangular sandwiches and tepid tea, and made efforts at conversation. Paige kept telling me that Tilda would need the love and support of her friends, that we must 'rally round'.

Robbie agreed and said it would help Tilda 'if she got stuck into some challenging roles. It's always good to immerse yourself in work during hard times, takes your mind off your troubles.' I was amazed by his presumption. How could he know what would be good for Tilda? I said I needed to eat, and moved away. I had spotted Francesca, sitting by herself at a table close to the food, and I took some sandwiches over.

'Would you like one? There's egg mayonnaise and ham. Are you Francesca?'

She gave me a sad, welcoming smile. 'That's right.'

'I'm Callie. Tilda's sister.'

'Ah… Poor Tilda. How long ago were they married?'

'Just a few weeks.'

'It's impossible to comprehend isn't it? Something this tragic…' Her voice was composed and dignified.

I was longing to ask her so much, but my questions were

too personal, too intimate, to say out loud, and I stood there like a lemon, blurting out, 'I love your dress,' then, more appropriately, 'There's so much I want to learn about Felix… about his life before he met Tilda.'

She didn't answer because, at that moment, we all looked at the door, at the crematorium contingent returning. Erik spotted Francesca, and he and Alana came over to us and as the three of them hugged each other, Francesca was whispering, 'I'm so, so sorry.' Across the room, Tilda was watching, a sort of wonder registering on her face – but then she turned her back, and talked to Lucas.

Mum appeared, coming to offer her condolences to Erik and Alana, walking towards our group in a black chiffon goth-like dress and a sparkly waterfall cardigan that looked out of place. She leaned in to kiss Alana, but Alana recoiled. Mum muttered, 'Felix was such a wonderful person. I was so happy to have him as a son-in-law.'

But Alana came right back, in a voice so small you could barely hear it.

'Of course, we wish he had never left Boston.'

Mum and I exchanged a glance and I guessed that, like me, she had heard 'Of course, we wish he had never met Tilda.'

'I understand,' said Mum. 'It's all so terrible. And not to have him with you in those final months…'

Alana whispered to Erik, 'Take me away.'

And Erik, in a deflated imitation of his former self, said, 'Do excuse us. We're both very tired.'

I watched as they left, seeing how old they'd become, realising that Erik would no longer set the world to rights with unbridled pomposity. I realised, too, that I would never see them again.

I returned to the sandwich table – for some reason I was rampantly hungry, and as I was leaning over, grabbing an egg mayonnaise, I heard, 'How are *you*, Callie?'

'Liam. It's nice of you to come. Did you only ever meet him at the wedding?'

'Yes. I didn't know him at all, other than from Tilda talking about him…'

'What did she say?'

'Well… she told me how much she loved him, of course…'

I had the impression that she'd confided a great deal, but that he didn't want to talk about it. Not here, at the funeral.

'Could I come and see you?' I said. 'I have things that I'd like to ask – but this is the wrong time, wrong place.'

'Sure, do that, I'd like it.' He reached into the pocket of his jacket to find his business card, and wrote his home address on the back. I put it safely in my bag, then noticed Liam staring across the room at Tilda and Lucas, who were deep in a conversation, sitting side by side, Tilda leaning her head on his shoulder.

'Have you had a chance to talk to Tilda today?'

'No… No, I haven't. I'd better do that now… I have to leave soon.' Something about his attitude suggested he was weighing up Tilda, assessing the way she was handling herself; and later, as I was on the train back to London, I kept thinking that Liam held secrets, that he could shed light on how Tilda really felt about Felix's death.

When I arrived home, though, I forgot all that, because I did my usual thing – sitting by my bedroom window, turning on my laptop, and I saw a message from Scarlet. It said simply, *30 October, 4 o'clock*. I wrote back: *Send me your address*. But she answered, *No. I'll send it on the 29th*.

37

I had no intention of waiting. Instead, three days after the funeral I took the train to Manchester, determined to find Luke. It was one of those dead Mondays, office workers trudging from Starbucks back to work, waiting in blank-eyed huddles to cross busy roads, and I stood with them, making my way from the station to Hollybank TV, wishing that I had a brilliant plan.

Hollybank, it turned out, was in a grey stone office block, along with insurance companies and legal firms with solid names like *Mackenzie and Singh*, and *Turner and Partners*. Clueless, I hung around by the revolving doors, watching people go in and out, pulling up the hood of my parka to keep warm. It was almost one o'clock and I had the absurd idea that Luke would come out for lunch, and I'd somehow recognise him. Which, amazingly, did in fact sort of happen – because a group of five young people emerged onto the pavement, looking scruffier and trendier than the office workers, and I thought *creatives*! I followed them down two streets and into a café called Red Onion.

You had to order at a counter, and a young woman started speaking for the entire group – saying, 'What do you want Lulu? Sanjeev?' and after she'd relayed the orders for almond milk lattes and quinoa salads, she called out, 'How about you, Luke?' to a skinny young man with black hair and dark circles under his eyes, who was talking with Lulu, discussing the next day's filming. He scratched the back of his head in a way that seemed both nervous and charming, and said, 'An espresso and a cheese-and-ham panini, thanks.' I noted his Manchester accent, and the way his Adam's apple moved up and down when he spoke.

The group moved to a table and sat down, while I ordered myself a hot chocolate then sat at the adjacent table. I couldn't hear everything that was said, but I gathered that they were working on a documentary about dangerous plants. At one point, Luke was talking about the 'dapperling mushroom… the amatoxin destroys your liver…' Then Lulu told the group about a whole family in Italy who died after the mother added death cap mushrooms to their soup, presumably but not definitely by mistake, and then the group started debating whether or not they'd recognise poisonous mushrooms if they found them in a wood or somewhere. I wished they'd stop discussing work, and switch to their social lives. But they didn't; they moved on to deadly nightshade.

When they left, I followed them along the street back to the office. Luke, I noticed, had a gangly, uneven walk, and he talked a lot, bending down, since he was taller than the others. It was impossible for me to get his attention, to take him away from the group, so I simply watched as he disappeared back inside the office building, and I was left once more hanging around outside. It was a cold day, but at least it wasn't raining, and I took up my vigil, leaning against a neighbouring shop window and waiting.

I was lucky. After twenty minutes Luke emerged again, this time alone, and I followed him down the street, where he stopped and stood in line to use a cash machine. I stood behind him, as though I was in the queue, then tapped him on the shoulder.

'Hi… Are you Luke Stone?'

He looked bewildered. 'Yes… Sorry, do I know you?'

'No… But I know your girlfriend…'

'Charlotte? You know Charlotte?'

I almost laughed out loud. Scarlet, Charlotte. Of course.

'Yes… I'm Callie Farrow. We know each other from ages ago…' I couldn't think of anything specific to say. *I know her from the internet?* Not good. *I know her from her acting and modelling days?* Implausible.

'Oh, okay…'

I stamped my feet, as though it was too cold to say outside, and said, 'Luke, do you have a minute to go for a coffee? There's something about Charlotte that I need to talk to you about…'

'What did you say your name was?' He stepped backwards, like he was trying to get away.

'Callie. Callie Farrow...'

'She hasn't mentioned you.'

'Oh. That's not surprising – we know each other from Narcotics Anonymous. We're not supposed to talk about it.' After having no ideas, that one just came to me from outer space, and I was pleased with my ingenuity. He'd be curious now.

'I see... Okay then, a quick coffee.'

We walked back to the Red Onion café and, as we entered, he said, 'Wait a minute – weren't you in here earlier? Have you been stalking me?'

'Yes. I'm sorry. It's just that there's something quite serious going on with Charlotte that you don't know about... that I thought you *should* know.'

'You're being extremely weird, Callie. You know that I'll tell Charlotte about this don't you?'

I didn't answer.

We ordered a coffee for him and a hot chocolate for me, and took them to two high stools next to a wooden counter by the window, so that we were facing out, watching the people on the street.

'I have to admit that I know some pretty intimate things about you and Charlotte,' I began, keeping my voice tentative and friendly. 'I know about the violence in your lives, and the sex games that you play...'

'What the fuck?'

'Luke... I know that this must seem really strange, but please, do listen to me. I want you to understand that I know Charlotte's secrets… That she thinks the only way to escape, to leave you is by destroying you, taking your life…' I touched his arm. 'Really. She's dangerous…'

He looked at me with wide dark eyes, trying to compute my words.

'I can't really explain,' I continued. 'But one of you *will* kill the other… I can see that. And the best thing you can do is get out of there, quickly. Please, Luke…'

He stood up, almost knocking his stool over. 'I don't know who you really are, but you're out of your mind. Just stay away from Charlotte, and from me. Otherwise, I'm going to the police. Do you understand?'

He was leaning over me, spewing his words into my ear, aggressive. The chatty charmer had gone, and I noticed for the first time that his eyes were red, bloodshot, and his skin a pallid grey. I tried to speak again, to tell him to take me seriously, but he left the café, striding past the window without looking in.

I remained at the seat, sipping my hot chocolate and watching the people on the pavement outside. Doubtless Scarlet would be furious with me now because I had no faith that Luke was going to follow my advice. More likely he'd go home and accuse her of terrible sins, of blabbing to me, of betraying him. God knows what the consequences would be.

38

She was totally mad, sending a torrent of emails, ranting, practically hysterical – *How could you! You're such a crazy bitch. You've no idea – the price I had to pay!*

Luke had gone home and accused Scarlet of sounding off at Narcotics Anonymous, of having secrets. How dare she talk about their private lives to people like me, whom she hardly knew! *You've no idea what you've unleashed,* she wrote, *he became turned on by the role he was playing – of a master reprimanding his slave, forced to punish me, forced to humiliate and hurt me… If I'm found strangled, or choked to death with some piece of rag rammed down my throat, Luke's to blame, and so are you!* Then she added, *How did you know? Luke's sensitive about drugs, because he was a user himself.*

I didn't know, of course. But it made sense. When I thought about how she wanted to kill him, with diamorphine in the arm, looking like it was self-inflicted. But

I didn't want to engage with that – instead I told her she was being unfair, and also that I needed to distance myself. But Scarlet said our lives were intricately bound together now, that there was no escape for me. That it was more crucial than ever that I kept my side of our bargain. *We made no bargain!* I wrote. *It's all in your head.* She came right back telling me that I was deluded. A deal had been struck – she had acted and I had to reciprocate. And the date she'd sent me earlier, would still work. *When you went to Luke,* she said, *you increased the urgency of your mission. Don't lose your nerve. Honour Belle.*

I'm not even convinced that you actually did what you said you did, I wrote back, sickened, and untruthful.

Remember the four-leaf clover. How else would I have it? It's proof.

I need more proof.

Okay – well I can tell you this. I brought him breakfast that day – a pain au raisin. What does it say in the post-mortem? Is that what he had eaten that morning?

I felt dizzy. She'd done exactly as I had asked and had supplied me with more evidence – it was almost too good to be true. I could go to Melody Sykes now, and say, 'Look what she wrote! How could Scarlet possibly have known they found raisins in his stomach?' Together with the cufflink, it was almost conclusive. At the back of my mind, though, I felt that one small piece of the picture was missing, some third sign that would place Scarlet at the

Ashleigh House Hotel that day – and I took the decision to go back there, to see Agnes again, the receptionist who'd taken photographs.

It was easy – a short train journey, and then a cab ride, and I was back in that stylish Georgian hotel, lawns stretching out to the woods.

I asked for Agnes. The young man on reception said that she was on her break. 'Who shall I say wants her?'

'Tell her Callie Farrow, the sister-in-law of Felix Nordberg.'

A few minutes later, she appeared, looking smart in her black uniform and perfect make-up, and her hair tied up in a neat ponytail.

'I wondered whether you could tell me about the day Felix died,' I said. 'And whether I might have another look at the photographs you took.'

'I sent them to your sister.' She sounded wary.

'I don't want to bother my sister. It's a difficult time for her.' It sounded weak, but I couldn't think of anything better.

'She asked me to delete them…'

'Did you?'

'Actually, I didn't. But they're very intimate, I haven't shown them to anyone.'

She wasn't budging, so I tried a new tack. 'It's possible that someone came to see Felix that morning, and I want to see if there is any evidence of that in the photographs.'

'Really? I didn't see anyone go to his room.'

'But wasn't the hotel busy? There was a conference going on.'

'That's true. One of his colleagues, maybe.'

That wasn't what I meant, but there was no need to elaborate, and I gave Agnes a half-smile that was meant to say *Well?* and at last she reached into her bag, telling me to come with her to the lounge area where we could sit down. She passed me the phone and I scrolled through the photos – once again I was struck by the pristine nature of the room – everything perfectly tidy. Of course, that was normal for Felix. Nonetheless there was a strange sense of the scene of his death being arranged for a viewing, the artistic way in which he was lying on the bed, his arm hanging down the side. Even his bath robe appeared to be draped in a thought-out fashion – and I thought of Scarlet's attention to detail, the way she planned things so carefully. I looked at the photographs a second time, hoping that something would unlock my thoughts, make me realise why I'd thought it so important to have come back here, to the hotel. Then, something struck me – the picture of the untouched hospitality tray. Nothing drunk and nothing eaten, not the wrapped up biscuits, nor the piece of fruitcake encased in cellophane.

'Did Felix have any breakfast sent to his room that morning?'

'No. Not at all. It was one of the reasons we thought something was wrong, when he hadn't left the room all day. He hadn't eaten anything, no breakfast, no lunch. Nothing.'

I thought about the pain au raisin. I supposed that Felix could have brought it with him to the hotel – but why? And if he had, why were there no used plates, no crumbs anywhere?

'Thank you, Agnes,' I said. 'Could you send me these pictures? As I say, I don't want to bother Tilda right now. She's too upset.'

'Okay…' She didn't sound sure, but she did it anyway. I checked that the untouched hospitality tray photo was in my inbox, and I thought *It convinces me, so surely it will convince Melody Sykes.* There was, though, still one element that was bothering me, that would be hard to explain to the police: Why would Felix have let Scarlet into his room in the first place? Did he know her from somewhere?

'The person who might have come to see Felix was a young woman, about my age,' I said, 'with dark hair, quite tall. Her name is Charlotte.'

'I don't remember anyone like that coming to reception, and I was the only staff member on the desk that morning. Although, we were busy, and I may have forgotten.'

'So it's possible that she came and asked for Felix's room number?'

'Yes. But we wouldn't give it out, just like that. We'd call up to the room, and check with the guest first. I'd remember that.'

'I see.'

Maybe Felix *had* known Scarlet; maybe she had known his room number. For an instant, something flashed into my mind. One thing they had in common was that Felix was angry and violent and controlling, and Scarlet liked sex games with violent men. But I dismissed the thought just as fast. For all his faults, I didn't see Felix as a cheater. Especially as he had only been married for a few weeks.

I thanked Agnes again and, as I left the hotel, I called a taxi to take me into Reading, to the police station.

39

A receptionist behind a metal grille was casually scrolling on her phone, not looking up as I said I wanted to speak to Melody Sykes. 'It's in connection with a death she investigated.' That was too strong, but I thought it would grab her attention.

Melody appeared two minutes later, clutching a Styrofoam coffee cup, propping the door open with a big hip. 'Come on through, we'll go somewhere private…' She sounded irritated, like I'd interrupted something important, and I almost had to jog to keep up as she strode down the corridor, swinging her large frame from side to side. She ushered me into a small, bare room, the sort you see in TV dramas when the police interview their prime suspect, and we faced each other across a table.

'So, Miss Farrow, how can we help?'

'It's about Felix Nordberg. The man who died at the Ashleigh House Hotel.'

'Oh yes. Heart disease wasn't it?'

'That's why I'm here. I don't think it was... I think the postmortem was wrong.'

'And what makes you think that?' She leaned back, scrunching up her face, looking sceptical.

'I know someone who says she killed him. Her name's Charlotte – and I think she went to the hotel and injected him with a lethal dose of diamorphine.'

'Mmm-hmm. Let's rewind... Who is this Charlotte? How did she know Mr Nordberg? Why would she want to kill him?' She did me the courtesy of opening her notebook, taking a pen from the pocket of her jacket.

'I don't know her well... I met her on the internet, and we'd discuss men who harm women, and things escalated until she said she would kill Felix for me, to protect my sister.'

'Why would she do that? It's rather extreme...'

I hesitated, unsure of how much to reveal about my own complicity, and then I said, 'She wanted me to kill her boyfriend, Luke. It was supposed to be a bargain. Like the film *Strangers on a Train*.'

'My goodness!' Her tone was disbelieving and annoyed. 'That's quite something. And you think she was serious? People often fantasise about murder, you realise – that's not a crime, it's just human nature.'

'I know... I know that. Really. And at first I didn't take her seriously... but now I think she's kind of insane. She sent me proof that she was actually there, in Felix's room.

A gold cufflink in the shape of a four-leaf clover. I can't see how she'd have it unless she'd been in Felix's room at the hotel. And, something else – she said she took him a pain au raisin for his breakfast... and at the postmortem, they found raisins in his stomach.'

'They also found that he died from hypertrophic cardiomyopathy...'

'That's what I don't understand. How come they didn't find diamorphine?'

'Well... the fact is they didn't do a toxicology report. It's not routine in a straightforward case like this.'

'What?' I could scarcely believe it. 'That's terrible! And now he's been cremated.'

'I think the point to focus on, Miss Farrow, is that the case was straightforward – so there was no need for a toxicology report.'

'Surely it could be a coincidence – that he had a heart condition, but that he was actually killed by diamorphine?'

She folded her arms over a large, protective bosom, exasperated, and not concerned. 'Well, that could happen,' she said. 'But it's unlikely... You seem to have got very caught up in your internet relationship with this Charlotte...' Then, in a kindly, patronising voice, 'The internet is a beguiling thing, relationships can become all-involving in such a short time. Is it possible that you've allowed your thoughts to get out of control – to run away with you?'

'I have considered that. Really I have... But you have to believe that I'm being serious.'

'So what would you like me to do? If it were up to you?'
Her brashness made it seem like she was saying, 'So what
would you like me to do, Young Lady? If it were up to you,
Young Lady?'

'I'd like you to interrogate Charlotte.'

'On what evidence? Do you have any actual evidence of
this *Strangers on a Train* bargain that you say you made?'

'You can look at our internet messages,' I said. 'They tell
you everything, but just not in straightforward language.
Everything is hinted at.'

I had made a print-out of the key conversations, and
I passed them across the table. Melody read everything
– slowly, carefully, running her finger down the text,
underlining extracts with a ballpoint pen. As I watched, I
felt a pain, like some stinging insect was inside my chest.
Yes, Scarlet had referred to 'our bargain' and 'the danger
Pink is in' and 'the need to act' – but I could see now that
Melody Skyes wouldn't be convinced. It didn't help that
I hadn't included the conversations in which I had gone
along with Scarlet, told her that I would keep my end of
the bargain.

She finished reading, and looked at me, a faint smile
on her lips, saying, 'You seem tired, Miss Farrow. I think
you need a good, long sleep. I understand that you've been
through a traumatic time – your brother-in-law dying so
suddenly like that… I'm not sure there's anything for me
to follow up on here. It just seems like, forgive me, it's the
only phrase I can think of – a bit of internet nonsense.'

Tears were pricking at my eyes. 'But you can go and see Luke Stone… He's Charlotte's boyfriend – so he can give you her full name. He's the one she wants me to kill!'

'And are you planning to go through with that?'

'Of course not.'

'Quite. That's my point.'

She picked up her coffee cup, and stood up, saying, 'I think this brings our meeting to a close. I've made a note of our conversation – do feel free to speak to me again if you need to.'

I could see that this was her standard way of ending meetings with members of the public. She didn't actually want to see me again.

*

At home later I drank half a bottle of Strongbow while I tried to figure out what I might do to convince Melody, and I kept arriving at the same conclusion – I needed to establish the connection between Scarlet and Felix. And the drunker I became, the more ready I was to dial a number I found online for Francesca Moroni, although the questions I wanted to ask were impossible, outrageous. I could hardly say, 'So how rough was Felix when you had sex? Did you ever think he would kill you?' But my head was filling up with a cloudy, optimistic recklessness, so I poured another glass of cider, and called anyway.

It was a good moment, apparently. She was alone and

could chat – and I explained that I wanted to ask her about Felix, that I was looking for closure – I winced at the word, but ploughed on, encouraged by her own slightly fuzzy diction, and pauses to sip.

'Fire away…' she said. 'I won't be offended. Seriously, I know that when someone dies you want to ask all the questions that you wish you'd asked when they were alive. Believe me, I've been there…'

So I questioned her about her relationship with Felix, how they met, and why they split up. She didn't come across as the 'poor Francesca' that Lucas had described – rather as a strong person who had had the courage to walk away when Felix had failed to commit.

We seemed to be getting along well, and I risked a more penetrating question. 'Did he want you to give up your career?'

'What are you getting at?' She sounded sharper now.

'I want to know if Felix was controlling with you? In an obsessive, harmful way.'

A pause, while she took another sip of her drink. Then, 'Like he was with Tilda? Is that what you're implying?'

'Yes.'

'I'm not going to bad-mouth Felix, Callie.'

'Please, Francesca, I have to know whether Felix harmed you – it's for my peace of mind. I'm trying to figure out if Tilda's better off now that she's free of him…'

'Stop it… It's disrespectful. Felix was demanding, yes… But he never harmed me. Our relationship wasn't like that.' She was speaking quietly now, and I couldn't tell whether she was being truthful, or whether she was simply protecting Felix's memory.

'I was worried that he might be seeing someone else, someone called Charlotte... For violent sex.'

'That's enough... It's ridiculous, you should stop making allegations...'

'Okay, I'm sorry.'

There was another pause on the line and I thought she was going to say goodnight. Instead, I heard, 'It's possible... just about. I once caught him accessing a website called illicithookups.com. But that's all. He was never violent with me. Never.'

40

Twenty-ninth of October – the day before I was supposed to kill Luke Stone – and late, just as I was going to bed, Scarlet emailed her address in Manchester, and reminded me of our *nice chat that day at Kenwood House.* There was no longer any need for me to humour her, so I replied, *Our chat was disgusting and I won't be following up on it.* A few minutes later: *You must follow up. It was agreed. Remember what I've done for you, at your bidding, and return the favour. You have no choice, actually. You're implicated.*

I was nauseated and didn't reply. But I'd had a bad night, lying awake and worrying. I thought maybe I should, after all, go to Manchester in the morning, to Scarlet's flat. If I found Luke in a comatose state then I'd be able to phone Melody Skyes. Luke could be revived, and Scarlet charged with drugging him. But the more I thought about it, the more doubtful I felt. Melody would probably suspect *me*, given that she seemed to think I was unstable. And I needed to concentrate on proving that Scarlet murdered Felix – her sick games with Luke were not my priority.

In the morning, I went to work even though it was a Monday. I think I just wanted Daphne's company. She was in a buoyant mood because Douglas was treating her to a holiday in Siena. 'I'd just mentioned to him that it's one of my favourite places – and he found us the most charming little hotel to stay in, and they're putting a table by the window, so I'll be able to write while I'm looking at the terracotta roofs and the winter sun. And I'll take breaks for us to walk the streets, exploring, stopping in cafés and bars. Oh, it'll be blissful.'

'I read in a magazine that your first holiday together can make or break your relationship,' I said. I didn't want to be negative, but I was aching from the contrast between her good fortune and my turbulent life.

'I reckon you're right.' She was untroubled by my sharpness, confident in Douglas, and she went back to pounding her keyboard, absorbed in *The Lady Connoisseurs of Crime*.

I had my laptop on the payments counter and I typed illicithookups.com into the address bar, then said I was looking for a man and hundreds came up instantly. Men who posted pictures of Brad Pitt and David Beckham instead of themselves, men who posted pictures of their hairy bellies, showing that their trousers were unzipped, men posting pictures of themselves in mirrors in grotty, dirty bathrooms, men in a variety of role-play costumes – babies, dolls, dogs, hangmen, you name it. A size-able minority, though, were hiding behind the stock photograph for the site – a suave city gent in a dinner jacket, with a cocktail in his hand. They'd be no way of finding Felix in this lot – so I tried being a man looking for an illicit woman, and in no time at all I was scrolling through pictures of women in lacy bras and thongs, stockings and stilettoes. Most of the images were like *Fifty Shades of Grey* – black fluffy handcuffs, leather whips pressed into rolling cleavage and buttocks and thighs. Anything more explicit, apparently, was only available if you paid £120 a month, a fee which would also allow you to message 'your fantasy girl', with a view to meeting her in the flesh.

I clicked on a skinny woman calling herself Playful Pandora lying across a bed; at least, the picture showed a sprawling, barely clad body, straining ribs, flung-back neck, but not a face, and I thought for a second that it could be Scarlet. But then I saw that she'd posted: 'Naughty nights with masterful sex god sought by luscious lovely 42-year-old.' I harrumphed with laughter, and Daphne looked pointedly at me. I read more, learning that Pandora really liked 'bondage, s and m, all exotic requests consid-ered'. When I clicked on other photos, Sexy-sexy, Betsy Bootylicious, Mistress Millie (alliteration was practically mandatory), I found women on all-fours, their bottoms in the air, doing *little ootsy-cutesy me* faces at the camera, and others that were the opposite, stern dominatrices in tight black rubber or leather brandishing so many different sorts of torture instruments that I wondered whether you could buy them on eBay. All the ads I saw were on the same theme – women touting sexual adventures involving pain and domination.

I opened up the dossier, and typed out hypothetical situations. Maybe Scarlet had learned from me that Felix was violent in the bedroom, and had gone looking for him on illicithookups – which was evidently the go-to site for rough sex. That was just about conceivable if she paid the £120 interaction fee. Or was it the other way round? Did Scarlet meet Felix on illicithookups a while ago – then go to controllingmen to see if he was on there as a Predator? Of course I quickly realised that that wouldn't work since I had simply referred to Felix as X, made him anonymous. I returned to illicithookups, scanning the profiles, trying to find Scarlet, and I spotted a few possibilities, but nothing that was truly convincing.

*

When I got home from work I phoned Wilf. It was my first attempt to contact him since he'd walked out of our lunch in the Albany, angry that I'd turned out to be insane. He didn't answer, and the phone went to voicemail, but I didn't leave a message. Five minutes later, he called back.

'Hey.'

'Hey.'

'Am I forgiven?'

'What for?'

'Walking out... I've been wanting to call you. I was knocked sideways by those things you said, Callie... but I want to know more. I mean, it sounds like you've been dragged into some horrible mire by unscrupulous people on the internet, like you could do with a friend by your side.'

I almost broke down. *'That's exactly what's happened! I'm finding it difficult to know what's real and what isn't.'*

'Would it help if I came round and threw you on the bed and made love to you?'

'I think that would help... It's certainly worth a try.' I was smiling – really, truly smiling – for the first time in ages. 'Come here – I'm at home.'

*

Making love with Wilf *did* help. It helped a lot. After so many months of struggling to establish some understanding, some control of the events in my life, it was a wondrous, joyous release to surrender myself to him, utterly. To be totally mouth-to-mouth, skin-to-skin.

Afterwards, I put on his shirt, savouring its earthy, rooty scent, thinking about poor Tilda putting on Felix's shirt after he died. I wandered into the other room, carelessly looking for my phone. We'd agreed that a Thai takeaway – green chicken curry with rice and lager would suit us very well, and I needed to order. My phone was on the sofa, wedged in a crack in the cushions, and I flopped down, intending to search for the restaurant number. I couldn't help noticing, though, a new email from Scarlet. I wanted to ignore it, to pretend that she didn't exist, but the pull was too great; and suddenly, against my will, I was back in the bloody riptide, wanting to see how angry she was at my failure to turn up at her flat, and I clicked.

Dear Callie,

I was sorry that you couldn't come to Manchester. It was disappointing. But all that doesn't matter now because a terrible tragedy occurred here today. The love of my life, Luke Stone, has died from a drugs overdose. I had known that he was a user, but I hadn't suspected that his life was in danger. I came home and found him dead. I'm setting up a memorial page for him on deardepartedfriends.com. I thought you'd like to know.

Yours,
Scarlet

Wilf appeared at the bedroom door, naked like a bear and grinning wickedly, until he noticed my expression.

'Look at this.'

He read Scarlet's letter, slowly. Then reread it. 'Fuck. I mean fuck… Callie, you need to go to the police.'

41

We went to the same room as before, a little interrogation cell, empty except for a table and four chairs. 'So, what brings you back?' Her tone was dog-tired. She looked like she'd slept in her clothes, a crumpled beige jacket over a yellow t-shirt with a coffee-coloured stain. 'Didn't I tell you to take a break from your amateur detective work?' She sighed loudly, for effect.

'Something awful has happened. You know I told you that Scarlet, I mean Charlotte, wanted me to kill her boyfriend? Well, he's dead. Luke Stone is dead...'

Melody scraped her chair in close, and leaned over, eyeballing me across the table like *this had better not be more of your bullshit, Miss Farrow.* 'You'd better explain yourself,' she said.

'Look at this.' I passed her a print-out of Scarlet's email. 'When she says, "I'm sorry you didn't come to Manchester," she means she's sorry I didn't come and kill

Luke. She had given me diamorphine and syringes, and told me to come and inject him... I didn't do it, so she's done it herself. See.'

She read it, and re-read it, and her tone changed. It was like she'd woken up. 'I'd like to call a colleague in. I think two of us should hear this.'

She left the room briefly and returned with a young man with lank, floppy hair. 'This is DC Ramesh Sharma. If you don't mind, I'll ask him to join us, and take notes. We'll also record our conversation.'

'I'd like that.' I sat up straight, like it was my first day at work, and I wanted to make a good impression.

'Okay. So let's go back to the beginning... You say Charlotte – you don't know her surname? – well, this Charlotte wanted you to murder her boyfriend?'

It was so complicated. I needed to explain about Felix at the same time – and I went through it all as best I could. Unlike last time, I showed Melody the photographs of Felix's room at the Ashleigh House Hotel, 'See how odd it is? Everything seems somehow *arranged*, and neat and tidy, and see how he hasn't touched anything on the hospitality tray – and yet they found he had eaten raisins that morning, which fits with what Charlotte told me. It's clear she was there, don't you think? And how come she could just go into his room, with breakfast for him? He hadn't ordered breakfast. And she must have spent time there, to somehow inject him... Isn't it obvious that he must have recognised her? I've found out that Felix went to a website called illicithookups.com, which is for people who like sadomasochism. Charlotte likes violent sex, I know that. And so does Felix. Could she have looked for him on this website? Befriended him? Isn't that worth investigating?'

She let me go on, and it was a wonderful liberation to be handing over my investigation to a professional person. At last! When she asked questions it was to nail down specific facts: What was the name of the hotel receptionist who took the photos? Did I have any more email communications with Charlotte? Could I give her Charlotte's address?

Thankfully, she didn't quiz me on my own complicity and, as I drew to the end of my account, she said, 'Okay, Callie. That's enough for now. We'll make arrangements for you to hand in the syringes and diamorphine that Charlotte gave you to your local police station.'

As she spoke, I felt like my insides were being eaten up, like parasitic worms were penetrating my intestines. 'I'm sorry… I binned them… it was so stupid of me…'

The look that Melody and Ramesh exchanged told me everything. The idiot witness had chucked the evidence. Or worse, she was, after all, a liar, a fantasist. Melody seemed to deflate into her crumpled, stained clothes.

'We have your contact details and you can expect to hear from me in a few days….' Her irritation was back, undisguised. 'In the meantime, stop your own activity. You have a wild imagination – keep it in check and we're more likely to get to the truth.'

'Thank you… Thank you. Will you see Charlotte today? Bring her in for an interview?'

'I can't discuss that. But take it from me that we're taking your claims seriously, and will investigate them thoroughly.' Her weariness had returned.

'I'm grateful.' And I was. Despite my stupidity, it seemed possible that Melody Sykes was taking over. That I'd offloaded a great burden.

42

Daphne said, 'You seem better, Callie. You've been looking knackered recently, but something's changed...'

'I'm pulling myself together. After Felix's death...'

'Good for you. Tell you what, I'm doing so well with *The Lady Connoisseurs* that I'll print off the manuscript and get you to read it. I'd value your opinion...'

I was flattered, and I spent most of the morning reading, and enjoying, her novel. I liked her private detectives, Maisie Fothergill and Hermione Swift, and the quiet treacheries of their circle of friends. There were big country houses, too, and steam trains and afternoon tea; time passed quickly until, just before lunch, Tilda came into the shop. She hadn't warned me that she was coming, and I was surprised that she looked different. More energised than recently. Eyes shining, rather unnaturally. Better clothes – not the big tweed coat or the hat. Just trendy jeans (XXOX, Paradise in the Park?) and a tailored jacket which looked expensive. Daphne said, 'Oh... I was so sorry to hear about Felix. You have my sympathy.'

Tilda was polite, but she talked too fast. 'Thank you. That's kind of you. We'd only been married a few weeks... it's still sinking in.'

'Of course.'

'I was wondering if Callie could come out with me for half an hour or so...'

'Yes, yes... we're not busy – that's totally fine.'

We went back to the Albany – only for coffee (her) and hot chocolate (me) because it was 11am, not lunchtime. I was bracing myself, preparing to come clean and admit to everything, to confess that I'd stolen the memory stick, read her letter to me. I didn't know exactly how far I'd go – to tell her about Scarlet, and my fears that Felix had been murdered, seemed too much at this stage, while her grief was raw... I sipped my hot chocolate and was about to launch into my speech, when, 'Callie, I've been making decisions... I've been so low, crying and crying, even thinking about taking an overdose – killing myself.'

She was making a tremendous effort to get her words out fast, speaking with a hollow, breathy urgency, all the time tracing shapes on the table with her finger.

'I miss him so much...'

She was bent up, staring up at me so hard.

'And it's so much worse when I'm at Curzon Street. He made it *his* place – choosing everything – the colours of the walls and the floors, the art, the bed, even the crockery and the cutlery. I walk around the place and I see him everywhere – cooking that damned squid in the kitchen, watching movies with us, lying in bed, and I can scarcely breathe – his ghost is in the brickwork there. And I'm not consoled by his presence – like those people who keep dead relatives' rooms just as they were left, like a shrine. I'm fucking tormented by it… Everything that tells me that he *was there*, tells me also that he's gone. Forever.'

She tried to pull herself upright, but couldn't manage it.

'Anyhow, Callie. Here's the thing. I've decided to leave England. I'm going to LA, to see if I can break into movies there. I've spoken to an American agent who says I have a good chance because of the scripts that are already being sent to me because of *Rebecca*, and also my role in *Envy* should help. You remember I told you about that? It's the one that reminded me of *Single White Female*. And this American agent says he can also help find me a good place to live in LA!'

She sounded wasted and manic at the same time.

'It's the best way forward for me… I need to move on. Not to forget Felix, of course. But to honour him by doing good work. Really *honour* him. Demanding roles in good films – the sort of thing that would have made him proud of me.'

I was so surprised that my brain felt numb. Eventually, I managed, 'I don't understand… How long will you be gone?'

'Oh, as long as it takes!' She spoke in a way that suggested a long sweep into the far future.

My thoughts stumbled towards practical things; obstacles. 'Don't you need a green card?'

'It's fine – Felix was American. And I'm his wife. Anyhow – it's easy with acting, if you're offered a good part. It's international.'

'What about money?'

'I can sell Curzon Street if I need to. But, in the short term, you can move in there. It's so much nicer than your flat.'

'You mean you're leaving soon?'

'Yes… I can't stand being here much longer… As I say, it's ripping me apart, being alone in that flat.'

'But that will look so bad. He dies, you leave.'

'For fuck's sake. I don't care how it looks. I don't care! I'm falling apart – and I need to save myself.' Her desperation was obvious now.

But still I said, 'Tilda… please don't go! I'll miss you too much.'

She got up and came round to my side of the table and gave me the deepest, warmest hug I've ever had from her. I sensed the enormity of her decision. She wanted to sever herself from everything, from England, from Curzon Street and from me. Inside, I was screaming *this cannot happen!*

'I know you'll miss me, little one. But I'll be in touch. And I'll come home sometimes… Come on… chip chip.'

'Can I come and see you?'

'Maybe… maybe, yes.' It sounded like no.

'I'm going next week. I'll get a spare key from Eva, and you can move in.'

I didn't tell her that I already had the spare key. I just sat silently, in shock, struggling to understand.

43

Tilda left for Los Angeles, and I moved into Curzon Street. Before I'd even unpacked, I went to the linen cupboard, rooting around, feeling for my fix. The memory stick was in its home – the corner of the last pillow case in the pile. So I extracted it, plugged it into my laptop, and was instantly rewarded.

Yes, Callie, I know you're reading this. I know you go through my things, looking for morsels of me to eat, searching for clues about my life; and you'd never miss my favourite hiding place. You think you know me, that you're under my skin – but I know you better!

I have one last message for you, little sister – let matters lie; stop your relentless prying. You think there's some mystery to solve about my life, but there isn't; I'm just a woman who's lost her husband – a grieving widow. Allow me that. Felix was a charismatic, flawed control freak who died tragically because of a random, cruel, idiotic heart defect. Yes, he was dangerous; yes, he manipulated me emotionally – I can see that now he's gone – and it might have been me who died first. But that's all over, and I need to move on.

Try to support my decisions. I'll have a new life, and new roles – my American agent is excited about my prospects in LA… I'll be able to lose myself in work, and maybe achieve some real success. It will be such a relief after the trauma of Felix's death. I'm hoping to do a fair amount of nothing also; lounging about in a villa in the Hollywood hills, catching up on sleep, swimming in my pool, maybe I'll even try to meditate!

As for you, Callie, nurture your own life now, think about your own ambitions. Go on – try to rustle up some! You can do it! And my offer stands – if you need therapy, I'll pay for it; and you can stay in Curzon Street as long as you like – I don't mind paying the costs. I can afford it, as Felix's money will come to me. He was too young to have made as many millions as he wanted, but there's enough – for both of us.

So, realise that our old lives are over – and that the future has begun,

Tilda x

While I thought about her letter, I wandered about the flat looking for something of hers to eat. She was right about that, at least. I searched in the bathroom, hoping that she'd left something behind – a used toothbrush that I could suck, or a lipstick that I could take a shaving from. But there was nothing. Apart from a few pieces of unwanted clothing, she had cleaned the place out, and there was little sense of her in the flat – it was all Felix, Felix, Felix.

I lay on her bed, re-reading the letter, marvelling at her change of tone. Distraught Tilda had gone – she was now digging deep inside, trying to be optimistic, imagining a new future, and I should have felt happy for her. But I didn't. It was too soon. I knew that, in truth, she was still in the first stages of grief, that her real emotions were a maelstrom of pain and anger. The upbeat force of the final words in her letter could only be explained by their heartbreaking falseness, and I thought that if she could make such an admirable, incredible effort towards survival, then I should be strong too. I shouldn't give in or rest, however weary or defeated I felt, and I opened up the dossier again, scrolling down, randomly stopping and reading words that I'd written at the beginning of the summer, concentrating on my observations of Tilda's appearance, the gaunt look of her face, her nervous eyes, her unkempt appearance. Then I read a note that I'd completely forgotten about: *Does Felicity Shore realise something is wrong? Have further information?* It seemed so long ago – that day when I'd searched the Curzon Street flat for clues, and listened to the answering machine, to Tilda's agent pleading with her, 'Come to lunch or something, and let's go through your options.' But I thought, one last push – for Tilda's sake, I'll see Felicity Shore.

As it happened, she said, she could spare a few minutes in the afternoon. So I walked across town to her office, which was in Soho.

'Hello, Callie.' She held out her hand, her manner warm, her plump palm slightly moist. She was a large lady, wearing large-lady clothes, a purple batwing sweater over a long green jersey skirt. And she was lavishly decorated: a statement silver necklace, with dangling ingots, vaguely African, fat silver bangles, oversized blue spectacles.

Her room was cluttered – photographs everywhere of her clients, some of them glossy headshots, others of actors acting in plays and films; I sat down in the comfy chair that she offered, mildly distracted by the cigarette smell and the photos, also thinking about how to explain myself, how to start the conversation. My mind was blank, but then she said, 'I've been trying to get hold of Tilda, but she's not returning my calls. So, I'm guessing that she's avoiding dealing with me directly – has she sent you as an envoy?'

'Yes, that's right,' I lied. 'You know she's gone to LA?'

'What? No, I didn't know that. Not at all…' She put her fist down on the table, not hard, but it made her bangles and bracelets rattle as they fell down her arm like a Slinky.

'Oh.' My embarrassment was obvious. 'She's only just left… Just a few days ago.'

She leaned forward, parking her big breasts on her

messy desk top. 'I see. Well that's what she wanted all along, isn't it? To make it in America? But she knows my opinion – she needs to mend fences here first… You know she alienated people on *Rebecca*? Behaving like a diva when you're just starting out – it's not a clever move. It's made it hard for her to get jobs.'

'But she has the *Envy* role coming up?'

Felicity laughed, in a derisive way. 'Really, that's all very well, but it's low budget, and Robert Galloway – he's an inexperienced director. It's not going to help… But she doesn't listen to advice these days…' Even though she was sitting down, she seemed out of breath.

'She *did* listen to Felix though…'

'What do you mean?'

'I mean he was tough with her. Telling her not to take second-rate roles…'

The bangles arm moved again, with percussionary sound effects, as she put her elbow on the table and her fingers to her chin.

'Is that so?' she said. 'She didn't give me that impression when she came to see me. Second-rate roles, as you put it, were all that was coming her way, and not very often. She seemed only too keen to take them.'

I had a sense, although I'd been in her office only five minutes, I knew that she didn't like Tilda. Also, she'd given me the information I needed, and I could leave now. In a business-like way, I said, 'Well thank you, Felicity. Tilda wanted me to tell you that she'll be away for a while, but will be back in eight weeks for filming on *Envy* and she'll call you then.'

As I was leaving, I looked around at the chaotic room – books piled up on chairs, posters of her clients untidily pinned and taped to the walls, a tapestry throw draped over a cupboard. Then I noticed a photograph propped up on a bookcase – it was of Tilda and a bunch of other actors from her student days. I studied it, Tilda with her arms around her two best friends at the Central School for Speech and Drama, looking relaxed and joyful. The three of them seemed so bright-eyed and optimistic – young people about to break free and make their mark on the world.

I hurried back to Curzon Street, and in the dossier I wrote: *Tilda wasn't honest with me about her career. It hasn't been going well – she behaved badly on* Rebecca, *and the only role she's managed to get since – Helen in* Envy – *is on a low-budget movie with an unknown director. She's gone to LA against the advice of her agent, Felicity Shore. It sounds like a desperate move, and I fear she is in one of her depressions, heading for a breakdown.*

44

It was 10am on a Saturday and I was at Curzon Street, lying in bed with Wilf, my legs across his, both of us staring at the ceiling, and in that moment I wasn't thinking of Tilda; I was in Wilf-world, feeling safe and cocooned. 'I love helping in the garden,' I said. 'I think it's because it stops me thinking. At the bookshop I'm thinking all day long, and that's how I become so obsessive and paranoid… But in the garden my mind shuts off, it's wonderful; I can enjoy the sense of things – without my bloody thoughts intervening and screwing everything up. I can just *feel*. The fresh air and the soft ground, the animal life, the earthworms and birds. There's always a robin that turns up when you start digging – I've noticed that.'

'I'm pleased that you *get it*,' said Wilf. With a finger, he was following the contours of my waist and stomach and hip bones.

'Oh, I do. Absolutely.' I rolled over, on top of him, and he held me in his arms, his finger now following the curves of my shoulder blades and my back. 'You know,' I said, 'when I was little, on my seventh birthday, I was in the Kent countryside, running down a long hill, and I fell right into a bush. I was stuck in there, and I put my hand deep into the earth and found the skull of an animal. Mum said it probably belonged to a lamb; I was so moved by it, it made me cry.'

'It was everything at once, birth and death, and you felt protective of a life that didn't last... And of the mother who lost her baby.'

I kissed him on his stubbled cheek for that, and then – across the room – my phone rang. I wrapped myself in a blanket and stumbled over to pick it up. It was Melody Sykes, working on a weekend.

'Callie, I hope it's a convenient moment... I want to tell you about our investigation. We've spoken to Charlotte Watts and to Luke Stone's friends and family, and we've reached the conclusion that there's no reason to investigate further. The postmortem confirms a drugs overdose, and his personal history with drugs suggests that they were self-administered.'

I turned my back to the wall, leaning on it for support.

'But you've seen the emails that Charlotte and I sent each other? How can you not realise what they mean?'

'I acknowledge that you *believed* you were entangled in some sort of murder plot, Callie. But I have to look at hard evidence, not at the fantasies that you and Charlotte dreamed up.'

She hung up and I relayed her message to Wilf, who sat up in bed and let out a long, guttural sigh. 'Well that's great news! Couldn't be better. Now you can forget about bloody Scarlet and her poisonous mind-fucking, and I can get you back – the real you.'

'Really? You really think it's all over?' I sounded sarcastic; but then I sighed too – wishing I could agree.

'I know her real name now,' I said. 'Charlotte Watts.'

Wilf got out of bed, and went into the bathroom to shave. He stood at the sink, running the tap, and I stood behind him, my arms around his waist, peeking out to study the two of us in the mirror, to see how we looked together, to see if we seemed a good match. And we did, his ginger hair was ruffled up, his eyes were receding and bloodshot from sex. And I looked like a jumbled mess too – messy hair, cheeks flushed with red, an old robe of Tilda's pulled around me untidily. I noticed a cocktail of scents, a concoction of his smell and mine, of bodies, and I felt happy. I looked around, the bathroom was scattered with used towels, opened toothpaste, bits of make-up – mascara, lipsticks, Wilf's dirty clothes on the floor. The flat's minimalist days were over.

'Let's get out of here and pick up some decent coffee at the Copernicus,' Wilf said.

'Okay.' I was drinking coffee now.

We sat at a table by the window, the one that I'd chosen

at the beginning of the summer when I'd been spying on Tilda. (I could admit it now – it *was* spying. I had been *the little stalker*.) Wilf tried to keep the conversation positive.

'Come with me to the Bishop's Avenue garden… you'll see the progress. There's actual planting now… camellias and hydrangeas and fruit trees; and I'm getting paid on Monday. It'll be enough to buy a new vehicle, with my name on the side! I'm going to call myself *Wilf Baker Gardens* – not very creative, I know. What do you think?'

'I love it. I love your name.' I leaned my head on my hand, gazing at him sadly, wanting to be the person he wanted me to be.

'What?'

'I'm thinking that you're going to do brilliantly at this, at gardening and business and everything – and I *am* going to support you as much as I possibly can…'

'But…?'

'Wilf, I can't give up my investigation into Scarlet, into Felix's death… I'm really close now, I know it…'

He shook his head. 'I don't think so, Callie. I think you're as far away as ever… And in any case, you're so worried about Tilda, that she's so unreachable and alone and mentally unstable… What do you think it would do to her to claim, on thin evidence, that Felix was murdered? It would be devastating…'

The way he spoke, firmly but not without kindness, made me slump in my chair, like someone who'd been thumped; it forced me to question my own judgement.

Was I so sure of myself that I was prepared to risk losing Wilf? We stared at each other, each silently assessing the strength of our convictions, each yearning to close the gap between us.

'Okay,' I said eventually. 'I can't promise anything... but I'll try to take a step backwards for a while, just until I can see things more clearly.'

45

I'm trying, so hard, to be a good girlfriend. Every day I try to focus on the future, and my relationship with Wilf, rather than obsessing about Tilda, Felix, Scarlet and Luke. I've even given in my notice at Saskatchewan Books, and I'm going to be the manager at Wilf Baker Gardens. It was time for me to move on anyway, and it will be exciting to try to make the business a success. Also, psychologically, it will be good for me to be *doing* rather than *watching*. 'I don't want to sound too New Age,' I said to Wilf, 'but I want to be connected to the earth.'

Yesterday Daphne gave me a leaving present, a lithograph by the illustrator Edward Ardizzone of people browsing contentedly in a bookshop. 'I hope you were happy here,' she said.

'I was *so* happy here! I love the books, and the customers and you.'

We had the longest, clumsiest hug, and promised to stay in touch.

'Every time I need a book, I'll come back,' I said.

She raised one eyebrow, signalling that she was about to make an announcement, and then, in a girlish voice, 'I'm giving your job to Douglas – he's retiring from the pharmaceutical firm.'

I laughed. 'That's so couply!'

'It'll be different, that's for sure. I'm only going to have the shop open three days a week, then we'll be down to his house in Somerset for the other four... I've always wanted that – a nice man with a house in the country. It's very Jane Austen of me, I know.'

I'm so pleased for Daphne that it makes me feel uneasy. Her happy ending (and beginning) with Douglas is so neat and perfect, unlike my situation with Wilf. As I say, I'm trying hard to make our lives harmonious – but the truth is that I don't always succeed. Sometimes I'm back online, researching.

*

At Curzon Street, Wilf and I are eating our supper in front of the TV. We're supposed to be watching *Antiques Road Show*, guessing the value of trinkets and paintings and old bits of furniture. But I'm not really concentrating on the contents of other people's attics; my mind is elsewhere and, bracing myself for Wilf's reaction, I say, 'I'm going to Manchester tomorrow.'

'Oh?'

'I saw on the internet that a group of Luke Stones' friends are meeting in a pub, to remember him, and raise a glass. It's an open invitation…'

I put my plate down and lie with my head on Wilf's lap, but he pushes me upright, grabbing my shoulders with his gnarly gardener's hands, making a 'grrrrrr' sound like the bear that he is.

'Really? Do you really want to stir things up? It's better to allow him to rest in peace, surely…'

'I don't think he is resting in peace… You know that…'

'But you're supposed to be letting go… Getting some perspective…' Even as I hear the anger in his voice, I register my love for its honest tone, the absence of vindictiveness.

'I know… I know. But Wilf, just this one trip? It might help me get closure, for all we know.'

'Get closure!'

He picks up our dirty plates and takes them to the kitchen area, scraping leftovers into the bin, standing at the sink, washing up in a horrible way.

'Please,' I say. 'Support me…'

'I can't. You know what I think – I think you were dragged into a dark world by poisonous people. You need to stay away from all that.'

'Belle wasn't poisonous… Far from it.' This morning

I read on the BBC website that Joe Mayhew had pleaded guilty to manslaughter, citing diminished responsibility, and had been sentenced to nineteen years in prison. Beside the report was a photo of Belle, her lop-sided grin, her head slightly on one side, looking so pretty, so cheerful.

'Go if you have to. I can't stop you,' Wilf says coldly.

*

The train to Manchester is overcrowded and late, and I'm stressed as I rush from the station, hoping I haven't missed the event, and in my haste I take a wrong turning, getting lost, wasting another ten minutes. When eventually I find The Green Man, I'm fearing the worst, sure they'll all be gone. But then I see, in the corner on small stools by a flickering fire, Luke's work colleagues, Lulu and Sanjeev, along with three other young people, who are introduced as Alistair, Poppy and Jill. Two bottles of wine are open on a table, alongside used glasses, signs of a bigger crowd that was here earlier, and I wonder whether Scarlet was amongst them.

I say that I saw the notice online, and have come up from London.

'That's nice of you… We're still in shock,' says Lulu, looking me up and down, checking me out. 'I guess you are too…' She crosses her legs, which are in scruffy but sexy fishnet tights, and holds her wine glass with a hand encased in a fingerless glove; her nails are varnished and chipped in black.

'I had no idea he was an addict,' I say. 'Did you? Was it obvious at work?'

'He used to look bloody awful sometimes. He got so thin, and sometimes his skin looked almost grey, and his eyes so tired… I'd say to him, "Another rough one?" and he'd laugh it off and say, "You know Charlotte, she keeps me up all night…"'

'Did she come this evening? Charlotte, I mean…'

'No…' She sounds disapproving. Takes a large gulp of wine. Flashes a scornful look with her kohl-rimmed eyes.

'That's a pity – I'd like to offer her my sympathy. Do you know if she's at the flat?'

'Actually, I don't think she's even in Manchester. She's acting weirdly. She's a fucking deviant.'

Lulu exchanges a glance with Sanjeev, and says, 'We found out about Luke's death from Charlotte; she turned up at the office to tell us. I guess it was the shock – but she was manic, describing everything in minute detail – how she found him lying across the bed on his back, his arm hanging down the side, a needle hanging out of his skin… It was grotesque. She was getting off on the drama of it.'

So Luke's position on the bed was identical to Felix's. It made a sick sort of sense.

'What makes you think she's not in Manchester?'

Lulu crosses her legs the other way. 'Well, she didn't come to the funeral, and the flat has gone back on the rental market. So, we reckon she's gone… How well do you know her?'

'Not well.'

'The thing is, Callie, she's not popular around here. We can't help thinking that she was a bad influence on Luke... Before he met her, he was fine.'

'How long were they together?'

'Three years. And in that time, he changed so much. You must have noticed? He became moody and depressed, and physically wasted, kind of crack-brained...'

She leans forward, jutted jaw, pushing untidy dreads of red hair out of her face – her manner suggesting that it's dawned on her, only now, to question who I am.

'How long had you known Luke?'

'Oh, not long.' That's truthful at least. Then I add, 'We met at Narcotics Anonymous,' realising at once that I'm making a mistake.

'I thought you said you didn't know he was an addict?' Now Sanjeev leans in to hear my answer.

'Oh, I meant I didn't know he'd relapsed...'

'Well if you're a recovering addict, you know how important it is to have positive people around you. And Charlotte was never that...' says Sanjeev, sounding annoyed.

'Did she or Luke ever mention someone called Felix?'

'I don't think so... why?'

'Oh, no reason... I just wondered if Luke knew my friend Felix...'

'Well, it's an unusual name,' says Lulu, flatly. 'And I agree with Sanjeev. I don't think Luke ever mentioned it.'

'I sometimes thought that Charlotte might have had

a fling with Felix – it's not that Luke told me so, but I wondered all the same.' I'm making it up as I go along, and there's a wild, anxious note in my voice.

'It's unlikely,' says Lulu. 'Charlotte's not that sort of girl – not at all.' She and Sanjeev exchange a look that I interpret as *She was only too keen on Luke, unfortunately.*

'And you've no idea where she went?'

'No. She could be anywhere. As far as I can make out, she didn't have friends. Not local friends anyway.'

'What about her work? Doesn't she work in a beauty salon?'

'Ha ha! No. She sometimes works as a model. At least, that's what Luke said. And she's trying to break into acting… not very successfully, I think. She's had a couple of theatre roles, in tiny venues, and nothing else. She'd consider herself way too good for a beauty salon… But, look, this evening isn't about Charlotte, it's about Luke.' Lulu's eyes become red.

'I'm sorry,' I say. 'I didn't mean… I didn't mean to distract you.' I can see that Lulu had feelings for Luke. I lean forward and whisper in her ear, 'I don't think Luke killed himself.'

She nods, giving me a sideways glance. It's not like I'm saying anything that surprises her. It's like I'm reflecting her own feelings back.

'I'm going to find Charlotte,' I say. I mean it. 'I know she's hiding, but I'll find her.'

46

Wilf's avoiding me, staying longer at work, going to the pub afterwards; while I revert to my old self, spending forever online, constructing new theories for the dossier. I give illicithookups.com one last try. Since Francesca had told me, so seriously, about the site, she must have thought it was significant. Maybe Felix was more than a casual visitor; maybe he was a regular.

I scroll through a hundred women or more, all the Naughty Nikkis and Sadistic Sadies, and stop to inspect someone calling herself Mystery Madam of the Night. In her photo she's kneeling on a bed, knees apart, skimpy underwear on her bony body and a black mask partially covering her face, leather, with cat-woman eyes. I study her. She could be Scarlet, it's just possible. I pay £120 for the privilege, and send a message:

Love your photo. But I'm new here. Don't know how it works.

Hello lover. It's easy. I'm here to listen. Tell me about your secrets, your fantasies and let's take it from there, Roxanna xxx

I'd rather tell you in person Roxy.

I'd rather that also. I adore a first-timer. What's your name?

Call me Felix. Have you been on here long? Met many guys?

Let's say long enuff to know how to turn you on gorgeous. How to satisfy your deepest desires. To give you what you want.

I can tell this isn't Scarlet. Scarlet's way of talking is so direct and uncompromising; and she would never call anyone 'gorgeous' or write 'enuff'. I move on, scrolling through other women… not finding anyone who's more likely to be her. The pictures are wrong – most of the women are too old and too curvaceous. Then something occurs to me, and I go back to Roxanna.

I have something to ask you. Has anyone on here ever wanted you to inject them?

Anything goes on here. Hahahaha!!! Anything. If you want, I can do that.

Has anyone else ever asked you to do that?

Yes. It happens. Heroin or crack. Is that what you want Felix?

Maybe.

Or something else? Some people just like injections. Vitamins hahahaha.

Who? Who likes them?

Oh punters… We can do that. I won't charge extra.

What else? What else do you do?

We can discuss when we meet. Can't wait to see you in person. Tell me what you look like…

I don't answer… I re-read our short exchange and as I do so it dawns on me that I don't need illicithookups.com any more – because, after Lulu and thanks to Roxanna, everything is starting to fall into place. My two short conversations with them have triggered something in me. Lulu saying she's 'not that sort of girl' – I know what she means now, I'm sure of it. And Roxanna's experiences with vitamin injections make me remember going through Tilda's bin early in the spring, at the start of all this, and finding that syringe. These revelations are the catalyst for a new clarity of thought. An ability to make sense, at last, of all my work, all my efforts; it's like a million unconnected musical notes have lined up, and arranged themselves into a recognisable tune. I don't feel enlightened, though. I feel, instead, that I'm falling in a dark space, and that I'll never stop.

I open up the dossier, scroll back, looking at all my notes since Tilda met Felix. I have so many of them now, thousands and thousands of words, almost a hundred chapter headings, thirty identified themes, for heaven's sake. I have recorded *so much* detail – the sharp tone of Scarlet's emails, the crucial timings of her first conversations with Belle and me, the sly little looks exchanged between Tilda and Felix, the sincerity in Francesca Moroni's voice when she said that Felix was never violent, the throwaway comments of Paige Mooney about Tilda's relationship with the Whisper Sisters and, above all, Liam. I know now that Liam is the key.

I check the time. It's 10.45. I don't care that it's late – I grab my coat, dash down the stairs and out of the house, and to Green Park tube. In my hand is the business card he gave me, with his home address in the corner.

I run down the steps, against the flow of people coming up, and I'm dodging and swerving until I reach the platform; then the train is crowded with drunken boys, singing raucously and swearing, swinging from the overhead handrails. They're driving me mad, because I'm trying to think about Liam, and the questions I need to ask. The final questions before I go to LA.

He answers the buzzer with a wary voice. 'D'you know what the time is, Callie? Can't you come back tomorrow?'

'Please, Liam. Please. It won't take long…'

He lets me into the sitting room, a pained look on his face, saying firmly, 'Five minutes. That's all.'

I don't even sit down. Neither does he, and we stand awkwardly facing each other. He's wearing an old t-shirt and sweat pants, and is gazing down at his bare feet. I'm willing him to look up at me.

'I have to know,' I say. 'About when you and Tilda split up, and she had that breakdown. You're a psychiatrist, and you understand what happened. I need details, Liam… It's important.'

'Callie, what I'm about to say, you know already. You've always known, deep down. Tilda is a narcissist...' He's speaking slowly, leaden-voiced.

My eyes tear up. 'Please, Liam, tell me.'

'It's basic... She has an ego so fragile, so damaged, that she has to believe in a fabricated identity... That's why she's always insisted on being a star. She has to be this exceptional person, or she's tormented, she's ripped apart. Your sister will do anything, manipulate anyone, to keep hold of her invented idea of herself, to save herself from that pain. And if she fails, well – she'd prefer obliteration. Actual death.'

He flops down now, into his grey comfortable chair, and I sit too, on the sofa opposite. He looks wrecked, like he knows how desperate this is – how it will change forever the nature of the bond between Tilda and me.

'You're right,' I say. 'I do know it... Perhaps I've always known. Your sin was to love the real, ordinary Tilda, not the girl with star quality. She would never have been able to handle that... And to leave her for Mary Strickland – who was so *normal*, but with a big idea of her normal self. I can see how that made Tilda collapse... And the Whisper Sisters? What about them?'

'Her claque... her sycophants. Always reinforcing her fantasy, endlessly under her control.'

'And me?'

'You're tricky – she's bound to you like no one else. She wants you as a sycophant, and if you don't oblige, well that's catastrophic for her. She can't simply reject you – as she can others who fail her.'

'I've always obliged.' I feel mournful, heavy with grief.

'It's best not to think of it like that, Callie. You were trusting and you loved her. You are a good and empathetic person, and sensitive and perceptive. When she was in pain, you felt it too, and you desperately wanted to take her suffering away. It's these wonderful qualities that make you an exceptional and beautiful young woman... Now, I'm going to bed,' he says.

'You think Tilda's dangerous, don't you, Liam? You love her, like I do. But you know the truth.'

'It's time for you to leave, Callie.' He stands up slowly, like he can't take any more of this.

I'm so drained, I can hardly walk through the rain to the tube station, so when a black taxi appears in Salusbury Road, I flag it down, and slump in the back seat.

'Having a nice evening?' says the driver.

I look out of the window. The rain is coming down hard now, shining rain, lit by lampposts, shop windows, headlights. People are running to take shelter, young men putting their arms protectively around their girlfriends, young women on tiptoe to protect their shoes, trying not to be splashed by passing cars. I close my eyes. I have no idea how I'll sleep tonight – but I know what I have to do as soon as morning comes.

Wilf is waiting for me. He makes hot chocolate, which we drink in bed, side by side.

'I've figured it all out,' I say. 'I know exactly what Scarlet did and why. I know how she got into Felix's room, how she injected him. It's taken me so long, and I'm so weakened by it, so wretched. But I can't leave it now… I have to take this thing to the end.'

He listens, stroking my hair as I tell him what I now believe, what I *know*, about Scarlet, and also about Tilda and Felix. And then Wilf and I make love, and Wilf tells me *the third thing*, the thing he didn't say in the bookshop that day. I tell him back, and we say how grateful we are that we found each other. It's two in the morning now and, before we try to sleep, Wilf says, 'I'm going back to Kensal Rise, and I'll stay away until it's over. It's better that way.' I agree, and I tell him that I understand.

I don't sleep. Not for a minute. And when I drag myself out of bed at 7am, and get dressed, Wilf's still dead to the world, lying on his back with one arm down the side of the bed. I can't bear to see that sickening pose, and I pull his arm back up, while he snuffles and mutters, 'Morning?' like he's not sure where he is.

I kiss him lightly on the forehead, and say I'm leaving now, and that I'll see him again after I've sorted everything out, after I've been to Los Angeles and found Tilda. He grabs me, and pulls me down onto the bed to kiss me properly, but he's not trying to keep me there; he knows that it's time for me to go, and I bury my face in his chest, briefly, before I grab my laptop, the bee bag and my coat. I have a busy morning ahead. I need to go back to Tilda's agent, Felicity Shore, and then buy my air ticket.

I walk to Soho. The rain has gone, and it's a bright morning, filled with silvery light, the sort of weather for making strides, getting things done, and I walk briskly up to the reception desk, asking to see Felicity, boldly, as though I have an appointment.

'Tell her that it's Callie Farrow, and I'm going to LA tomorrow, so I'd like to see her urgently about Tilda.'

Five minutes later, Felicity escorts me into her office. She's wearing batwinged clothes again, and heaps of her jangly jewellery, and she has her hair up in a messy bun, a silky scarf tied, turban-like around it. Her style, I figure, is supposed to exude a tone of creativity and friendliness – but the look on her face is one of pure annoyance.

'I only have a few minutes…' she says. 'But I'd like you to take this message to your sister – tell her to get in touch with me. She's still not returning my calls or my emails. Frankly, Callie, I don't have much to offer her right now. It's thin pickings. But she *does* need to stay in touch. It's the professional thing.'

'Absolutely,' I say, trying to think of some appropriate small talk, before I get to my real reason for being here. 'I'm going to LA tomorrow, and I thought you might want to give me a message for her, that's why I've stopped by…'

'What is she saying about her UK work? Is she even available at the minute?'

'Oh, definitely…' I'm improvising. The truth is Tilda

hasn't been returning my calls either. 'And she'll be back for *Envy*, of course…'

'But I've had the producers on the phone telling me she's backing out.'

I don't show how shocked I am by this news. 'Oh, she hasn't totally made her mind up yet.'

'It's unacceptable, Callie.'

'I'll tell her.' I get up, saying, 'Do you mind, I just want to look at this photo again…' And I stand, staring at it, my heart beating against my ribs. 'Who's this girl, standing next to Tilda?'

'Why do you ask? What's this got to do with anything?'

'I need to know… I think Tilda's back in touch with her…'

'That's Lottie Watts. She was on my books once… I don't know what happened to her.'

Lottie, Charlotte. Charlotte, Lottie. 'My girl crush'. That's all I need to know. I leave in a hurry; Felicity Shore making no secret of her irritation at my visit.

47

I should have gone straight home and bought my air ticket. But I didn't. I lost my nerve. I knew the truth now, but I couldn't handle it. I couldn't face Scarlet, and I dreaded seeing Tilda again. It hit me as I was sitting there, staring at the British Airways website and its pictures of sunny Santa Monica beaches, of turquoise swimming pools belonging to white-washed hotels. All that brightness seemed like an impossible choice.

Instead, I felt stuck in dark, wintery London; I opened up the dossier, and started to write everything down. That pitiless, penetrating insight from Liam, and the confirmation from Felicity Shore that Scarlet was Lottie from Tilda's drama school days. Everything was explained, all the loose ends tied up neatly, just like *Strangers on a Train*. It took me more than an hour to think it through and type it up – and when I'd finished I transferred the dossier to a memory stick and then, with Tilda in mind,

I hid the memory stick in the corner of a pillow case, and put it at the bottom of a pile in the linen cupboard. And that's where it stayed, month after month, as I worked on suppressing all thoughts of Tilda and Felix and Scarlet and Luke. Belle was the only one I allowed myself to remember, the only one who made me feel better inside.

I distracted myself by concentrating on my new life with Wilf – who was relieved by my inaction, and moved himself back into Curzon Street. I worked hard as his manager at Wilf Baker Gardens, booking new business, making sure that we were paid on time, checking that the crew were in the right place. And often I'd go along at lunchtime to see Wilf at work, bringing ham sandwiches and a flask of strong tea, and sitting with him while he explained his planting ideas – 'A perennial meadow, blocks of colour, that's the idea, with gravel paths.' Or, 'White roses and raspberry bushes – purity and blood – it's what Catholics used to plant hundreds of years ago.' Sometimes I'd lend a hand, under Wilf's guidance, and dig and plant, like I did on our first proper date, thinking of long ago when I was seven, running down through the blue sky, into the bush and the earth, where the skull was.

In the New Year Wilf grew a big ginger beard; I became a better cook; we both resolved to get out of London more, planning to see Mum in Wales in the spring, and then travel down to Cornwall to go surfing. Also, we moved out of Curzon Street. All the costs of the flat had been paid by Tilda, direct debit, and for a while we were grateful to be able to live somewhere so central, I'd even say glamorous, for nothing. But I was always less comfortable there than Wilf was, seeing Felix everywhere – in the choice of furniture, of crockery, even of the bathroom taps. And my feelings about Felix had become horribly painful. I knew now that he wasn't a monster after all. He just liked order in everything, was a run-of-the-mill control freak. In Curzon Street it was hard to suppress such thoughts, but we couldn't go back to my flat, which had been let out to someone else, and I was pleased when, in January, Wilf and I viewed a one-bedroom first-floor apartment back in Willesden Green. The kitchen was tiny, and the bedroom filled up totally by the bed – but the sitting room was a decent size with a balcony and a view of a garden. When I stood out there I could hear the sound of trains.

Wilf resigned from Willesden Estates so that he could do gardens full-time. He worked longer hours than before, sometimes gardening from first light until after dark, and he would arrive home sweaty, dirty, exhausted and never quite free of the garden smell, even after he showered. He'd collapse onto the sofa with me, and we'd sit there with our chili con carne and beers watching *I'm a Celebrity* or *Bake Off*, making occasional comments about the contestants, or about the rain outside, which was going sideways. Not real conversations, just enough to feel companionable. I loved those evenings and I could see that he did too.

One time, I was lying with my legs across his, TV on, and I looked over, catching a slightly dazed expression on his face. I asked, 'What are you thinking?' He smiled and said, 'Never ask me that. Life's better when you don't have to spell it out.' In total agreement, I kissed him, thinking only for a second about my dossier and its horrific catalogue of secrets; only for a second about Tilda and her extraordinary career in Hollywood. *It ends here,* I thought. *This is my life now.*

48

Everything has changed, because of the body of a girl floating, face down, in a swimming pool in California. The image is so clear inside my head. I see those long thin arms outstretched, those parted fingers; and that bloated white skin taking on a tone of greyish-blue. I see too the long hair radiating out like a distorted halo, signifying something that I can't articulate. Something toxic. She's wearing that diaphanous golden dress, the one with the delicate straps that criss-cross all the way down her back. It's the dress that I tried on that day in Curzon Street, the one that I pulled off so quickly that I split the seam. Is it split now, I wonder, as it clings to her lifeless body, and winds around her skinny legs?

When Felix died, the hotel manager said he was reminded of the painting of the death of Thomas Chatterton; now I think of another painting – of Ophelia, a beautiful floating corpse, caressed by the softness of her dress, seeming as though she might be gently sleeping. But this Ophelia is inverted, her blank eyes gazing at the bottom of the pool. All I see is the back of her head, the radiating hair, and I wonder about her last thoughts. Was she regretful, or remorseful? It's two weeks ago now, but I haven't stopped thinking of the scene, turning it over in my mind, trying to make sense of it.

I slump in the back of the taxi that is taking me from Los Angeles airport to Tilda's villa in the Hollywood hills – to that cursed place, that pool. It's my first visit to America, but it's hard to be curious about my new surroundings. The road starts to twist and climb, and I'm dimly aware of the hazy sky, the strange, waxy vegetation, the low, white-washed buildings set back from the road. It's merely an unfamiliar backdrop for my grim mission here.

'Come for a vacation?' says the driver.

'No – nothing like that.' He doesn't hear, and in any case my mind is elsewhere – I'm thinking of the dossier, and the section that I wrote after my visits to Liam and to Felicity Shore.

Before I left London, I had opened it up, and re-read those final words one last time. I wanted every detail to be fresh in my mind when I arrived in America. I've brought the laptop with me, of course. It's in the bee bag on my lap, and I hold it tight, clinging to my dreadful words, the loathsome truth that I put into a letter that wasn't sent.

Dear Tilda,

I know now that you met her at drama school – your 'girl crush', the young woman who is Scarlet, Charlotte, or Lottie. And you made such a pretty couple: your willowy beauty, her dark intensity. I imagine that *you* were the sisters then, the twins. But afterwards, Charlotte failed at acting and modelling, while you picked up decent roles and were stunning in *Rebecca*. You had the beginnings of the glittering career that you so desired, whilst she was stuck in Manchester with horrible, sadistic Luke, occasionally picking up some role in a tiny theatre production. What did you promise her, Tilda? A life together in LA, where she could make a fresh start?

But I'm getting ahead of myself. I want to go back to the beginning – and that night when you invited me to Curzon Street to meet Felix for the first time. I remember you in my flat, half out of the door, saying, 'How can you stand it? All those broken fingers tapping at the glass.' I should have realised that you weren't really talking about the twigs tapping at my windows, you were thinking of the painful self-doubt in your head, the needles in your brain. But I wasn't thinking deeply enough then, not like I am now, and I turned up at Curzon Street, bright and sunny, with my bottle of Strongbow, noting that Felix was in charge of everything – the wine, the kitchen. But I was wrong. I see that. You were in charge, not Felix, making us watch *Strangers on a Train* – the film that was an inspiration not just for your acting, but also for a path in life that you had dreamed up, a path that involved me and Charlotte, and the death of Felix.

You must have felt smug, self-satisfied, as you lay on the sofa watching us innocents, taking everything at face value. Remember, we talked about Hitchcock putting his good people on the right hand of the screen, and the evil characters on the left? You explained that that made you the evil one, because of where you were sitting. Felix and I were enjoying your joke, but you were laughing at us really, at our gullibility. And when Felix said he was 'in the middle, could go either way', you must have thought *he has no idea! I'm going to send him clearly in one direction!* And from that day onwards you did exactly that – you set about making him seem dangerous, sinister, a threat to your life. I realise now that the only time I ever actually saw Felix appear to be harmful was that day on the river, when he held you under the water. How long were you down there, I wonder? Was it truly long enough to justify your state when you came up for air? You were heaving, and limp, and sank into his arms as though you were about to expire. But, Tilda, you were acting weren't you? That's what I believe now. And I have to acknowledge that you're very good at it – a real professional.

From then on, it was all about the bruises on your arms, those little ink spots. Not just the fact of them, but the way you hyped up the drama, dashing into the bathroom when I pulled up your shirt sleeve, emerging sort of spacey, as though you were covering up deep distress. And I recognise now, Tilda, that you were always capable of desperate measures when you were on a mission, that you have a long history of extreme behaviour. Liam made me realise the truth about your self-harming at school – that you did it in order to gain admiration from your friends, to show off your troubled soul to an audience. You're a narcissist – covering up your self-loathing with a fragile, empty show of how special you are, deeper than the rest of us, emotionally, even spiritually. Well, it's crap. That's what. Total garbage. I'm angry with myself for falling for it so completely, and think of those times that I snapped and raged at Felix, even drawing a knife on him. No wonder that, by the end, he wanted to keep me at a distance.

I see now that all your behaviour is deception. You're endlessly acting. That time when you went out of Curzon Street, for fags, and I surprised you with a tap on the shoulder. You started, like you had been stung by a wasp, immediately turning it on. You seemed so ragged, distracted, distressed – it was hard to get your attention for ordinary things, and I blamed Felix. Always, Felix. I didn't see the artifice, not for a moment. And I have to ask myself why that was. Partly it was you, and your craft, so excellently executed; but mainly it was me. I had bought into your narrative, weakly, naively, and now I was looking for corroborating evidence. I was alive to it. My heart was open. And every time I found something,

I felt somehow vindicated and motivated to rescue you. Just as you wanted, Tilda.

How lucky that Felix had obsessive compulsive disorder, categorising his shirts in white boxes, arranging the crockery and cutlery so perfectly, everything painstakingly clingfilmed. Once I might have seen all that and thought *how eccentric!* I might even have found it endearing. But, guided by you, Felix's peculiar habits became sinister – your message was always the same. *Look how weird he is. Look how he controls me.* You added violence to the mix, and I was hooked.

I even think this – that when you went to France and I asked to stay at Curzon Street, you planted the memory stick in the pillow case especially for me to find. You knew I would, because of our childhood mind games, because of your history of hiding things in pillowcases. And what did I discover? An account of your strange psycho-sexual relationship with Felix, of you surrendering to his control, emotionally and physically. Of violent sex. But none of it happened, did it, Tilda? You were riffing for my benefit. Having fun. No purple vase was ever hurled at your head. You made it up, along with the cracked mirror, the thousand shards of glass. I realised this when I spoke to Francesca Moroni, who told me that Felix was never violent, and I believed her. So, dear sister, you made a stupid error. You were relying on me being nosy, ferreting about in your flat, finding the memory stick. But it's my nosiness that made me go one step further than that – seeking out

359

Felix's ex, and asking her embarrassing questions, the sort of questions that most people would never ask. I suppose it's possible that he became violent only after he met you but, when you think about it, really think – the evidence is rather thin, isn't it?

It's funny – I got to the truth by working out that I was the obsessive one, far more so than Felix. When I used to eat your things, it was because I felt a compulsion not just to be part of you, to be synthesised with you, but paradoxically, also to resist being dominated by you. It was logical, at least according to my way of looking at it – my act of devouring your hair and your teeth showed that I owned you just as much as you owned me. These days, I've displaced the urge to eat bits of you, with the obsession with *understanding* you. I'll never be able to do that, not completely. You shine too brightly, and dazzle me, so that I can never see inside your head. I know it, and yet I try and I try – and maybe arrival doesn't matter; maybe the quest is enough – because it has taught me one crucial fact – that you are malevolent. I know what you did Tilda – and I know how you did it.

49

The taxi rounds a steep, shady bend, and pulls up alongside a white wall in a patch of late-afternoon pinkish sun. I see a metal gate, an entry-pad, and the house number – 1708. The cab driver grunts the fare at me, and after I pay he drives off without a goodbye, so that I'm left standing in the road, my parka over my arm, my heavy bag weighing me down – I'm a refugee from a wintery place, disconcerted by the sunshine and some foreign insect that's making a high-pitched, rasping sound.

The buzzer is answered by a man with a familiar American accent – like Felix's, but slightly looser, a more conciliatory tone.

'Lucas? What are you doing here?'

He buzzes me in, and I heave my bag along a narrow terracotta path overhung with heavy foliage which only partly masks the pool, a blue flash over to my left, one level down. At the end of the path Lucas waits in the doorway of the house, leaning on the frame with one arm, seeming weirdly nonchalant. He's wearing a pink linen shirt, and for a second I think I recognise it as Felix's, worn as Felix never would, ostentatiously unbuttoned, not tucked in.

'I want to say hello, sister-by-marriage,' he says. 'But are you my *former* sister-by-marriage now?'

'Oh, I don't know.' I don't care either, and I drop my bag on the floor. 'Where is she?'

'Upstairs. She's getting ready, beautifying, for a movie premiere – it's later this evening. She said to send you up, but not straight away because she's in the shower, so come on through and let's give you a drink of something. You must be shattered. What would you like, Callie? A cup of tea, or a lime soda, or a glass of wine? All we have is sparkling, Tilda likes it.'

I notice *all we have – we*, like he's living here. And *Tilda likes it*, like he knows her habits. I take the sparkling wine, an attempt to settle my nerves, and we sit side by side on a low, squarish sofa, while I look around, assessing Tilda's new home. It's darker than Curzon Street, dark tiles on the floor, wooden kitchen cabinets, trees and shrubs advancing on the French doors. Would Felix have liked it? I think not. It's not exactly jumbled, but the lines aren't clean, and there are cushions, and curtains with swags, paintings on the walls of hills and sunsets. Not as crazy as Mum's, but not a million miles away either.

'Were you here when it happened?' I may as well come to the point.

From his attitude on the sofa, I can see that he doesn't register the tension in me. He thinks I'm merely curious. 'Yes. I've been staying for a few weeks – I have a job here. Another house.'

'Congratulations.'

'So, yes, I was here. She seemed like a nice girl. A bit intense and moody maybe, and quiet. But basically nice.'

I think that nice is the worst possible word for her. 'So what happened, exactly? I mean, I only know that she died in the pool. Tilda emailed me, about the fuss in the press and so on, but I don't know any details.'

'Oh – okay. Well, she pitched up here wanting to stay, and I don't think that Tilda had been expecting her. After all, they didn't know each other well. They'd been students at drama school, as I understand it, but that was a long time ago. Charlotte seemed to think that she and Tilda had some special bond, and that Tilda would be delighted to have her as a house guest. Tilda didn't have the heart to turn her away – and Charlotte just settled in. She made herself useful, I guess, going down to the grocery store each morning, buying food, making our meals. And she'd work out which movies we'd watch in the evenings. She reckoned she could make it here as an actress – like thousands of young women before her, of course – but she didn't seem to realise that she and Tilda are leagues apart. Tilda has something special about her. Charlotte didn't.'

I'm noticing the differences between Lucas and Felix.

He's put his feet up on the coffee table, and is drinking his wine too fast. And there's something about the way in which he talks about Tilda, an element of admiration in his voice, and of supplication, that makes me realise that she has him under her control, and I pity him.

'So, that night...' he says. 'Charlotte and Tilda were down at the pool. Charlotte, I remember, was wearing a long dress of Tilda's, a gold-coloured silky thing – it had a split seam, and Tilda said she didn't want it any more, that Charlotte could keep it. They'd been drinking, Charlotte had taken some coke, and they were swimming. It's a famously lethal combination, of course. And they'd swum in their clothes, which, at the time, they'd thought was an amusing thing to do. Kinda crazy, in a good way. I was here, up at the house, making dinner for once. Anyways, Tilda came up from the pool, drenched, dripping wet skirt, making footprints on the tiles. She went upstairs for a shower, came down again, and was surprised that Charlotte hadn't appeared. We called her from the terrace, but she didn't come, so we walked down to the pool together, Tilda and I, and there she was, floating face down, her black hair radiating outwards, the dress tangled up around her legs. I kinda went into emergency mode, jumping into the pool, and together we pulled her out...'

We sit silently, and I put my feet up on the coffee table, next to Lucas's. I can hear my sister upstairs, the snap of a closing door, the scrape of a chair, and I say, 'Do you blame Tilda?'

It's a while before he answers. 'No, not at all. Why would I?'

Then she calls out, 'Come up, Callie!' in a voice that is too light, too fresh. So I leave Lucas on the sofa and ascend the stairs, to find Tilda waiting for me, standing at the door of a bedroom, bathed in a pinkish glow that is coming from an open door behind her, a door to a balcony. She's wearing a thin, white cotton robe over her naked body, and her feet are bare. Her long fair hair is freshly dried and glimmers at its edges, as do tiny specks of dust in the air. Her expression is sweet, a sort of tender bemusement.

'I told you not to come, little one. There's far too much going on, and it would have been better to wait... It's been difficult...'

She pulls me to her and kisses my cheek, not barely brushing it in her usual way, but pressured and long, like she's missed me, and I'm not sure whether to feel cherished or used.

In any case, I don't want to pull away. She smells of geranium and of orange, which I suppose is her shower gel or her shampoo, and I bury my face in her neck, to get more of it, as I hug her and say, 'I've hardly slept... It's making me feel strange, like you're not real, like this house isn't real.'

'LA is a little like that – it deals in fantasy.'

'I don't mean that... I think it's more that you are your fabricated self here, in an unnatural habitat.' Something

I could never have said before Liam brought it into the open and made it true.

I look around her dark-wood bedroom, at the table with her make-up on the top, lipsticks and mascaras and foundations untidily scattered, the tops left off; at the bed, which is oddly low, the covers thrown back, the sheets and pillows dented; at the open glass doors, the balcony beyond, with a view of nothing other than deep, waxy foliage, and the tiniest glimpse of the pool.

'You're funny, Callie...' she says. 'If you're so tired, why don't you lie on the bed? Actually, I might join you – I have time before the hair and make-up people arrive, I may as well rest.'

She unbelts her robe, lets it drop to the floor, so that I'm gazing at her naked body, finding myself filled with embarrassment, but unable to look away. Apart from a quick glance that day on the Thames, I haven't seen her without her clothes since we were children, since we were pre-pubescent and shared an evening bath, and I'm unable to speak as she crosses the room towards the bed; I'm noticing everything about her as if for the first time, jutting little hips, the soft cupping curve of her breasts, the waxed skin down between her legs. It's too much to take in, but I want to touch her white, white skin – no little ink-spots now, just a few freckles clustered here and there, and the mole on her shoulder.

She gets in, pulling up the sheet, and I take off my shoes and my jeans, and I join her.

'Can I hug you?'

'Of course.' She opens her arms, and I move in, resting my head low on her shoulder, practically on her breast, and for a few blissful seconds I close my eyes and imagine what life would be like if my sister was an innocent person. I wriggle to get comfortable, moving my arm under her back, the other across her stomach, entwining my legs with hers, until we are one amorphous being, and Tilda says, 'We're like the babes in the wood.'

'I know everything.' I stroke her stomach with my finger, and then her bony hip.

'Really?' It's that tender attitude again. 'That's good. You're me and I'm you – so I guess it's important that you know.'

'You didn't always think that…'

'No – but then I didn't realise how well my plans would work out.'

'You were lucky.'

'I'm a lucky person, Callie.'

'This is how I understand it…' I move my hand up her body, caressing the side of her breast, then stroking her face and her hair. 'You got the idea from the *Strangers on a Train* movie… the idea of swapping murders. If you could get someone to kill Felix for you, you'd kill in return…'

She laughs gently, a tiny sparkle of a laugh. 'And why would I do such a thing? Why would I want Felix dead? My darling boy.'

'Oh, you never loved Felix. You wanted his money…

Your career was foundering – Felicity Shore told me that – you'd been behaving badly in London, like a prima donna, losing jobs, and you were desperate to make a fresh start, here in LA. So you married Felix, made sure you would inherit…'

'I'm proud of you, you know. I always have been, actually. You see things that others don't. It's your sensitivity…' She kisses the top of my head, pulls my hair back away from my face, almost roughly.

'But you didn't mind using me, did you?' I say. 'You're ruthless, Tilda… When I told you about controllingmen. com you saw how to haul me in – you told Charlotte to join up, and to befriend me, to take me further and further into my obsession with dangerous men and vulnerable women. That way, I'd keep quiet about Felix's death – and you thought I'd be persuaded to kill Luke for Charlotte. You were outsourcing your side of the bargain to stupid me.'

'Oh, you haven't got that bit quite right.' Now she's whispering. 'Charlotte was practically psychopathic… She was keen to kill, she saw it as exciting… So I knew that if you didn't go through with Luke's murder, she'd do it anyway. There was no real reason for Luke to die, you see, other than Charlotte's belief that if she and I were both bereaved, sharing a lethal secret, that we'd be bonded together for good. That we'd both have brilliant careers, sharing success. That's what she wanted. She was a fool, Callie.'

I pull away, so that I can look at her face and she gives me the sweetest smile.

'Charlotte told you about Belle, and how she was a nurse,' I say, 'and you came up with the injections idea.'

'I'm so clever, don't you think?'

'Then you introduced Felix to Charlotte – you told him she was a medic who could administer your vitamin injections. And, what? She came round to Curzon Street a couple of times – in my imagination she's wearing a white cotton coat and has her hair pulled back in a ponytail, looking so professional – and you both had harmless injections, it didn't matter what was in them… You were simply getting Felix accustomed to the idea that Charlotte was authorised to inject him. And when he said he was going to attend a conference at that hotel, you seized your chance. You told him that Charlotte was nearby, that she could come round for his injection, that it would be good for him, keep him at the top of his game.'

'You're right. I even used that cliché – *You'll stay at the top of your game, darling.*'

I rest my head on the pillow so that we are face to face, so close that our lips are nearly touching, our eyelashes almost brushing each other.

'It was all so perfect,' she says. 'When Felix died, the police suspected nothing. That stupid Melody Sykes woman called me up and asked me about the marks from the injection, and I told her – vitamins, both of us had vitamin injections. And she accepted it – I could scarcely believe it. Then it turned out that Felix *did* have some sort of heart condition. Sykes told me that they do cause of death on a balance of probabilities – nothing more. I thought that was utterly hilarious.'

I think of her playing the grieving widow, grey with suffering, scarcely able to stand, struggling to formulate words. I remember her bearing at the funeral, the melancholy bride, the excruciating sorrow. Tilda is a brilliant actress, I have to give her that.

We are so close now that I feel her breaths on my face, and I realise that this moment is rare, special, because for once she isn't acting, she's being honest.

'It's such a relief,' she says, 'to be with you… I could fall asleep in your arms I feel so relaxed and happy.'

But I'm not going to let her get away with that, and I ask, 'What happened with Charlotte? Did you hold her down under the water… was it difficult?'

She kisses my lips, whispers, 'It was so, so easy, Callie… She was out of her head, drugged and drunk, and I think she wanted me to do it. Deep down, she knew we couldn't be together, that she'd always be inferior… that'd she'd feel forever bitter, betrayed even. And I didn't want her around, reminding me of our dirty little secret.'

I move in closer still, holding her so tightly that she gasps, then I release her and turn onto my back, staring at the wooden ceiling as I think about what to do.

'What about me?' I don't look at her as I speak. 'Don't I remind you of your secret? Won't you resent me for that?'

'No, little one. Of course not. You're an extension of me... you know that.'

'I'm wondering whether I should go to the police. If I call Melody Skyes and tell her everything, all the detail of it... She'd have to believe me.'

'Really? You think so?' She's getting out of the bed now, and is walking towards the open doors, saying, 'Watch this – this will tell you what you need to know.'

She doesn't pick up anything to cover herself up, walking outside, onto the balcony – it's dark out there now, just a faint silvery light, unnatural, like it's from a lamp in the garden. I get out of bed too, following her. In the corner a thin pole connects the side of the balcony to an overhanging roof – and Tilda climbs up onto a chair, holds the pole, and then steps up onto the metal rail that runs the breadth of the balcony. Holding on with one hand, she swings herself outwards, towards the black trees and the foliage, and she's balanced precariously there. I automatically step forward to look down, and see that the drop is a long one, that there's concrete below, and nothing to break a fall.

'I'd rather you pushed me,' she says, 'than go to the police. You see, I'm not afraid – I'm exhilarated when I think of death – I *do* like to flirt with it, just as I told you on the memory stick... That bit was true.' She's swinging back and forth now, recklessly, seeming not to mind that the slightest slip would kill her.

I don't feel alarmed as I watch her wild movements,

her rocking white body; instead, I feel comforted. This is the Tilda I recognise, so deeply, like I recognise night or grass or sky, something that would make you die if it was taken away. This is the impulsive, crazy girl, who can mesmerise you whenever she wishes, who will switch from ethereal to intense in a second, who believes that she has a God-given right to be a star.

She laughs as she pulls herself back to safety, clambers back down onto the chair, and the floor, saying, 'Well that's enough of that! I think you get the point… Now, scoot, Callie. The make-up person will be here soon. Go and chat to Lucas.' She picks up her cotton robe, and covers herself up, saying again, 'Go on!' So I do. I leave her alone so that she can preen and beautify, create the person that she so admires.

50

I'm standing on a pavement, squashed in a crowd, straining to see the stars who parade the red carpet, pausing for the cameras, lit and sanctified by white flashing lights. Knowing poses, shining eyes, a flick of hair and a backward glance, again and again, a parade of goddesses in flimsy gowns and impossible shoes. Tilda appears and, like the rest, she has that entitled, self-regarding smile, always for the cameras, scarcely registering the fans crammed behind the metal barrier, the contemptible civilians.

'It's Tilda Farrow,' says the obese woman next to me, her breath smelling of gum. 'She was in the press – some girl died at her house, and now she's got this big new role in a movie called *The Stranger...*'

Tilda hadn't told me, but I'm not surprised. Of course her dream has come true. It was inevitable, I suppose, because of her determination, her power. I stand on tiptoe, to get a better view, hoping she'll spot me. But she doesn't, she's concentrating on giving an interview to a man in a tux, holding a microphone. I can't hear, but I can imagine what she's saying. 'Yes, I'm excited about this new part. It's challenging, but I'll be working with some amazing people.' All the deceiving platitudes of her profession delivered with ease and self-absorption. Then she turns to go into the building, and it's only now that I realise that she's wearing the golden dress with the criss-cross straps going down her back. She rescued it from the pool, had the seam repaired.

I turn my back on the revolting scene, and make my way back through the crowd. I'm going home, to England, and Wilf and gardens, to Mum and her bad paintings, to Daphne and Willesden Green, even to Liam. Now that I've found him again, I'm not going to let him go. I plan to live the life that Tilda imagined for me all those years ago, back in Gravesend, when she identified my 'calling'. One day I'll be in a house with a good man, maybe Wilf, with children and dogs, and I'll give myself to ordinary things, everyday loves.

But I do know – how could I not? – that I'm the keeper of a secret that puts sinfulness at the heart of me, that I'm eternally tainted. I'll have to live with that, because I'm not going to betray my sister. It would kill her if I did; she'd fall off that balcony, stage a beautiful death. I can't allow it. Instead I'm choosing to believe that she's done her harm; that now she's moving on.

She'll discard Lucas, of course – he's a temporary crutch – and thanks to Felix's money she'll become a film star, surviving on my silence, on the absence of normal life, endlessly craving the adoration that sustains her in the darkness.

ACKNOWLEDGEMENTS

I'd like to thank my brilliant publisher Lisa Milton and fabulous editor Sally Williamson for their perceptive editorial contributions. Also, the *White Bodies* copy-editor Jamie Groves for his light touch and wry comments. As always, I'd like to thank my agent, Natasha Fairweather, for her wisdom and guidance, Lucy Kellaway for her encouragement and advice, and Kate Wilkinson for her many vital editorial adjustments. The other Wilkinsons and Molly Robins, over glasses of prosecco, helped me choose a title and reject several others including The Train on the Girl, Oughtn't it Be and What I Didn't Know; Agnes Makar was a first-class PA and reader; Dr Stuart Hamilton gave me valued advice on heart conditions and forensic pathology; and Paula Southern and Andy Banks once again allowed me to write in their room with a glorious view. This is my first novel and I could not have made the switch from non-fiction without a Fellowship awarded by the Royal Literary Fund. At home, where most of the novel was written, Tom McMahon kept me going with his love, intelligence, wit and kindness.